SF

DOCTOR WHO

ROBERT PERRY & MIKE TUCKER

Ypsilanti District Library
5577 Whittaker Road
Ypsilanti, MI 48197

BBC

Published by BBC Worldwide Ltd,
Woodlands, 80 Wood Lane
London W12 0TT

First published 1999
Copyright © Robert Perry and Mike Tucker 1999
The moral right of the authors has been asserted

Original series broadcast on the BBC
Format © BBC 1963
Doctor Who and TARDIS are trademarks of the BBC

ISBN 0 563 55577 7
Imaging by Black Sheep, copyright © BBC 1999
Krill depicted on front cover designed by Mike Tucker

Printed and bound in Great Britain by Mackays of Chatham
Cover printed by Belmont Press Ltd, Northampton

For Steve Cole

Thanks to:
Sophie and Sylvester
Andy
The Staff of the Sheesh Mahal, Croydon
Chris Parr
Sue Cowley
and
Mark Morris
(for making us find a title without 'Deep' or 'Blue' in it!)

'Later on BBC1, *The Generation Game*. But first, the start of a new four-part adventure for – *DOCTOR WHO*.'

Trad.

Part One

'Oh I do like to be beside the seaside.'

Chapter One

High above the oceans of Coralee, NavSat Nine drifted in an elegant orbit that took it over every point on the planet's surface. Checking and rechecking data from the hundreds of colony uplinks, transport shuttles and oceangoing craft that scattered the surface, its navigation transponders sent a trillion messages out into the void – a steady stream of information for the colony ships that used Coralee as a way station *en route* to the frontier.

Delicate sensors scoured the planet for data, relaying oceanic current changes and atmospherics to Coralee control. A sensor beam swept over a weather system forming in the northern hemisphere and NavSat Nine sent a possible hurricane alert to the Coralee meteorological data mainframe.

Attitude thrusters flared into life and the satellite turned as it crossed the equator. A routine pulse bounced up from a ship in the deep ocean. Recognition software identified the transponder code as that of the *Hyperion Dawn*. The correct signal at the correct time from the correct place.

NavSat Nine sent back its confirmation codes and drifted on, lost against an ocean of black scattered with a billion stars.

Holly Relf took a final bite from her sandwich and hurled the remains into the sky. It had barely left her hand when the iridescent shape of a gull flashed past and snatched the bread from the air. Holly watched as the gull spiralled higher and higher, pursued by a shrieking flock of other birds. She pulled a pack of cigarettes out of her jeans and stared out at the glittering ocean. The morning suns were harsh and high, the reflections dazzling. She pulled her shades down, swung her legs over the edge of the *Hyperion Dawn*'s control cabin and shook her battered lighter into life.

Taking a deep drag Holly stared out over the water of the planet that had been her home for the last four years. She never failed to be fascinated by the ocean. Scarcely a day went past when she didn't see something new in its constantly shifting surface.

A gust of wind whipped the ash from the tip of her cigarette and out to sea. She stared after it. The distant horizon seemed perilously close, a long, unbroken line of blue. It was no wonder that ancient mariners on Earth feared that they would fall off the edge of the world. She wondered what those explorers would have made of Coralee. There was no chance of concluding that it was flat; at less than half the size of Earth, the curve of the planet was plainly visible. It was 98 per cent water, and the only dry land a broken line of islands strewn around the equator like a necklace.

She craned her neck back, staring up at the clear blue sky. High above the soaring gulls the rings of Coralee arced from horizon to horizon. On clear nights the rings outshone everything else in the sky, sending ragged reflections skittering over the waves. She pitied the colonists that had chosen to settle on drier worlds. The ocean planets were breathtaking as far as Holly was concerned, fascinating, and Coralee was the best of the bunch.

She knew she wasn't the only one to feel that way. All the water worlds were inhabited – by a very individual bunch of settlers. The oceans seemed to attract frustrated explorers and hopeless romantics. Holly, however, was feeling far from hopeless at the moment. Coralee had been nothing short of miraculous for her love life. She squinted through the blazing sunlight at the shape of Jim, struggling with a seized engine filter on the far side of the deck. She smiled as his curses drifted across to her. She'd finish her cigarette and go and give him a hand.

The *Hyperion Dawn* was showing its age. Twenty years ago it had been a top of the line cable-laying platform; now the sea had done its work and it was worn and scruffy, the polycarbide hull showing the scars of too many storms. It was long overdue for a refit but the colony was expanding fast and they had to get the communication and power cables laid to the outer islands before the winter storms started to set in.

A sudden swell lifted the platform and Holly snatched at her coffee cup as it toppled from the edge of the wheelhousing. There was a bang from the deck and a burst of swearing from Jim. The autopilot gave a brief electronic burble and motors whined into life as the automatics repositioned the craft.

There was a harsh shriek from the communications console. Holly stubbed out her cigarette and clambered back into the cabin. She picked up the microphone.

'*Hyperion* to deep crew, go ahead.'

'*Are you planning on letting that crate drift all over the frigging planet? The cable just jumped a foot out of its housing.*'

'Stop moaning, Auger. We had a short on the starboard thruster. Jim's on it. Besides, I hear that with you, anything over four inches qualifies as a foot.'

'*Don't you just wish, Bruiser. Don't you just wish.*'

Holly grimaced. She'd been christened Bruiser after an incident at her last company, OMC. She'd rather hoped that the whole thing would be forgotten but everyone on Coralee seemed to know about it.

She'd been with OMC for seven years and had worked her way up to a position of considerable authority. Planetary engineers with oceanic specialities were something of a rare commodity – how do you train divers when your planet's oceans are so choked with sewage and pollution that it barely qualifies as water?

She'd only seen the sea on Earth once, when she was in her teens. She'd defied the curfew and, under cover of night, had slipped past the guards and scrambled under the fence, creeping down to the narrow strip of concrete that looked out from New Oslo over the North Atlantic. She remembered her shock at the vast expanse of liquid heaving back and forth, a thick viscous slime, flecked with grey scum.

This wasn't what was shown on the broadcasts. Sure, everyone knew that all the cetacean life forms had had to be shipped to the settlements near the pole because of the pollution but this... This was obscene.

She had crawled back to her living unit in a daze and vowed that she would get away from Earth, make for the colonies and see an unspoilt ocean. She'd joined the planetary engineering course shortly afterwards, directing all her energies to the study of the water worlds.

OMC had snatched her up as soon as she had graduated and within a year she was part of the team terraforming Hobson's World out in the Cerelis cluster. A good relationship with her team and a genuine love of the sea propelled her up the company ladder faster than anyone expected, and before long she was sitting in on colonisation meetings at the highest level.

Extra responsibility brought duties that Holly would rather have done without. Paperwork, courses, endless, pointless meetings. By far the worst was the annual company ball. Big social affairs had never been Holly's thing. She was far happier in overalls than ball gowns. Her flame-red hair and deep green eyes would have made her an imposing woman at the best of times, but years of diving had toned her figure and given her a set of shoulders broader than those of most men. She knew she could turn heads when in her work clothes and in a party dress she could bring a room to a standstill.

The OMC dinner on Kandalinga had been no different. As always it was hosted by the chairman of OMC, Trantor Garpol. Holly had only spoken with Garpol once before – a company dinner back on Earth – and she hadn't been impressed. He had been all over her like a rash, telling her what an asset she was to the company and promising bonuses. Then his fussy little assistant, Blint, had whisked him away, informing him that there were far more important people waiting and he hadn't spared her another glance.

Garpol always threw a party on his new colony worlds, partly to let the colonists know how much they owed OMC, partly to gloat at the competition. Holly had watched his expensive personal shuttle glide down to the colony pad and a skimmer whisk him to the reception. She had been in a bad mood from the start of the evening. She was fed up with spending more and more time behind a desk and less and less time out at sea, and she had spent all night fighting off the advances of faceless, suited creeps and drinking far too much expensive champagne. When Garpol had spotted her through the crowds and started fawning over her she was less than polite. When his hand had strayed to her backside her tension had exploded in a punch that sent him sprawling into a table of hors d'oeuvres.

As officials ran around in blind panic Holly had smoothed her dress down, crossed the room to the head of InterOceanic, and asked for a job. She'd been hired on the spot.

Another buzz from the communicator woke her from her reminiscing.

'OK, Bruiser, we're ready for the next cable length.'

Holly crossed to the cabin window, stuck two fingers in her mouth and whistled hard.

Jim looked up from the deck, sweat dripping off him. Holly grinned at him.

'You're soaking!'

He shrugged. 'Well perhaps if the skipper would lend a hand instead of gazing at the rings like a first timer...'

'OK, OK! I'll be there. Send Trevor up to take over in here. The guys are ready for the next cable length.'

Jim gave her a thumbs up and began shouting orders to the men on the deck. Holly crossed back to the communicator.

'It's on its way, Auger.'

'Cheers, boss.'

'Oh, and Auger...'

'Yeah?'

'Call me Bruiser one more time and I'll put a knot in your airline. *Hyperion* out.'

Fourteen fathoms below the *Hyperion Dawn*, the thick rubber-coated cable snaked down on to the seabed, guided into its moorings by two suited divers who crawled over the sandy sea floor like huge metallic crabs. Auger and Geeson were experienced company divers; they'd been part of Holly's team on Hobson's World and Kandalinga. They had transferred to InterOceanic the day after she had, and had been top of her list for the Coralee crew.

As the cable slipped into its final mooring Auger thumbed the stop stud on the arm of his suit. The cable glided to a halt and the two divers lumbered forward to lock the couplings in place.

Tony Auger was in a bad mood. He'd been on shift for five hours now and he was tired and hungry. As he grappled with locking the coupling the spanner slipped from his grip and tumbled on to the silty floor.

'Goddamn it!'

His partner, Geeson, looked up. 'What the hell is it now?'

'These frigging suits!' Auger held up a gauntleted hand. 'You tell me that a diver designed these!'

Geeson grunted. This was an old argument. Deep-diving suits for frontier worlds were rugged, tough and functional; they hadn't been designed with fine work in mind. He sighed. Working under water had all the problems of working in space and none of the advantages; it was just as claustrophobic with little of the manoeuvrability. Even so, he wasn't about to give in to another bout of Auger's griping.

'You whinge too much. Just get on with it.'

He watched as Auger pulled the spanner out of the mud, batting aside the fish that had drifted over to investigate. There were always fish at engineering sites, darting in to catch anything stirred up by the machines. A great shoal of them hovered nearby, their multicoloured fins glinting in the weak sunlight that filtered down from the surface. Geeson was always surprised at their variety. He was a veteran of dozens of ocean colonies and the fish were always uniquely different. Now they darted in, jaws gulping at the tiny shrimps disturbed by the cable. He waved them away from the front of his visor and tightened the final bolt.

'Right. Done. Let's get the cable unhooked and get the hell out of here.'

'I'll do it.' Auger lumbered over to the end of the cable run and began unscrewing the guide wire.

There was a sudden flurry of movement in the water. Geeson turned his head inside the bubble of his helmet in time to see the cloud of fish sweep past him like a rainbow wave. 'What the hell...?'

He looked over at Auger. The other diver shrugged. 'Beats me. They've gone. All of them.'

Holly was down on the deck helping Jim with the starboard motor when she heard the communicator shriek again. She hauled herself up into the cabin. Trevor handed her the mike.

'Thanks, Trev. Go give Jim a hand, would you?'

She settled into the pilot's chair. 'What is it now, guys?'

'*Holly, it's Geeson. Anything strange going on up there?*'

Holly was puzzled. 'Strange? How d'you mean?'

'*I don't know exactly. All the fish just quit the area.*'

'You're worried about the fish?'

'*They're all gone, Holly. Now something sure as hell scared them off. You got anything on the radar?*'

She glanced at the screen. The two tracer blips of the divers

7

were bright and glowing, their low pings keeping steady time in the small cabin.

'Only you two on the screen.'

'*Well, keep an eye on it, will you?*'

Holly frowned. Geeson didn't usually get this freaked. 'You sure you're OK, Martin?'

'*Yeah.*' There was a short barking laugh from the speaker. '*Just been down here too long, I guess. We're packing up now.*'

'OK, Martin. I'll keep an eye on the screen and let you know if anything shows up.'

She glanced idly over at the small radar screen and her eyes widened with horror.

'Jesus Christ!'

The screen was suddenly alive with signals moving through the water with impossible speed. The tracers of the two divers were swamped. The cabin was filled with a cacophony of electronic noise.

She snatched up the microphone. 'Auger! Geeson! What the hell is down there with you?' She could hear screams over the speakers. '*Martin!*' There was nothing but static now. She raced on to the deck. 'Jim! Get them up!'

He looked up at her, puzzled.

'Auger and Geeson are in trouble! Get them up! Now!'

Jim slammed the emergency winch button. Klaxons blared out over the platform. The winch mechanism screamed as the divers' safety lines reeled in. Holly threw herself at the rail, her eyes scouring the water for the first sign of the divers. Jim spotted them first. 'There!'

Holly followed his gaze. A smudge of light was rising from the deep – the high beam from one of the suit helmets. The helmet broke the surface of the water and Holly stepped back from the rail, fighting down the bile rising in her throat.

Geeson's suit was nothing more than a collection of shredded metal lumps. She could see his face through the visor, but the rest of him... It was scarcely possible that the lumps of ragged meat could once have been a man. Jim hauled the other cable from the water. The end was severed. There was no sign of Auger.

Holly stared across at Jim. All the crew were looking at her, waiting for her to give an order.

She never got to give it. The platform heaved suddenly, sending them sprawling across the deck. There was a ragged tearing noise.

'That was the hull!' Jim was on his feet now. He darted across the deck and punched buttons on the winch control. 'I've got to release the cable!'

The platform lurched again and the engines whined in protest as the autopilot laboured to keep the craft level.

Holly struggled to her feet. 'I'll take us off auto! See if I can get us out of here.'

She staggered over the deck as the platform pitched again. Two crewmen tumbled against the rail. Holly's head snapped up in shock as something reached up and snatched the men over the side. Their screams mingled with a guttural, bubbling roar.

The remainder of her crew were struggling to help Jim with the cable controls. They hadn't seen the... thing. Holly was about to call out to them when the deck was punched up from below. Several shapes punctured the steel and began to tear it back, peeling it apart as if it was paper. Holly was shaking her head. They couldn't be claws... they just *couldn't* be. There was a deep, throaty roar from beneath them. She could see wet flesh glistening under the torn deck plates. Her mind was a whirl. There were no predators on Coralee. The colonisation survey would have said...

She stared helplessly across at Jim. The two other crewmen were backing away, desperately searching for something to defend themselves with. One of them passed Jim an axe. The ship rolled again and Holly caught a glimpse of several huge shapes surging up from the water. She turned and fled. She could hear the cries of Jim and the others from behind her, high agonised cries and wet, tearing noises. She tried to blot them out with her own screams. She scrambled through the control cabin, not daring to look back. She could hear claws dragging on the deck plates, sense things swirling through the water.

There. Ahead of her. The escape bubble. She launched herself at the hatch. Long, painful seconds passed as the hydraulics creaked open. She could hear something behind her, dragging across the deck. Harsh, laboured breathing.

The hatch opened and she dived through, kicking at the door controls. The hydraulic rams had started sliding the door shut when the arm came through the gap.

Holly pulled the fire axe off the wall and swung it down on the pale, fleshy limb that thrashed and flailed in the confinement of the bubble. Thick ichor sprayed over the walls. She screamed and swore at the things that had taken Jim, taken her crew and swung the axe again and again. The door mechanism crushed home and the severed arm thumped to the floor. With a lurch the bubble launched from the platform. Holly didn't notice. She continued to hack at the writhing arm until the floor was littered with flesh and blood.

Only when the last piece stopped moving did she stop and give in to her grief. She collapsed on to the floor with tears streaming from her eyes. She huddled into a corner rocking herself back and forth, the sound of her sobbing echoing around the walls of the escape pod.

Then the claws began to scrape along the hull.

Chapter Two

The beach stretched for miles, a huge white curve of sand glaring under the twin suns. White crested waves tumbled on to the shore in a constant hiss and the soft wind carried the distant screech of gulls.

At the edge of the beach tall palms curved elegantly towards the sky, providing some shelter from the burning suns. In the shadow of one of the palms the air began to blur and take on a bluish tint. With a series of rusty arthritic groans the tall shape of the TARDIS struggled to gain solidity. That achieved, with a loud thump it materialised fully and the door creaked open.

The Doctor stepped out on to the beach, took a deep breath, and smiled. His trousers were rolled up to the knees, he had a huge kite under one arm and was clutching a bright red plastic bucket and a spade with a curious question-mark-shaped handle. He propped the kite up against the palm tree and rummaged in his pocket. Pulling out a large paisley handkerchief he began knotting the corners.

'Come on, Ace! Surf's up!'

Pulling the handkerchief on to his head, the Doctor hoisted his kite back into his arms and began to amble towards the sea, licking his finger and testing the wind direction.

There was the sound of a scuffle inside the TARDIS and his companion emerged into the sun, adjusting the straps on her swimsuit. Ace stared at the beach ahead of her and gave a sigh of deep satisfaction. Truth be told, she hadn't believed that they would ever get here. Too often the Doctor's promises of a relaxing holiday turned into just another nightmare, and they had been through enough nightmares recently. She had to hand it to him, though – this time it looked like he'd really done it.

Ace hauled a huge baggy T-shirt on over her swimsuit, then slipped on her sunglasses, hoisted her ghetto-blaster on to her shoulder and followed the Doctor on to the beach.

He was busy putting his kite together when she dropped on to the sand next to him. She leant back and stared at the huge sweep of the rings cutting across the sky.

The Doctor smiled at her. 'Impressive, isn't it?'

Ace nodded. 'Wicked.'

'It used to be a moon – a very long time ago.'

Ace stretched back on the white sand. 'What happened?'

The Doctor stared up at the rings thoughtfully, shading his eyes. 'I'm not sure. I should pop back one day and find out.'

'But not today.'

'No.' He held his kite out proudly. 'Not today.' He clambered to his feet. A bunch of kids thundered past him down the beach, splashing into the sea. Ace could hear the chatter of their parents lounging under the palms. All around there were scattered groups of people, swimming, sunbathing, generally having a good time. On the edge of the shoreline a small group was setting up a sophisticated sail board. Ace stared at them. Humanoid but definitely not human. Too many limbs for one thing.

The Doctor answered her unasked question. 'Dreekans. You find a lot of them on the ocean planets. Very good swimmers. Having four arms does help, I suppose.'

As if to prove the point two of the Dreekans launched themselves into the water and within moments they were little more than dots heading for the horizon.

The Doctor began to trot down the beach, reeling out the kite's tail. Ace rummaged in her beach bag and pulled out a cassette tape. Courtney Pine. God, it had been a long time ago when she bought this. Another nightmare. She peered at the small shape of the Doctor. It was so strange seeing him in a relaxed environment. Too often they were in the thick of things as soon as they landed; and the last few weeks had been worse than most. The Blitz. Victorian London...

The events of their last adventure had shaken the Doctor badly. Things had been awkward between them since then, and they hadn't talked about it properly. Not yet. Ace scratched idly at the small scar on her neck. The scar where the Doctor had tried to...*

She shook her head angrily. She was on holiday for God's sake! They had come here to heal things. To relax.

She slipped the cassette into her ghetto-blaster and hit play. Soft jazz drifted over the beach. One of the Dreekans on the shoreline cocked his head, listening. He turned and gave her a dazzling smile.

Ace grinned back.

'I wonder what else you've got four of,' she murmured.

There was a sudden cry of delight from the kids she had seen earlier. The Doctor's kite had leapt into the sky, sending gulls scattering in alarm. The Doctor sent it soaring higher and higher, weaving in intricate patterns against the distant rings.

Ace settled back on the soft sand and closed her eyes. The suns were gorgeously warm on her skin. Everything was turning out perfectly.

Brenda Mulholland sipped her third coffee of the morning and stared out of the huge, curved window that dominated her office. The island chain stretched away into the haze of morning light, a thin line of green among the endless blue. Below her the colony stretched down the headland, already alive with traders and tourists. Tourists, for God's sake! Only four years since the first colonists had arrived on Coralee and they were already attracting tourists from the outer worlds. Not that this was a bad thing, of course, it was good for the economy – she could just hear the chatter from the market quarter and the harbour.

The colony was already beginning to struggle with the rapidly expanding population, which was well over the projected

* See Doctor Who – *Matrix*.

figures. They had to start developing the other islands fast if they were going to keep up with demand. Most of the infrastructure was in place, the reactor was more than capable of coping with the extra demand and one of the smaller islands had been fitted out as a halfway decent shuttle port. She could see a distant transport droning across the sky. As she watched, its main thrusters kicked in and it surged upwards, vanishing towards one of the sister worlds.

They had to get power to the outlying clusters though. When that was done then the engineers could move in and they could take the next batch of colonists. Earth was screaming at her to get things hurried along.

There was a tap on her door, and the rugged face of Phillip Garrett, the colony's chief engineer, peered into the room.

'Still trying to come up with names?'

Brenda grimaced. 'If I ever meet the genius who decided that it was a great honour for me to come up with names for over two hundred islands...'

'You could always name one after me. Garrett Island. Got a nice ring to it, don't you think?'

Brenda smiled. The initial orbital survey had classified all the islands by size and with reference numbers. According to the manual the colonists currently inhabited Coralee island cluster 262704K, but within weeks of planetfall they had christened their new home the Grayson Islands, after their pilot. Now, as colony co-ordinator, it was Brenda's duty to name the remaining islands.

She smiled as she stared over at two large pillars of rock that dominated the bay. Damn and Blast It; the first islands she had named. That had caused an uproar. *Typical of the flippant attitude that taints all of Brenda Mulholland's decisions.* She still had that memo taped to her notice board.

The islanders liked her, though. Apparently several of the tavernas ran a book on which island she would name next.

Someone had won over two hundred credits recently by correctly guessing that she would call one of the smaller islands Trigger, after her dog.

She took another sip of her coffee and slumped into the chair behind her desk. 'What have you got for me, Phillip?'

Garrett lumbered across to her desk and handed her a data-pad. 'Supply request from MacKenzie for the next quarter. The dig is taking longer than expected and he's running out of essentials.'

Brenda scanned the list. 'We're going to struggle to get these approved. He's already way over his weight quota for the next cargo shipment.'

Garrett shrugged. 'Then he stops. He can't work without this stuff.'

Brenda slumped into her chair. 'OK, leave it with me, Phillip. I'll talk to Central, see what I can do.'

There was a sharp buzz from the console on her desk. She snapped it on.

'Yes?'

'Sorry to disturb you, ma'am, but we've got a problem.'

'I'll be right out.'

Garrett gave her a sympathetic smile. 'It never rains...'

The two of them stepped into the huge control room. After the brightness of the office the control centre was like a huge, dark cave. Slatted blinds hung over the windows allowing shafts of light to lance across the room, glinting off the screens of dozens of monitors. Dreekan and human technicians sat hunched over read-outs, the Dreekans' hands flying over multiple keyboards. The entire room throbbed with an air of quiet efficiency.

Brenda peered through the gloom, her eyes adjusting rapidly. A young traffic controller looked at her expectantly. She crossed the room, settling into the seat alongside him.

'What seems to be the problem?'

'It's the *Hyperion Dawn,* ma'am. No contact for over twenty minutes.'

Brenda frowned. 'That's Holly's ship, isn't it?'

The technician nodded.

'Did they make their last routine call?'

'No, ma'am. That's when I tried them, but there's no response.'

Brenda leaned over the console. The small transponder signal that was the *Hyperion Dawn* blinked steadily on the screen.

'Any distress signal?'

The technician shook his head. 'Nothing from the NavSats, either.'

'It could just be a faulty com system.' Garrett, as usual, sounded confident. 'That crate is well overdue for retirement.'

Brenda sank her chin into her hands, staring thoughtfully at the screen. Suddenly she shook her head. 'I think we'll be safe rather than sorry. Get the flyer airborne.'

The klaxon shattered the peace of the control room. Suddenly there were people everywhere, settling into a well-practised routine. Brenda crossed to the window and pulled the blinds apart. The bulky yellow shape of the coastguard flyer lifted clumsily from the shuttle pad, engines roaring. She watched as it soared out over the sea.

'I've got a bad feeling about this, Phillip.' She turned round, looking for him through the gloom, but the engineer had gone.

Ace drifted through crystal clear waters, watching the sandy ocean bottom, which rippled with reflected light. Coral bloomed from rocky outcrops – a riot of colour amidst the gentle blue. She kicked out with powerful strokes and swept across the sea floor, sifting through the pebbles nestling in the sand.

Fish drifted around her, sometimes darting in between her fingers as she disturbed the sand, mostly just contemplating her with huge, unblinking eyes. She was picking at a cluster of bright polished stones when the fish suddenly exploded away from her in a furious flurry of scales.

A sudden shadow drifted over her and she turned her head upwards. Something huge and yellow passed overhead. Ace struck out for the surface.

She broke through the waves in time to see the coastguard flyer thunder into the distance, the roar from its engines echoing around the cove. Shading her eyes she watched as it vanished over the horizon.

Flicking her wet hair over her shoulders she turned back to the beach. She had drifted out further than she had intended. The shore was a distant white stripe, the people on it no more than colourful dots. She picked through the selection of pebbles in her hand and pulled out a vivid green one. Popping it into her mouth for safekeeping she discarded the rest and struck out for the beach.

Out in the deep ocean it had drifted, swept for miles by the currents, every system on shutdown. Now vibrations through the water revived it. Gradually its senses opened up – light dazzled it, sounds and smells bombarded it. There was prey here. It could taste it through the water, feel it struggling towards the shore.

Every sense heightened, it targeted its prey and surged forward.

Ace's head jerked up at the sound of something loud and fast approaching her. The speedboat was little more than a red blur as it sliced past, the wave from its bow sloshing over her head, momentarily blinding her. She pulled the pebble out of her mouth and waved angrily at the pilot.

'Wanker!'

The boat sped on, oblivious. Suddenly there was a loud thump, and a protesting roar from the engine as the hull struck something under the water.

Ace could see the pilot wrestling with the controls – the boat was jerking as if it was caught on something. The engine screamed as he wrenched on the throttle. With a sudden torrent of spray the boat was free again, lurching forward through the waves.

As Ace watched, it circled for a few seconds, the pilot scouring the waves for the obstruction, then sped off across the endless blue.

Ace glowered after it.

'Hope your prop shaft's bent.'

Popping her pebble back into her mouth she resumed her swim back to shore.

Ace waded up on to the beach to find the Doctor sitting in front of a huge sandcastle – really huge. It must have been about four metres square and nearly a metre high. The Doctor was tinkering with a collection of electronic spares while the local kids were further along the beach, shrieking and playing with his kite.

The Doctor was running a long cable to the top of his sandcastle where he had constructed an impossibly slender tower.

Ace sauntered over to him.

'Wom's at em, ampon cut?'

He stared at her. 'I'm sorry?'

Ace pulled the pebble out of her mouth. 'I said what's that then, Hampton Court?'

The Doctor looked indignant. 'Certainly not! It's the City of the Exxilons, one of the Seven Hundred Wonders of the Universe!'

He pressed a button on the collection of junk in his hand and the top of the sand beacon began to pulse with light. He beamed at Ace. 'I was able to stimulate the silica in the sand and make it light-emitting.'

Ace shook her head in disbelief. 'Professor, you're in a class of your own.'

She slumped down on to the sand next to him and began towelling her hair. 'Did you see that flyer that went over earlier?'

The Doctor nodded. 'Coastguard. Search and rescue. There's quite a big town at the end of the bay.'

He handed Ace a pair of opera glasses and pointed down the beach. Ace peered through the glasses. Through the palm trees she could make out gleaming white buildings bordering thick green jungle. The town swept out along a natural peninsula with a small harbour at its tip. Ace could see sails and expensive-looking cruisers. It reminded her of the Greek islands; except for the rings of course, and the extra sun.

She lowered the glasses. 'Professor...'

'Hmm?' The Doctor was hunched over the circuit board, poking at it with his screwdriver.

'Do you have any plans? I mean, are we rushing off anywhere?'

'Not especially, no. Why?'

'Well...'

The Doctor looked up from his work, his eyes twinkling. 'Well...?'

'Could we stay for a couple of days?'

He grinned. 'I was hoping you'd say that.'

Ace lay back on her towel. 'Wicked.'

The Doctor returned to his tinkering. 'If we've got a couple of days I'll have time to magnetise the sand and get the doors to open.'

Ace was about to tell him that he was a sad git when a shadow suddenly blotted out the suns. Before she had a chance to shout out a warning the Doctor's kite came hurtling out of the sky and crashed into the City of the Exxilons.

Chapter Three

The *Hyperion Dawn* drifted quietly in the swell of the ocean, with no indication on her decks of the violence of the morning. She suddenly bucked in the water as the coastguard flyer dropped over her in a low hover, its engines churning the sea into boiling foam.

Sensors swept over the craft and the ship's log automatically uplinked to the hovering flyer. The pilot began a slow circle of the ship. His co-pilot suddenly pointed at the ragged holes torn in the deck plates.

'What the hell d'you think did that?'

The two men looked at each other grimly.

'Coastguard to Coralee Control.'

Brenda was at the communications console before the technician had a chance to raise his hand.

'Go ahead.' Her heart was pounding.

'We've found the Hyperion Dawn. *She's at her original coordinates. Looks like she's still tethered to the com cable. She's taken on a lot of water, barely afloat.'*

'What about the crew?'

'No sign of life. And there are... marks.'

'Marks?'

There was a pause. *'It looks as if something tore the bottom out of the ship.'*

'You mean she ran aground?'

'No. No, she's too far out for that. I don't know what in hell caused this.'

A low mutter began to run around the control room. If there was something that Brenda could do without it was a mystery at sea.

'Quiet!' Her voice was like a gunshot. She glared at the technicians around her. 'Leave the rumours to the market traders. We've got a rescue in progress, remember.'

She turned back to the console.

'Is the escape bubble still there?'

'Hold on, we've just got to swing aft... No. No, the bubble has been launched!'

'Then there may well be survivors. Get on to it.'

'Do you want us to tractor the ship back in?'

'Yes. No, wait.' Brenda tapped her teeth. It sounded likely that the ship had been attacked by someone or something. If it was a natural phenomenon then it would be under her jurisdiction but if it was a deliberate act of piracy...

'Send a drone down. Full data sweep. When it's done I'll send a salvage crew out. You get after that bubble.'

'Roger that, Control. Coastguard out.'

Brenda crossed to the video wall that dominated one side of the control room. A Dreekan technician powered up the sensor array, his hands dancing over the keyboards.

'Drone online. Receiving data.'

The screen glowed into life with the startup icon from the drone, then flickered briefly with static.

Brenda frowned. 'What's wrong?'

The Dreekan looked puzzled. 'It's as if the signal is being split.' He punched at a series of controls. 'Got it!'

The picture swam for a moment, then suddenly they were seeing the *Hyperion Dawn* from the air as the drone dropped from the belly of the coastguard flyer. Brenda leaned close as the remote swooped over the deck, zeroing in on the gashes that criss-crossed its metal surface. Machinery whirred and hummed around her as sensor data was received and decoded. She couldn't take her eyes off the gouges in the metal.

'Jesus Christ, Holly... where are you?'

* * *

In another part of the colony a huge, lumbering figure watched with satisfaction as telemetry and pictures from the wrecked ship scrolled across a small screen. Reaching down with clumsy, club-like hands the figure pulled a squat communications relay from a case and punched a series of studs. The machine chattered into life.

Leaning close, the figure barked a short, guttural message into the machine. It chattered again then gave a series of rapid clicks.

The figure resumed watching the screen, its harsh breathing echoing around the darkened room.

The Cythosi ship hung in the asteroid field, huge and ugly. Like a great whale it drifted slowly with the thousands of tumbling rocks, its hull rough and barnacled, pitted with countless meteor scars and blaster burns. Low-power force fields flickered around it, nudging the ship clear of the larger rocks, deflecting the smaller ones, keeping the vessel moving without giving its position away.

In the observation blister slung low under the belly of the ship, Commander Bisoncawl sat watching the huge chunks of space debris tumble gracefully past. He shifted his bulky frame in his chair, scratching idly at the hair that tufted from his neck.

Functionary Bavril stood to attention just behind him and to his left, as operational regulations required. Cythosi didn't like to have to look at their humanoid slaves. Aesthetically unpleasing, they said. Some Cythosi had been known to execute on the spot any humanoid who had the temerity to make eye contact with them. General Mottrack was like that. He was one of the worst.

Then again, summary execution wasn't the worst fate that life on the Cythosi ship promised for Bavril's people...

Bisoncawl, Mottrack's number two, wasn't so bad. Bavril knew he was lucky to be appointed to serve him.

That having been said, it was never entirely possible to relax in the presence of any of the Cythosi – they could all be vicious and unpredictable. Particularly at the moment. For days the ship had drifted, waiting, waiting for the signal, its Cythosi crew getting bored and vindictive, its human crew suffering as a result. There was nothing they could do – not now. This had been a long voyage. When they'd started out, Bavril's people had outnumbered the Cythosi by six to one. Now they were practically down to essential personnel only. Everyone else had been taken below...

Bisoncawl was concerned, Bavril knew. Silent running was difficult to maintain at the best of times, and was practically impossible over long periods. The ship had been in the asteroid field for nearly twelve cycles now, with no sign of the signal and no sign of the enemy. The crew were becoming complacent and General Mottrack had responded in predictable Cythosi fashion by getting brutal. Only yesterday a careless human communications operator had triggered a sonar buoy and been shot down on the spot. If the signal didn't come soon...

Bisoncawl's communicator blinked. He was required on the bridge.

'Come,' he said, heaving himself from the chair and stepping out into the corridor. The battle cruiser was typical of Cythosi design – bleak, functional, uncomfortable. Clouds of vapour hung in oily patches down the length of the main walkway. Bisoncawl thrust his head into one of them and breathed deeply. Bavril shuddered. The smell always reminded him of rotting meat, and made him feel nauseous.

'I've been out on frontier duty too long,' Bisoncawl rasped. 'I'm ready to go home.'

Bavril dropped his eyes. These little intimacies, officer to adjutant, frightened him. A lesser officer would never get away with it – although it would of course be the functionary who suffered. Bavril could never decide whether Bisoncawl was being friendly or cruel.

A cluster of growling Cythosi troopers turned the corner. Bisoncawl straightened and the troopers fell silent, saluting him as they lumbered past.

They approached the command area and Bisoncawl pressed his thick, clawed hand on to the security access panel, growling with impatience as the door ground open. He stepped through and something spitting and vicious clamped itself on to his shoulder.

He clawed it off in one swift movement, slamming it to the floor and pinning it there with a booted foot.

The service robot writhed and spat, tearing at the fabric of the commander's boot. Bisoncawl drew his blaster and pumped three shots into the robot. With a metallic rattle it sparked and lay still. Bisoncawl swore under his breath.

A low chuckle drifted across the darkened control room.

'Problems, Commander?'

Bisoncawl holstered his gun and saluted stiffly. The huge form of General Mottrack loomed over them. Even by Cythosi standards Mottrack was ugly. A veteran of a dozen campaigns, the general wore the evidence of battle like medals. One side of his face was a mass of scar tissue, one eye buried in deep folds of raw flesh, the other wide and staring, its burning red pupil never resting. The heavy bone of his forehead was pitted and bent, giving him a constant glower.

The red emergency lighting of the bridge glinted wetly off the oil on his battle fatigues and the huge plasma blaster that hung ominously at his side. Bavril had noticed that Mottrack's hand was never far from the butt of the blaster.

As usual Mottrack totally ignored Bavril. He leant close to his second-in-command. 'Well, Commander,' he growled, 'I asked you a question.'

Bisoncawl returned his glare. 'Nothing I can't correct, sir,' he said. 'The protocols on the service robots seem to have been reset to defence posture. An oversight in maintenance, no doubt.'

'No oversight, Commander. My orders.' Mottrack kicked the remains of the service robot. 'We had a security breach on one of the lower decks last night.' Mottrack glared at Bavril. 'The security team found no one, but I'm taking no chances. Besides, it will keep my scum of a crew focused on their duties.'

Bavril could tell Bisoncawl was struggling to contain a rising anger. 'Am I to understand then, sir, that the protocols on *all* the maintenance robots have been set to hostile?'

'Yes, Commander, that is what you are to understand.'

Mottrack leaned closer, his breath hissing in Bisoncawl's ear. 'The phase one signal has been received. I need the crew to be at battle readiness. You will return to engineering and prepare the engines for warp jump.'

He straightened and turned back to his command position. 'Dismissed,' he said.

Bisoncawl saluted and turned.

'Oh, and one more thing, Commander.'

'Sir?'

'I have released all the reserve service robots into the interdeck ducting, so be careful on your way back to engineering.'

Bavril groaned inwardly. He had no doubt as to who was responsible for the security alert. Peck. Now the Cythosi would be jumpy, and that would only mean more deaths among his own people.

He followed Bisoncawl from the bridge. Mottrack's booming laugh was abruptly cut off by the command-deck door slamming shut behind them.

Ace squatted on the beach helping the gang of children rebuild the Doctor's sandcastle. The straight lines of the City of the Exxilons had now been replaced by towers and turrets, by outbuildings and keeps. It even had a moat, fed from a small stream that bubbled down the beach from the jungle.

The Doctor had tried to get the kids to build the castle according to his original plans, but he was no match for half a dozen enthusiastic twelve-year-olds and had eventually gone into a sulk. Ace looked over to where he was paddling in the shallows, his checked trousers rolled up around his knees. She smiled inwardly. He was nearly a thousand years old and he could still act like a schoolboy. Reminding herself that making sandcastles wasn't exactly the most adult of pastimes, Ace filled another bucket with sand.

The Doctor mooched through the waves wiggling his toes in the sand. He could hear the screams of the children echoing down the beach, and Ace's happy laughter. This had been a good idea. They both needed a break. He hadn't realised how used he had become to deciding her life for her; finding wrongs that needed to be righted and launching her into the midst of them. Too often she had followed him blindly into situations that he could barely control, her blind faith in him giving her courage. That blind faith had nearly got her killed by him; nearly left her as a mutilated corpse in Victorian London.

He stared down at his toes, distorted through the rippling water. It had scared him, what he had so nearly become. Scared him more than he cared to admit to Ace – or himself.

There was a splash in front of him. He looked up to see a young boy sitting in the shallow water, washing shells and placing them in a large plastic bucket. He was absorbed in his task and didn't hear the Doctor approach.

'Hello.'

The boy looked up, squinting in the bright sunlight. "Lo,' he said.

He returned to his shells. The Doctor squatted down next to him. He remembered that the boy hadn't joined in with the kite flying, preferring to scrabble through the soft sand. A loner. The Doctor let his mind drift back a long way, to his own childhood. His own magpie nature.

'I'm the Doctor. And you are...?'

'Troy.' The boy continued scrubbing at the shells. Then he stopped and stared at the Doctor. 'What sort of doctor?'

The Doctor shrugged. 'Every sort.' That seemed to satisfy Troy, and his attention wandered back to the task in hand.

The bucket was full of shells, a huge collection of different shapes and colours. The Doctor picked out a cowri-like shell, admiring it. 'You've been busy.'

Troy nodded. 'I collect them from all over the place.' He looked at the one in the Doctor's hand. 'That one's good, but it's not the best.'

He rummaged in the bucket, pulling out a long twisted shell. He swished it in the shallow water, making it glint under the suns.

'This one's the best.'

He held it out to the Doctor who took it gingerly, his brow furrowing. The shell was long and concave, the tip wickedly sharp. It was a dull ivory colour and felt cool – more like a piece of metal than a shell. The Doctor turned it over in his hand, running his fingers over the grooves in its surface.

'Where did you get this?'

'Over there.' Troy pointed to the far end of the beach. 'The sea brings all sorts of things in. They get caught up in the old shuttle wreck.'

The Doctor stared down the beach, his eyes narrowing. He turned the shell over and over in his hand.

'I don't suppose I could keep this, could I?'

Troy snatched the shell back. 'No! I told you, it's the best one!'

The Doctor fixed him with a piercing stare, his eyes twinkling wildly. 'I'll swap you for it!'

Troy eyed him suspiciously. 'Swap it for what?'

The Doctor rummaged in his pocket and pulled out a large fluff-covered toffee apple. He held it out proudly then noticed the fluff and began cleaning it in the water. Troy looked at it with distaste.

'If that's the best you can do...' He began to put the shells away.

'No! No, wait a minute!'

The Doctor proceeded to pull a variety of increasingly alien and increasingly useless objects from his pocket, his frustration mounting as each was inspected meticulously by Troy and then discarded with a curt shake of the head.

Eventually the Doctor could pull nothing more from his trouser pockets and slumped back on the sand in exasperation.

'Well, is there anything that I've got that you do want?'

Troy turned and solemnly pointed up the beach.

The Doctor sighed.

Ace watched as Troy vanished down the beach, a huge smile on his face and the Doctor's kite clutched in his arms. The other kids gathered around him like a cloud, pleading with him to let them play.

'How to win friends and influence people, eh, Professor?'

'Hmm...?'

The Doctor had his eyeglass in and was examining a shell. His brow was creased with concentration and he had a look that Ace knew all too well.

'Professor...' Her voice was accusing and the Doctor looked up.

'What...?' His face was all innocence.

'You've found something, haven't you? Some plot, some... *thing* that's going to ruin our holiday.'

'No, no, no, Ace! It's just a very unusual shell, that's all. Our young friend there found it and I'm intrigued.' He bustled over, handing Ace the eyeglass. 'If you look at the linear ridges down the convex side you'll see...'

Ace pulled her sunglasses down and peered at him over the top of them. The Doctor shuffled awkwardly and pushed the shell and eyeglass back into his pocket. 'Yes, well it'll give me something to do of an evening in the hotel.'

'Hotel?'

The Doctor clapped his hands together. 'Yes, there are a few big hotels in the colony, and, as I remember telling Tegan once, it's hardly a holiday if we just stay in the TARDIS. So pack a bag and we'll go and check in.'

Twenty minutes later Ace had changed into her cycling shorts and vest top and was struggling out of the TARDIS with a bulging rucksack full of T-shirts, shorts and underwear. She hauled the door shut and crossed to where the Doctor was waiting for her in the shade of a palm. He was looking cool and comfortable in a white linen suit, his battered straw hat perched untidily on his head.

He was sitting on his umbrella, its handle opened out flat like a shooting stick. Ace frowned at him. 'Surely you won't need that?'

The Doctor stood up and snapped the handle shut. 'You never know. All set?'

Ace nodded at the small Gladstone bag at his feet. 'Is that all you're taking?'

The Doctor beamed at her. 'Oh yes. Come on.'

He set off at a trot. Ace slung her rucksack over her shoulder, cursing at the weight, and set off after him nursing a suspicion that his bag was probably dimensionally transcendental.

The coastal path meandered through the edge of the jungle and soon the two of them were marching along arm in arm, whistling tunelessly, the Doctor doffing his hat at every passer-by and occasionally pointing out some unusual specimen of flora or fauna with his umbrella.

A sudden thundering roar made Ace look up. Through the canopy of trees she could see the boxy shape of a freighter silhouetted against the rings.

'What do they export here, Professor? Fish?'

The Doctor stared at the rapidly vanishing ship, pursing his lips. 'I doubt it. Salt, probably.'

'Salt?'

'Yes. Very important on these frontier worlds. And not always easy to get hold of.' He nodded at the sea. 'Unlimited supply here.'

He set off along the path again. Ace followed on. She never failed to be amazed at how much information the Doctor seemed to be able to cram into his head. Whether it be the complete schematics for an alien battle cruiser or a recipe for a Baked Alaska, he seemed to have useless facts for all occasions.

Soon the jungle began to give way to the edge of the colony – prefabricated buildings were being assembled by teams of service robots, the metal of their casings glinting under the twin suns. There were more and more people and before long Ace and the Doctor were walking through streets lined with market stalls and stores.

The inhabitants seemed mostly young and tanned, and Ace marvelled at how quickly she was feeling at home in this bright, lively colony. The Doctor seemed content too, peering at junk on stalls, occasionally swapping a few words with the locals, completely unfazed by the variety of life forms that swarmed around them.

The street opened abruptly into a wide square dominated by a tall statue of a woman looking over her shoulder. Water bubbled up around her feet in a constant cascade, leaving a glittering white deposit.

Ace crossed to it and read the plaque at its base.

'Lot's Wife.'

The Doctor crossed to the fountain and ran a finger over the white deposit. He peered at his finger for a moment, then stuck it in his mouth.

'Salt.'

Ace rolled her eyes.' OK, Professor. So you're right, as always.'

She spotted a ragged symbol scrawled on the clean white stone. Long red slashes of red, their outlines dripping.

'What d'you think this is, Professor?'

The Doctor bent and peered down. 'Some cabalistic symbol of sorts. Can't say I recognise the design. Curious...'

'Well, curious or not, it can wait for the moment... Now where's this hotel?'

The Doctor pointed across the square. Ace turned. Ahead of her the hotel stretched elegantly up the side of the hill, each balcony fringed with tropical plants. One side of the building faced a broad, open garden, terraced as it climbed the hillside, beyond which lay a square surrounded on three sides by imposing buildings. On its other side, the hotel stretched into a huge terrace overlooking the bay. Ace could see people seated around clusters of tables, sipping at drinks.

She turned back to the Doctor with a huge grin on her face. The Doctor extended an arm to his friend.

'Shall we check in?'

'Peck?'

Bavril's voice echoed around the hold of the Cythosi ship. 'Peck, where are you?'

There was a movement in the shadows and a thin-faced man shuffled forward.

'What are you doing here, Bavril?' Peck didn't disguise his contempt. 'It's dangerous.'

'And sneaking around restricted areas isn't? What the hell were you doing?'

'I needed to check the layout of the lower decks.' Peck thrust his jaw out defiantly. 'It was necessary.'

'Really?' Bavril grasped the front of Peck's tunic. 'The Cythosi have put all the service robots on hostile settings. Hostile! Do you know what that means?'

Peck angrily shook himself free, but his face went pale.

'How do you know that?'

'Because I work on the bridge! I hear things. You are going to get us all killed, Peck!'

'Well at least we will have *tried*!'

There was a muffled clang from the other side of the hold and the two men scurried into the shadows, pressing themselves against the wall.

The noise faded.

'I've got to go, I'll be missed.' Bavril glanced around the bay. 'No more stupid risks.'

He scurried off. Peck watched him go.

He shook his head. He was tired of waiting.

In the service tunnels beneath Coralee Control, Roz Walsh cursed as the torch slipped from her headband for the millionth time. Snatching it off the damp floor she thrust it back into position, and turned back to the power relay.

Roz was not in the best of moods. She liked the sea, she liked the sun and she had thought that Coralee was the best posting she was ever likely to be offered. What she hadn't counted on was spending most of her first month underground. What was the point of a posting to an ocean planet if you never saw the sun? But she was a senior engineer with a specialisation in power relays. The power relays were all underground and therefore so was she.

She poked a sonic probe into the coupling housing in disgust. The Coralee power grid was a mess. In her opinion the design team, headed by Phillip Garrett, should have been shot, or hung, or at the very least poked with cattle-prods. Not that the colonists shared her view. Oh no. Garrett was God as far as they were concerned. The man who, almost single-handed, had designed and built the most advanced colony in the frontier.

The engineering corps had a different opinion of him. They thought he was a jumped-up nobody who had appeared from nowhere and brown-nosed his way into a senior position. Sure, his organisational skills were impressive – he'd got the place up and running in record time – but Roz and all her colleagues knew what a rush job it had been. If any credit was due, it was due to the engineering teams who'd coped with his unreasonable schedules, who'd struggled to make his vision a reality, who regularly plugged the gaps when something went down.

Only last week a major heating conduit in central admin had blown itself apart. The police, at Garrett's suggestion, had put it down to vandalism. Roz knew this was impossible – the conduit was far too sturdy for someone to just walk in and wreck it – and besides, it was in a restricted area. Only the engineers and senior administrative staff had access.

She snorted. The police always took Garrett's line. He spent more time across the square in police HQ than he did in his own offices. Garrett was a politician at heart, not an engineer. He was shrewd, and was always willing to show his gratitude to his loyal team with a few judicious bonuses, a few glowing commendations at company dinners. He knew how to buy silence, if not love or loyalty.

Roz returned to the damaged power coupling, grinding her teeth in anger. She'd been one of the recipients of Garrett's latest round of bonuses, mouthing her thanks with all the others. It wasn't that the money wasn't useful – far from it – it was just the principle of the thing. She jabbed angrily at the fused relay. Still, with any luck she wouldn't have to put up with the man for too much longer. Holly Relf was on the planet and Roz had already made it plain to her that she was willing to jump ship. As soon as Holly got back from her assignment...

The light slipped from Roz's headband again, rolling down the access conduit.

'Goddamn it!'

Roz hurled the sonic probe away in disgust and sat back heavily, eyes closed, trying to relax. She breathed deeply, and tried to consider the cool dark as beneficial. What did she want to be up top for? It was too hot, too crowded; people crammed into shops, into bars, having nice cool drinks...

Her daydream was interrupted by a muffled thump further down the access corridor. She looked up in time to see a shadow flicker over the far wall.

'Hello?'

She peered into the darkness. There was nothing. But she was sure she had seen movement. She reached down for her fallen torch.

There was another thump. She flashed the light down the corridor, clambering to her feet. 'Jarrel, is that you?'

There were definite scufflings now. There shouldn't be anyone down here except the engineering detail – her and Jarrel – and he'd gone off shift hours ago. She began to back towards her tool kit. There was a large wrench poking out of the top and, however stupid she might feel afterwards, at the moment it was the best weapon she had.

She thought she could see movement in the shadows. Was that a person? It seemed too big, too bulky. There was a smell, musky and harsh, and a ragged, rhythmic, breathy sound. She brought the torch beam up, and screamed.

Chapter Four

The Doctor strode across the foyer of the hotel and took great delight in pressing the old-fashioned bell that sat on the reception desk. A tall, thin robot unfolded itself from underneath the desk.

'GOOD AFTERNOON, SIR. HOW MAY I HELP?'

The Doctor raised his hat. 'I'd like to book two rooms please, one for myself and one for my friend.' He waved Ace over.

The robot swivelled to look at her then swung back to the Doctor.

'CERTAINLY, SIR. WILL YOU BE STAYING LONG?'

The Doctor waved airily. 'Oh, a couple of days.'

The robot chittered to itself for a moment, then slid a large book over the desk.

'WE HAVE TWO ROOMS ON THE ELEVENTH FLOOR. IF YOU WOULD SIGN THE GUEST BOOK...'

The Doctor signed with an elaborate flourish and passed the book over to Ace.

'HOW WILL YOU BE SETTLING YOUR BILL? WE ACCEPT MOST RECOGNISED FORMS OF CURRENCY.'

The Doctor rummaged in his pocket and pulled out what looked like a small metallic scarab beetle. 'Will this do?'

The robot bleeped happily. 'THAT WILL DO NICELY, SIR.'

It whirred across to a complex terminal. The Doctor placed the 'beetle' on the desk. As Ace watched it sprouted tiny legs and scuttled over to the terminal, clambering up it and settling into a little recess. The computer hummed into life and figures flashed across a screen. Tiny lights flickered over the back of the 'beetle', then it disconnected itself, scuttled across the desk and hopped back into the Doctor's hand.

The robot nodded towards the lifts.

'YOUR ROOMS ARE THAT WAY. THE SERVICE ROBOTS WILL BE HAPPY TO TAKE YOUR LUGGAGE. HERE ARE YOUR DOOR ENTRY CODERS. ENJOY YOUR STAY AT THE CORALEE HILTON.'

'Thank you.'

The Doctor took the offered plastic cards, raised his hat once more and turned towards the lifts. Two spider-like robots scurried over and the Doctor placed his Gladstone bag on the back of one of them.

Ace eyed the other spider nervously. 'I hope they don't expect a tip.'

'All paid for.' The Doctor waggled the scarab at her. 'We won't need to pay for another thing while we're in the hotel.' He handed her keycard to her.

Ace was about to point out that he'd never seen her with a hotel mini-bar before, then decided against it. She shrugged and dumped her rucksack on the back of the other hovering robot. The two spiders scuttled up the stairs at speed. The Doctor watched them go.

'I think we'll take the lift, don't you?'

'Monsters in the service tunnels? Really, Brenda, are you taking this seriously?'

Brenda shrugged and lit up another cigarette. 'The girl's pretty shaken up, Phillip. Claims that she got a good look at it. I've got the security detail doing a sweep.'

Garrett threw his arms up in disgust. 'I don't believe this! Monsters for God's sake...'

'Well at least I feel as though I'm doing something, damn it!'

Garrett stared at her in surprise. Brenda wasn't the fiery type. She turned away. 'I'm sorry, Phillip. It's been a long day.'

'Still no news about Holly?'

Brenda shook her head and stared out of her office window

over the sea. 'The flyer is still out, but they're running low on fuel, they're going to have to come back in the next hour or so. I've put out a general bulletin asking all incoming freighters to run a sensor sweep, and I've put NavSat Nine on continuous alert. If she's out there...'

'Then they'll find her.' There was an awkward pause. Garrett shuffled uneasily. 'I'm off shift now, if you fancy a drink later...'

Brenda smiled at him. 'Thanks, Phillip, but I think I'll turn in early. I'll see you in the morning.'

Garrett nodded and opened the office door. He paused in the doorway. 'I'll ask my teams to keep a look out for anything... suspicious in the service corridors. A monster head would look good on your office wall, wouldn't it?'

With a wry smile he closed the door.

Brenda blew a cloud of blue smoke into the room, then turned her attention back to the sea.

Ace placed her pebble on the chest of drawers and then hurled herself on to a bed that was practically the size of a football pitch. Her room was huge; the bathroom alone was bigger than her mum's old flat. Plush rugs were scattered over the pale wooden floor amid tall, lush plants. A complex entertainment console was set into one wall, elegant curved wardrobes lined another.

She clambered to her feet and bounced on the bed a couple of times, giggling, then sprung off and stepped out through the picture window on to the balcony. Her room overlooked the bay. She could see the beach where they had landed. She tried to pick out the tree where the TARDIS was – she'd have to borrow the Doctor's opera glasses again. A breeze brought the smell of the sea across the bay. She breathed in deeply. This was fabulous.

Turning back into the room, she hauled her rucksack on to the bed and began pulling her clothes out. They seemed dwarfed once they were hung in the wardrobes and she was suddenly aware that everything she owned was getting tatty. She was meant to be meeting the Doctor for dinner at eight – the restaurant had looked quite posh.

Suddenly she made a decision and, snatching up her keycard, she stepped out into the corridor.

The Doctor had the room next door. She rapped on the door.

'It's open.'

The Doctor's Scottish-sounding lilt drifted from inside. Ace pressed her palm on the entry panel and the door slid open with a soft whoosh.

The Doctor was sitting on his balcony, watching the activity in the harbour. Ace crossed the room. Somehow the hat stand from the TARDIS was standing in a corner, and a small electric train set wound its way round the bed and into the bathroom. The wardrobe was full of identical sets of clothes, jackets, checked trousers; there were at least six of those blasted question-mark pullovers. She shook her head. She'd been right – that bloody bag *was* bigger on the inside. Stepping over a speeding Eurostar she joined the Doctor on the balcony.

'You've made yourself at home, I see.'

'A few creature comforts. Everything all right next door?'

Ace nodded. 'Fantastic, but I wanted to ask a favour....'

'Hmm?' He looked at her quizzically, his eyes shaded under the brim of his hat.

'I was going to pop into the town, I need something for tonight but, er, well...' She shrugged. 'I've got no dosh, Professor.'

'Ah!' The Doctor sat back in his chair, rummaged in his pocket and pulled out the scarab. 'And you'd like to borrow this.'

Ace tried to put on an endearing expression. 'I won't go berserk, Professor, honest.'

The Doctor stood up and looked at her sternly. 'If you lose this...' he broke into a huge grin '...then I'll have to steal another one!' He tapped her on the nose and held out the scarab. Before

40

Ace could reach for it the 'beetle' had hopped off his hand and attached itself to her vest, clinging there like some elaborate brooch.

'Thanks, Professor!'

Ace bounded out of the room. The Doctor watched her go and then settled back into his chair. Reaching into his pocket again, he plucked out the curious shell and placed it on the rail in front of him.

His expression darkened.

'No. Something is definitely wrong.'

The first of the suns was already sinking below the horizon when Brenda Mulholland finally turned away from the sea.

The search had been called off an hour ago and she had watched the coastguard flyer lumber back over the waves and settle on the pad, its searchlights blazing. If the colony had been bigger they might have had more search and rescue vehicles, but Earth Central had plenty of other, more important, colonies, and her request for another coastguard crew had been denied.

She snapped her computer shut angrily. Executives from Central were all too keen to take the supralight transport when they wanted a holiday, or when they wanted to impress some ambassador or other with a trip around their showcase colony, but when it came to shelling out hard cash...

More and more people came to Coralee every year, and yet the hastily assembled infrastructure was designed for a population half the current size. If ever they had a major disaster they were in real trouble.

She shut off the lights in her office and stepped out into the main control room. The dull red lights of the artificial night had just kicked in and she could see technicians swapping consoles with the next shift, handing over data-pads and pointing out anomalies to be watched. Tired people stretched and yawned and prepared to head down to the waterfront, to meet loved ones, pick up the threads of their social lives. Coralee seemed to be conducive to relationships. Brenda had performed three wedding ceremonies this month alone.

She nodded her goodnights and crossed through the security gate, her ID card bleeping softly as she checked out. She set off towards the main exit. The corridor was warm after the air-conditioned calm of the control centre. She stopped. Her apartment was a good walk away on the east side of the colony and she wasn't sure she had any food in anyway. Perhaps she'd join Garrett for that drink after all. It would be better than moping around on her own.

Hoisting her computer bag on to her shoulder she turned about and headed back the way she had come. Garrett tended to drink at Sullivan's bar on the west quay. If she cut through the lecture room she could leave the building through the loading bay and save struggling through the market.

She jogged down the stairs to the lower level and tapped her access code into the lecture room door. After the warmth of the corridor she shivered as she entered the cavernous hall. Ranks of tiered seats stretched around her in a semicircle. Coralee boasted one of the finest lecture facilities in the colonies. It was due to host a major conference for the Braxiatel Trust next year.

She closed the door, plunging the room into darkness once more. She could see the exit sign on the other door glowing from the far side of the room. She set off across the podium, using the backs of the front row seats to feel her way.

Suddenly she crashed into something and cursed as she overbalanced and tumbled to the floor, her computer flying from her hand. She struggled upright, clutching at her bruised shoulder. That would teach her to try and take short cuts. She delved into her bag and flicked her lighter into life. The flame sent huge shadows dancing over the lecture room walls. Brenda retrieved her computer from the floor. It didn't look damaged. She'd have to get Phillip to look at it when she got to the pub.

Holding the lighter high she tried to see what it was that she had tripped over. She frowned. Someone had set up a desk. The floor was littered with textbooks, maps. She had just reached down to pick up one of the books when something moved at the back of the auditorium.

'Who's that?'

The flickering light made it impossible to make anything out. Brenda began to move up the stairs.

'This is a restricted area. What the hell are you doing in here?'

She could hear something now. Breathing. Rasping and heavy. One of the shadows seemed too solid. She thrust the lighter forward and something darted through the edge of her vision. She got the impression of a rough hide. There was a smell; oily, musky.

Goose bumps suddenly ran up Brenda's spine as she recalled the description the engineer had given of the monster she'd encountered in the service tunnels. She had mentioned a smell.

Suddenly frightened, Brenda began to back slowly down the stairs, her eyes raking through the dark. The breathing seemed louder now, it seemed to be all around her.

Brenda screamed as the video wall burst into life, the InterOceanic anthem blaring from the speakers. Eyes streaming, she tried to see through the blaze of sudden light. There was a shape moving across the room, silhouetted against the screens. Brenda turned to run, but something huge and powerful slammed into her.

The Doctor stepped into the restaurant and looked quickly around for Ace. She wasn't there. Good. He hadn't wanted her to wait for him. Smoothing down his waistcoat and brushing fluff from the lapel of his burgundy jacket, he crossed to the bar and hoisted himself on to one of the stools. Catching the eye of the robot waiter he ordered himself a glass of wine and swivelled to watch the rest of the clientele.

As with all colony worlds, the bar was full of representatives of dozens of different species. Most of the humanoids were indeed human, but there was a fair percentage of Dreekans, Chimerons, Metalunans and Martians. A large pool bordered the bar, dolphins bobbing in the cool water. Elsewhere in the bar he could see a scattering of familiar alien shapes and one or two arachnid life forms that he couldn't place; and judging by the noise coming from the table tennis room there was a party of Alpha Centaurians in the hotel.

'Marvellous, isn't it?'

The Doctor turned at the sound of a plummy voice behind him. 'I'm sorry?'

A rotund man in a casual suit was lounging at a table near the bar, a bottle of wine in front of him. He waved expansively around the restaurant.

'I said it's marvellous, all this peace and harmony, all these species working together in the common pursuit of a single goal. Leisure.'

He raised his glass in a toast, took a good swig of his wine, and beckoned the Doctor over.

Plucking his own glass from the bar, the Doctor hopped off his stool and slid into a chair on the other side of the table. He held out his hand. 'How do you do. I'm the Doctor and this...' He gestured to his left and suddenly realised that Ace wasn't with him. 'This is where my young friend Ace will be joining us.'

The man shook his hand vigorously. 'Edwin Bryce. Delighted to meet you.'

He pulled his chair in closer and refilled his glass. 'Couldn't help noticing you. So few people take the time to sit and look these days.'

'Look?' The Doctor smiled apologetically. 'Look at what?'

'Anything! Everything!' Bryce tapped him on the knee. 'I took one look at you and thought, Edwin, there's a man of the world. There's a man who knows a thing or two.'

The Doctor took a sip of wine. 'You're very perceptive Mr Bryce. It wouldn't surprise me if *you'd* seen a few things in your time.'

Bryce waved his hand airily and took a huge gulp of wine. 'Well, when you've travelled the colonies as extensively as I have...'

'What brings you to Coralee, Mr Bryce?' asked the Doctor.

Bryce poured the rest of his wine into his glass and leant back in his seat, waving at the robot wine waiter for another bottle. 'I'm writing a book on the colonies, Doctor. A gazetteer. *Walking the Final Frontier; The Travels of Edwin Bryce*. I've already been published, of course. *Androgum Cookery for Novices: How to Master the Boomerang Spoon*. Perhaps you've read it?'

The Doctor shook his head. Bryce failed to disguise his disappointment.

'Ah, well – no matter.' The robot waiter arrived with a fresh bottle and Bryce took great pains to check the wine, sniffing it and sloshing it around theatrically before shooing the robot away. He snatched the Doctor's glass from him and filled it, then filled his own again. 'This new book will collect some of the fascinating stories from these colonies, both from those intrepid terraformers and from some of the aboriginal species that still exist. Coralee is the last world on my grand tour.'

He leaned forward conspiratorially. 'It's a planet with quite a history. All the neighbouring worlds have stories and legends about it, some of them quite explicit. I've seen records referring to Coralee as far out as the Cachalot system.'

The Doctor's curiosity was piqued. He fingered the shell in his jacket pocket. 'What sort of legends, Mr Bryce?'

Bryce looked over his shoulders, as if expecting someone to be lurking in the shrubbery. 'War,' he hissed. 'Violence. Genocide.' He threw back another glass of wine. 'The indigenous species here were among the most warlike that the galaxy has ever seen. Planets light years away lived in fear of them, but they seemed to spend most of their time fighting among themselves. Then, suddenly, overnight...' Bryce drew his hand across his throat. 'All of 'em. All gone.'

The Doctor frowned. 'The entire species?'

Bryce was beginning to sway in his seat. He waggled a drunken finger at the Doctor. 'All that's left are the cities, out in the sea. And for years afterwards every ship that set down on Coralee was destroyed.' He gestured upwards. 'The locals wouldn't go near the planet. For centuries no one except the Dreekans would come here at all. Until us, until the indome... intimotob...' He hiccuped. 'The unstoppable human race.'

He sloshed more wine into his glass and raised it in a toast. 'Here's to us. Here's to humans.'

The Doctor's mind was already sifting through the information he had been given. 'Do any of the legends say how these ships were destroyed?'

'Ah...' Bryce tapped his nose. 'Now you want to know about the Krill.'

'The Krill...' The Doctor's hand strayed once again to the shell. 'Yes, tell me about the Krill, Mr Bryce.'

Bryce shook his head. 'Nothing to say. There are no pictures, no fossils, just the stories of their savagery.'

The Doctor sat forward eagerly. 'Tell me the stories.'

Bryce waggled a finger at him, his other hand reaching for the bottle again. 'Ah, now you're going to have to buy the book, Doctor. Can't give away too many free samples now, can I?'

The Doctor was about to argue when he noticed Bryce staring over his shoulder, open-mouthed. The Doctor turned in his seat.

An elegant young woman stood before them, and it took the Doctor a couple of seconds to realise that it was Ace. She was wearing a long dress of some silk-like material, deep blue fading to sea green, that wound around her in a delicate swirl. Her shoulders were bare, a fine filigree of shells trailing around her neck and down one arm. Her hair was wound in an elaborate bun, pinned with another shell. She smiled shyly.

'Is this all right, Professor?'

The Doctor rose to his feet and beamed at her. 'Wicked.'

He turned back to the table. 'Mr Bryce, may I introduce my young friend Ace?'

Bryce rose and took Ace's hand, kissing it with a flourish. 'Charmed. Will you please join us, Miss Ace?'

Ace curled herself elegantly into one of the wicker chairs as Bryce relieved a passing waiter of another glass and poured her a drink. The Doctor settled down next to her.

'Mr Bryce has just been telling me some of the legends of this planet, it's really quite intriguing.'

Ace stared at the red-faced man in front of her. 'Are you an expert, Mr Bryce?'

'Oh yes, my dear. I have quite a reputation, you know. And please, call me Edwin.'

They continued to talk about the planet's history, the Doctor trying to prise more information out of Bryce, the writer becoming more evasive and more drunk. Ace began to tire of the conversation.

Suddenly there was a commotion at the bar. Ace turned to see two of the spider robots grappling with a bare-chested Dreekan man. He was waving his arms wildly and had daubed the walls with a garish red swirl.

'Extraordinary.' The Doctor peered at the swirl with interest.

'Oh, a little local bother, Doctor. Nothing to worry about.' Bryce waved his hands dismissively. 'The local religious zealots flex their muscles now and again. Keeps the constabulary on their toes.'

'There is a local religion?' The Doctor leant forward inquisitively. Ace nudged him. 'We were going to eat, remember?' she whispered.

The Doctor pulled out his pocket watch and stared at it in shock. 'I had no idea it had got so late.' He jumped to his feet and shook Bryce vigorously by the hand. 'Well, fascinating as this has been, Mr Bryce, I'm afraid that we have a table waiting, so if you will excuse us...'

Bryce's face fell. 'Oh, what a shame. I was going to see if I could tempt you to a game of chess...' He pulled a small chess set from under the table and Ace watched the Doctor's face light up. She quickly caught him by the sleeve and flashed Bryce a dazzling smile.

'Another time perhaps. Thank you for a fascinating evening.'

Hanging on to the Doctor's arm, she dragged him into the restaurant. 'Where did you find the lush, Professor?'

The Doctor stared back into the bar. 'He found me, actually.'

The head waiter, a rotund Frenchman, bustled over and ushered them to their table, passing the Doctor the wine list while holding the chair for Ace. The Doctor had booked them a table on the terrace. The clink of glasses and the murmur of quiet conversation rose from a dozen or so tables.

Ace stared at the sunset. One of the suns had vanished completely, the other was a pale orange orb on the horizon. The sky was a patchwork of colour, the rings like dull gold.

Ace was suddenly aware of the Doctor looking at her. The light was reflected in his eyes making them sparkle and dance. He nodded at her dress.

'If this is how you're going to dress from now on, then I'm going to have to find a better calibre of villain for us to fight.'

Ace blushed. 'You don't look too bad yourself.' She ran her hand over the shoulder of his jacket. 'I thought you only wore brown.'

The Doctor looked hurt. 'I'll have you know that back on Gallifrey I was renowned for my sartorial elegance!'

Ace held his gaze for a moment, then the two of them dissolved into giggles.

A waiter scurried over and looked at them expectantly. Ace wiped the tears from her eyes and picked up her menu. 'I think we'd better order, don't you?'

* * *

The meal was one of the best Ace had ever tasted. Not surprisingly, Coralee's oceans provided a wealth of seafood and she and the Doctor tried seaweeds and shellfish, exotic undersea salads and sweet corals, washed down with a delicate sea-green wine. As a small robot cleaned away the last of their plates Ace pulled her chair over to the Doctor's side and the two of them stared out over the rolling ocean.

Sunset had given way to a velvet night, the moons of Coralee distant and bright, the rings – silver-blue now – dominating the sky.

They sat in silence for a while, sipping their wine and watching the stars, then the Doctor said, 'You don't regret it, do you?'

Ace looked at him, puzzled. 'Regret it?'

'Coming with me. Leaving Iceworld. Heading for Perivale by the scenic route.'

Ace laughed. 'Are you kidding! What on earth made you think that, Professor?'

The Doctor didn't look up. 'Because sometimes I forget how dangerous my life can be. Because sometimes I just drag people into the vortex before thinking about what that can do to them. And... because sometimes people die.'

He looked at her now. 'I nearly got you killed, you know. I nearly killed you...'

'Stop!' Ace held her hand up. 'Professor. The last three years have been... well, I still can't believe what they've been like. You've taken me to my past and my future, you've shown me planets that I couldn't have begun to dream about. I've met monsters and criminals, I've held Excalibur...I've travelled in time! Do you really think that if someone had given me some warning, that if someone had sat me down and told me a strange man was going to turn up in a police box, and he was going to take me travelling in time and space, I would have said no?' She squeezed his arm. 'Yes, there are dangers, but... for God's sake, people die crossing the road. Life's too short to live like that. I stay on my own terms, Professor. If ever I've got a problem with it, I'll let you know.'

She reached for her glass and held it up, the delicate green wine sparkling in the ringlight. 'To us, Professor. Champions of Time and Space.'

The crystal glasses clinked and the Doctor smiled.

They chatted on, about adventures and people, about friends, and the atmosphere that had dogged their relationship since they had left Whitechapel finally dispersed. At last, Ace rose from her seat and stretched. The food, wine and atmosphere of Coralee had finally caught up with her. 'I think I'm going to call it a night, Professor.'

She leant down and gave him a peck on the cheek. 'Thank you, for a fabulous holiday. This place is absolutely perfect.'

The Doctor watched her make her way through the restaurant, an elegant young woman far removed from the fiery teenager he had first met. He placed his glass on the table and crossed to the railing of the terrace. He stared down at the sea, watching the patterns in the waves.

The head waiter appeared at his shoulder.

'Was everything satisfactory, sir?'

The Doctor nodded. 'Oh yes, very nice, thank you.'

The Frenchman joined him at the railing. 'Good weather tomorrow.'

'Really, how can you tell?'

The head waiter pointed up at the rings. 'When they're that colour, we always have weeks of good weather. It's a sure sign.'

The Doctor turned and stared him full in the face, his eyes a steely silver-blue like the rings.

'Oh no. You're wrong,' he said. 'There's a storm coming.'

Chapter Five

Ace awoke early. The sun streamed in through the window, seagulls screeched from the harbour. She lay in the huge bed for a while listening to the sounds of the colony drift into her room, enjoying the opportunity to lie in.

Yawning, she slid from the bed and padded over to the bathroom. A note had been slid under her door. She reached down and unfolded it.

Gone for a wander. I expect we've got different itineraries.
See you for dinner tonight.
The Doctor.

Ace grinned. That was the Doctor's way of saying that he had things to do and didn't want her in the way. Still, it suited her. She fancied exploring on her own.

She showered quickly and wandered down to the restaurant in search of breakfast. Once again the Doctor's scarab credit card seemed to have worked wonders and waiters scurried around her as if she was royalty.

Draining the last of her coffee she strolled out into the suns. The island was abuzz with traders and tourists, the beach already full of holidaymakers. With a grumbling roar the yellow shape of the coastguard flyer swooped low over the colony and out to sea. Ace frowned. They obviously had a problem somewhere. It was difficult to imagine tragedy in this vibrant place.

Pulling her sunglasses from the top of her head, she meandered down to the waterfront, rubbing the sleep from her eyes. The harbour was awash with boats of different shapes and sizes – trawlers, tugs, pleasure cruisers. A huge salt processor drifted out on the horizon. There was a crowd at the end of one of the jetties, and with nothing better to do Ace wandered over.

The crowd was gathered around a small submarine. The crew were setting up a gangplank to the jetty. Ace suddenly felt a hand clamp on her shoulder.

'Good morning, my dear.'

Ace groaned inwardly. Bryce. She slid out from under his hand. 'Wotcha, how's the head?'

Bryce shook his head dismissively. 'I'm fine, my dear. It takes more than a few bottles of cheap colony plonk to dampen my spirits. Besides, I've got work to do. Lots of research.' He gestured at the submarine. 'Are you joining us? Exploring the ruins, delving into the past?'

Ace was about to decline politely when her eye was caught by the man clambering out of the sub. He was about her age, tall and slim – Indian by the look of him – muscles rippling under his vest. He looked over at her and smiled.

Ace patted Bryce on the arm. 'I may well be, Mr Bryce. I may well be.'

Bryce followed her eyeline. 'Ah, young Rajiid. Our captain.' He waved at the young Indian. 'Rajiid, come and say hello to our new guest.'

Rajiid hopped up on to the jetty and sauntered over, grinning. 'Who have you found to bother now, Edwin?'

'Bother? My dear young man, Miss Ace is a keen explorer and companion of an excellent fellow by the name of the Doctor.' He looked around in surprise. 'Where is the Doctor by the way? I wouldn't have thought he'd want to miss this.'

'Oh he'll catch us up later, don't you worry.' Ace held out a hand to Rajiid. 'Hi.'

The submarine pilot shook it firmly. 'What brings you to Coralee, Miss Ace?'

'Not a lot, and it's just Ace.' She nodded at the sub. 'Does that make you a scientist?'

Bryce laughed. 'Him? No, he's an entrepreneur. Now if you will excuse me, I must get my usual seat.'

He bustled off down the gangplank. Ace looked after him, puzzled. 'What did he mean, an entrepreneur?'

'He means that I saw an opportunity and took it. Tourists are flocking here so we set up a tourist attraction.' He nodded at the tall blond guy helping people down the gangplank. 'Greg and I do tours of the ruins. The mysteries of ancient Coralee. The sub's not big but she does the job.' He grinned at her cheekily. 'Fancy a trip around the bay? On the house, of course.'

Ace nodded. With no monsters to fight and the Doctor out of her hair until dinner, a day with a gorgeous bloke seemed just the thing. 'Why not.'

The two of them walked over to the sub. 'Is it just the two of you running it?' asked Ace.

'Three.' Rajiid corrected her. 'R'tk'tk is our tour guide.'

'R'tk'tk?' Ace looked around the jetty. 'I don't see him.'

'That's because you're looking the wrong way.'

Rajiid pointed over the edge of the jetty. In the clear blue water a dolphin floated near the bow of the sub. As Ace knelt down it swam over to her. Its grey skin glistened in the morning light. Ace could see a tiny headset set into the skull behind the dolphin's ear. A translator unit. The Doctor had told her about the cetacean life forms that had settled on the colonies. Earth was far too polluted for them these days, and dolphins and whales comprised nearly a quarter of the colonists on ocean planets.

The dolphin squeaked at her, and Ace felt a slight tingling in the back of her neck as the telepathic translators kicked in.

'I'm the brains of the outfit, darling. Greg and Rajiid are just the brawn.'

She shrugged. 'Nice brawn though.'

The dolphin gave a series of harsh clicks. 'All right if you like that sort of thing. Give me a nice set of fins any day.'

R'tk'tk turned to Rajiid. 'Hull seems fine. That boat yard may be full of crooks but they seem to know their job. Are we ready to go yet? Tides on the turn, you know.'

'OK, OK!' Rajiid ushered Ace over to the waiting submarine. 'He's terribly bossy. Gets it from his mother.'

Ace bounded down the gangplank and clambered through the hatch. The sub was about the size of a small bus. Everything was arranged around a central airlock bordered with portholes. Two long windows ran down the curved metal walls and rows of seats lined the central aisle. The cabin in the nose contained two chairs for the pilots and was crammed with controls. Greg had already squeezed himself into one of the control seats and had started powering up the engines.

R'tk'tk suddenly popped up out of the airlock, sending water sloshing across the floor.

'Ladies and gentlemen, if you would please take your seats and strap yourselves in, we will be leaving shortly.'

Ace looked around. To her dismay the only free seat was alongside Bryce. Most of the other passengers were human, but the two rear seats housed a couple of the octopoid aliens that the Doctor had told her were from Alpha Centauri.

The two aliens were chattering excitedly in shrill, squeaky tones, trying to ignore Bryce who frequently interrupted with fascinating facts about Coralee.

Rajiid clambered down the ladder behind Ace. 'Put the headphones on,' he whispered. 'That way you get R'tk'tk's commentary instead of Edwin's version.'

He winked at her and pulled the heavy hatch closed. Ace slid into her seat, watching the Indian as he clambered into the pilot's position.

Ace could see Bryce turning to talk to her. Quickly she clicked her harness home and pulled the headset from the back of the seat in front of her, slipping it over her ears. Bryce mouthed something at her but she shook her head and pointed at her headphones. There was a slight vibration and Ace pressed her nose to the window as the sub spiralled away from the jetty and into the depths of the ocean.

* * *

The Doctor stared up at the buildings that surrounded the elegant square on three sides, dominating the colony. They looked just like the hotels which dotted the island; the same bland, welcoming architecture. Only a few discreet signs gave them away: Central Administration – Coralee; Soames Institute for Historic-Scientific Research; Coralee Medi-Centre. Evidently nothing here was allowed to disturb the languid-yet-exhilarating, tropical-yet-tame ambience of the island.

He had already identified the window of the control centre and peered at it through his opera glasses. Now his problem was how to get past the security guard who sat hunched behind his desk, sweltering in his uniform.

A small tabby cat that had been sunning itself on the wall when the Doctor arrived was now curling its way between his legs, purring happily. The Doctor scratched its head idly.

'Now how am I going to get in there, hmm?'

He patted his pockets and pulled out his UNIT pass. It wasn't going to be much use to him here, but at least it had a photo of his current incarnation on it; something that the Brigadier had insisted on.

A noise from the other side of the square made him look up. A tubby, middle-aged man in a shabby cotton jacket and straw hat was making his way past the fountain, scrabbling in a heavy leather bag. Papers and folders were hauled out as the man searched for something. 'For God's sake! Where is the blasted thing?'

The man stopped and squashed a pair of half-moon glasses on to his nose. With a cry of triumph he held a small plastic card aloft, clamped it between his teeth and resumed his journey across the square, trying to push the assorted folders and documents back into his bag.

The Doctor looked from the man to the door of the admin building and back again. If he timed this just right...

He reached into his pocket and pulled out a small clockwork mouse. He wound it up and waggled it at the cat. 'Nice kitty.'

The cat looked at him expectantly. The Doctor placed the mouse on the floor, did a quick calculation, and let it go. Mouse and cat raced across the square, the clockwork motor whirring furiously. The man barely had time to register the noise before the cat thundered between his legs, batting gleefully at its new toy.

With a loud thump and muffled obscenities the man crashed to the dusty ground, papers scattering everywhere as his bag split open.

The Doctor was at his side in a moment. 'Are you all right?' He hauled the man upright and began dusting him down with a small clothes brush.

'Yes. Yes I'm fine, thank you. Blasted animal.' He scrabbled for his spectacles.

The Doctor scurried around the square, plucking papers from the ground and piling them into the man's arms. 'Well, I must rush.' Doffing his hat, the Doctor vanished into the foyer of the admin block, the man's ID card clutched in one hand, some scissors and a tube of glue in the other.

The guard nodded as the Doctor entered the building. The Doctor smiled broadly. 'Good morning.' The ID card bleeped softly as he passed through the turnstiles.

'Excuse me, sir.'

The Doctor's heart sank as he heard the guard get up. He turned with his most innocent expression. 'Yes?'

The guard took the ID from him and clipped it on to his lapel. 'If you could wear your ID at all times while in the building.'

The Doctor beamed at him. 'Of course. Silly of me.'

He trotted off down the corridor. As he rounded the corner he could hear heated voices from behind him.

'But for heaven's sake man, you see me come in here every day!'

'I'm sorry, Professor, but those are the rules. I can't let you on the premises without a valid ID, unless you are signed in by somebody.'

With a pang of guilt the Doctor peered down at his stolen ID. The picture from his UNIT card was slipping. He readjusted it, getting glue all over his fingers. Wiping his hands on his handkerchief, he scuttled away.

The building was quiet. Most of the offices were still empty. The Doctor scampered down the stairs to the lower levels. Checking that no one was around he pulled a hairpin from his pocket and within moments an office door opened with a soft click. The Doctor slipped inside and settled himself in front of a computer terminal. He hit a key and the machine chattered into life.

'Now then.'

His hands were a blur over the keyboard. He started his search with legends of the Krill and then began to expand it outward, accessing data from all over the colony.

He scribbled frantically in his diary, jotting down anything he could find about the Krill, noting with interest a big archaeological expedition currently based off the coast. He cross-referenced his data to the coastguard records. When the video files from the coastguard drone came up he stopped, leaning close to the screen, scrutinising every frame. Suddenly he heard something, a movement in the corridor. He quickly printed out all the data on the dig then, as an afterthought created a new ID card for himself – Dr John Smith, senior investigator for InterOceanic. Shutting the computer down, the Doctor slipped over to the door. There were scrapings outside it, and something else. A smell. The Doctor frowned.

Carefully he eased the door open and peered out into the gloomy corridor. The smell was harsh in his nostrils and he could hear laboured breathing. One of the shadows detached itself from the wall. The Doctor could hear it scraping along the corridor.

He tried to peer after it, but the door creaked sharply and the shape gave a harsh growl and lumbered off.

The Doctor stepped out into the corridor and stared after the mysterious shadow. He was about to set off after it when a groan drifted through the doorway.

The Doctor stepped through the door, flicking the lights on. He was in a lecture room, ranks of seats surrounding him in an elegant semicircle. A middle-aged woman was struggling to her feet. The Doctor hurried over to her.

'Let me help.' He caught her arm as she staggered, and led her over to one of the chairs. She slumped into it, clutching at her head. The Doctor brushed her hand away and made a quick examination of her scalp.

'The skin's not broken, but you're going to have quite a lump.' He took a glass from the lectern and filled it with water. Pulling his handkerchief from his pocket he dipped it in the water and pressed the cloth to the back of the woman's head. She winced. 'Thank you, Mr...'

'Doctor.' The Doctor beamed at her. 'Doctor John Smith, Senior Investigator, InterOceanic.'

'Brenda Mulholland, colony co-ordinator.' Brenda held her hand out and the Doctor shook it vigorously.

'Who did this to you?'

Brenda shook her head. 'I didn't see...'

The door to the lecture room suddenly pushed open.

'Brenda?'

She looked up. 'Phillip...'

The big man crossed to her side. 'What the hell happened to you?'

Brenda smiled grimly. 'Our mysterious monster took a dislike to me.'

The Doctor frowned. 'Monster?'

The man rose, peering at the Doctor suspiciously. 'Who the blazes are you?'

Brenda rose unsteadily to her feet. 'This is Dr Smith, Phillip. Doctor, Phillip Garrett, senior engineer.'

The Doctor doffed his hat cheerily. Garrett eyed him curiously. 'What brings you to Coralee, Doctor?'

'Oh, this and that.'

Garrett was about to question him further when Brenda suddenly swayed unsteadily.

The Doctor grasped her by the shoulders. 'I think we'd better get you somewhere more comfortable, don't you?'

Brenda nodded. 'My office.'

With Garrett following, the Doctor steered her out of the room and towards the lift.

People were beginning to drift in to work, coffee cups clutched in their hands, weary hellos being called through the corridors. They stared curiously as the Doctor led Brenda Mulholland by the arm into the lift. With a swift whir it sped them to the top floor, to the control centre. Brenda pushed open the door to her office. The Doctor could hear raised voices inside it.

'Blasted impudence of the man! He sees me every day. I've a good mind to talk to his superiors!' The man from the square.

'He is only doing his job, Professor.'

'Damn it, so am I, and I've got more than enough problems with the dig without your security people compounding them!'

'Oh come now, Professor MacKenzie...'

'What the devil is going on?' The secretary looked up with relief as Brenda pushed open the door.

'Professor MacKenzie has had a little trouble with security, ma'am. He lost his ID card...'

'Damn it, I did not lose it, I...'

'Professor!' Brenda's voice was like a whipcrack. 'I've more important problems than you to worry about at the moment, if you don't mind.' She pushed past him to her desk, and called Garrett over. 'Phillip, I want a security detail out here now.' As the two of them crowded over the communicator, MacKenzie rounded on the Doctor.

The Doctor scurried forward and shook him warmly by the hand. 'Delighted to meet you, Professor. I'm the Doctor.'

'Doctor...?'

'Just Doctor. The work you are doing out at the ruins looks most interesting.'

MacKenzie beamed, his face softening. 'Ah, so you know of our work. Well... Doctor... our latest findings are really quite fascinating...'

'Yes, I've been studying your notes.' The Doctor pulled his printout on the dig from his pocket. 'These inscriptions that you've found, some primitive history do you think?'

'Undoubtedly, but if you study the culture as a whole...'

There was a cough behind them. The Doctor turned. Brenda was staring at them over the top of her spectacles. 'If you two have quite finished with the science seminar. Doctor, why wasn't I informed of your arrival?'

The Doctor looked apologetic. 'I'm sorry you weren't told Miss Mulholland, but when we received the video data from the wreck...'

'You've seen that?' Garrett looked concerned.

'Yes, Mr Garrett.' The Doctor tried to sound officious. 'Passed on from Earth Central. They are most concerned. I'd like to get a look at the wreck as soon as possible.'

'You've some idea what caused those marks?' Garrett looked at him suspiciously.

The Doctor held his gaze. 'I've a few ideas, but I would really like to say no more until I've had a chance to confirm my suspicions.' He turned to MacKenzie. 'I'd like to look at your site as well, if I may, Professor.'

The Professor nodded enthusiastically. 'Yes. Yes, of course.'

'Good.' Brenda pushed open the door to the control centre. 'That solves the problem of transport for you, Doctor. The Professor has a skimmer heading out in the next half-hour. You can make a detour to the *Hyperion Dawn,* can't you, Alex?'

'Yes, yes. Come along, Doctor. I'll introduce you to my crew.'

Grasping the Doctor by the arm, the Professor began to bustle towards the lift.

'Doctor...' Brenda was framed in the doorway of the control centre. 'A friend of mine is still missing from that wreck. If you find anything, anything at all, you will report back to me immediately?'

The Doctor caught her gaze and nodded, then the door to the lift slid shut.

MacKenzie and the Doctor walked quickly through the now-bustling marketplace towards the harbour, the Professor babbling excitedly about the dig. The Doctor smiled inwardly. He began to wonder if he need have bothered about trying to prise information from the computer. The Professor was anything but reticent.

Eventually MacKenzie stopped and gestured proudly to the end of the jetty.

'There she is, Doctor. The *Zodiac*.'

Even among the multitude of craft in the docks, the *Zodiac* was impressive. More submersible than boat, the slender lines of its hull glinted under the suns. The Doctor was about to make a comment when something large and mechanical clattered over the bow. 'Ah, there's Q'ilp.' The Professor waved frantically and raced off down the jetty.

The Doctor followed, staring in fascination at the mechanical monstrosity that clicked its way over the deck on six delicate legs. He could see a dolphin shape nestled in the spider-like exoskeleton and two pincer arms waved in front of it, clutching a variety of tools. There was something sticking out of the blowhole in the top of the dolphin's head. As the Doctor got closer he realised with surprise that it was a cigar.

MacKenzie beckoned him over. 'Doctor, may I introduce my assistant, Q'ilp.'

One of the mechanical arms plucked out the cigar. 'Assistant?

Dogsbody more like it. Be warned, Doctor, he'll have you up to your neck in it before you can blink.'

MacKenzie tutted.'Come, come. Now, are we ready to go yet?'

'Some of us have been ready for the last half-hour.' The dolphin stubbed his cigar out on the jetty wall.

'Yes, yes, yes. All right. I had to get my seasick pills, didn't I.' MacKenzie bustled up the gangplank.'Come along, Doctor. We should get going.'

The Doctor followed him and settled into a seat in the control cabin as Q'ilp clicked his way along the jetty, the mechanical arms unhooking magnetic cleats. As the Doctor watched, the spider shape lowered itself on to its 'knees' and the dolphin slipped into the cool waters of the harbour. Moments later there was the roar of powerful engines and the *Zodiac* powered away from the colony.

Mottrack sat in the moist gloom of the interrogation cells. In front of him the scattered remains of one of his Zithra prisoners quivered in the dark. Mottrack enjoyed interrogating Zithra. They were always so... responsive. He twisted one of the creature's bioelectric implants off its head, watching with morbid satisfaction as it twitched and drooled on the blood-splattered floor.

The creature hadn't told him anything useful, but then Mottrack hadn't really been after anything specific. The prisoners in the holding cells were there more as a diversion than for any strategic value.

Bisoncawl didn't approve of course, but that was why Bisoncawl would never command a ship of his own. Too soft, too lenient. Mottrack twisted the implant savagely and with a harsh rattle the Zithra shuddered and died, the light fading from the metallic sheen of its eyes.

A guard appeared in the doorway.

'Yes?' Mottrack snarled.

'There is an incoming coded message, General. For your eyes only.'

'Route it through to my console here.'

Mottrack threw the implant to one side and wiped his hands on his overalls. He turned to the communications station, brushing the Zithra's head aside. The cell filled with static. Mottrack leaned close to the speaker, drinking in the information.

The com system went quiet and he leant back in his chair, pulling at his beard. Unexpected developments. Investigators from InterOceanic. Phase two brought forward.

He slammed his fist down and gave a guttural laugh of triumph. No more skulking in the dark. The battle could start.

He opened the cell door and bellowed at the guard.

'Tell Commander Bisoncawl that I want warp power in two cycles.'

The guard saluted stiffly and vanished into the fog of the corridor. Mottrack turned back to the cells. He would celebrate with another interrogation.

Chapter Six

Ace had watched the gentle green of the ocean give way to a darker, more mysterious blue as the sub spiralled deeper and deeper. Eventually the exterior floods had kicked in and a different world was revealed. Now she was lost in a kaleidoscope of plant life and fish – and the towering structures of an enormous city.

With R'tk'tk's commentary in her ears, she stared out at streets and colonnades that stretched for miles across the sandy sea floor. She had been expecting the suggestion of a city, a few impressions in the sand; maybe a ruined wall or two, but this... She shook her head in amazement.

'Impressive, isn't it?'

Rajiid was at her shoulder. Ace pulled off her headphones. 'How much of this is there?'

Rajiid shrugged. 'Difficult to say. Until the first engineers came down to set up the reactor we didn't even know the cities were here. As far as we can make out they're all over the planet.'

'A huge empire, hidden from human gaze...' Bryce gave a deep theatrical sigh. 'What secrets these stones could impart if only they had a voice.'

Rajiid rolled his eyes. 'He'll go on like this for hours,' he whispered. 'He's been down every day for the past week. Not that we can get him to go out in a suit, mind you. The closest Mr Bryce gets to water is soda in his whisky.'

Ace grinned and turned back to the window.

With a slosh of water, R'tk'tk suddenly popped up through the open lock. Rajiid looked at him in surprise. 'Hey, boss, what's up?'

R'tk'tk beckoned Rajiid over. Ace strained to hear what they were saying.

'Getting something on my transmitter,' the dolphin chirruped.

'Sounds like an InterOceanic beacon, but it's faint.'

Rajiid pulled himself back into the nose of the sub. 'Anything, Greg?'

The big Australian held his hand briefly up for quiet. His fingers danced over the controls of the com system and after a moment he nodded.

'R'tk'tk's right. It's a standard InterOceanic distress beacon, broadcasting on a very narrow band. It must be that pod they've been looking for. Signal's almost too faint to pick up. We're lucky to find it.'

Rajiid slid into his chair and snapped home his harness.

'OK, Greg, get me a bearing. R'tk'tk, get out there and see if you can spot the pod. Keep an open com channel.'

The dolphin vanished into the dark.

'Everyone in the back, strap in and keep your eyes peeled.'

The sub banked sharply and searchlights lanced out into the dark water. Ace watched as R'tk'tk became a dark blur circling in front of them, darting through the ruins of the city. She strained her eyes in an effort to spot the pod in the tangle of ancient stone, but the lights kept throwing long confusing shadows across the seabed and the glinting of thousands of fish kept distracting her.

There was a sudden cry from up front.

'Found her!' There was a series of excited clickings from R'tk'tk's communicator.

Ace pressed her nose to the window. The dolphin was circling a dull grey sphere that nestled in the sand. As the sub dropped lower Ace could see ragged tears along the pod's skin, huge dents in its hull. A small river of bubbles streamed from one side of it.

'Dear God...' Rajiid had gone pale.

Greg pointed at a tangle of torn metal on the pod's hull. 'No wonder the signal's weak. Look at the communications relay! Those pods are meant to be indestructible. What the hell could have done that?'

Rajiid shook his head slowly, then regained his composure. 'The docking ring looks sound. Let's see if we can get a link-up.'

The sub dropped lower, engines whining as Rajiid tried to line up the airlock. R'tk'tk darted between the two craft, barking instructions. There was a sudden clang and the sub lurched as locking clamps snapped home.

Rajiid and Greg unclipped themselves from their seats and crossed to the lock. There was a sharp hiss as the pressure equalised and Rajiid unclamped the hatch.

The inside of the pod was dark, and there was a sharp smell of something rotting. Rajiid peered nervously inside. 'Hello...'

There was no sound from the interior.

He reached behind him. 'Somebody get me some light.'

Ace unhooked a heavy rubber torch and handed it over. Rajiid snapped it on, playing the powerful beam over the inside of the pod. 'We've got a survivor!' Ace and Greg crowded at his shoulder. The woman was huddled in a corner, her breathing fast and shallow.

Suddenly her eyes snapped open and she began to scream.

And scream.

And scream.

The Doctor stood on the deck of the *Hyperion Dawn*, steadying himself with his umbrella against the swell of the ocean. A stiff breeze was blowing in, flecking the sea with white foam. He stared down at the holes torn in the deck plates. MacKenzie was crouched next to them, running his hands over the shredded metal.

'From the way this is folded it must have been done from underneath!'

He was incredulous.

The Doctor stared out to sea. 'Are there any indigenous predators that could do this, Professor?'

MacKenzie shook his head. 'There are a few primitive

cetacean life forms, but no... nothing that could do this.'

The Doctor crossed the deck and hauled himself into the control cabin. MacKenzie followed him. The control console was wrecked, instrumentation smashed and twisted, the walls buckled and scarred. The Doctor bent and ran his fingers over the floor. They came away sticky with blood. MacKenzie covered his mouth. 'Oh, my God.'

There was a cry from outside. Q'ilp was bobbing in the water at the platform's stern.

'What do you make of this, Doctor?'

The Doctor crossed to the hollow where the escape bubble had nestled. The breeze brought a fetid smell across the deck. His nose wrinkled. The pod-release mechanism was covered with a thick black ooze that had splattered across the deck. Pulling a small bottle from his pocket the Doctor scooped up some of the slime. He held it up, raising his eyebrows quizzically at MacKenzie.

'I found this as well.' Q'ilp flicked his head and tossed a small metal container on to the deck. 'It was hooked on to the hull, well below the water line.'

MacKenzie went to retrieve the container, but the Doctor stopped him.

'Just a moment, Professor.'

He delved into his jacket pocket and pulled out a small gun-like device. He pressed the trigger and the machine crackled like a machine gun.

MacKenzie was puzzled. 'Radioactive?'

The Doctor nodded.

'But why would there be a radioactive source attached to the bottom of the platform?'

The Doctor said nothing. Suddenly he crossed back to the cabin. Its metal walls were criss-crossed with deep, narrow welts. The Doctor reached into his pocket and pulled out the shell that Troy had given him. He leant forward and drew the shell along one of the tears, then stepped back and pushed it on to the end of his fingertip.

MacKenzie's jaw dropped. 'You're not serious...'

'I'm afraid I am, Professor. I think an old predator has woken up, and I think it's hungry...'

Ace pulled the blanket over the woman and smoothed the hair back from her head. She looked up at Rajiid. 'She's sleeping now.'

Rajiid nodded. 'The shot I gave her should keep her calm until we get back to the colony.' He lifted up the woman's identity tag. He turned to Greg. 'See if you can raise control. Let them know that we've found the pod, and Holly Relf with it.'

'Rajiid...' Ace straightened. 'What do you think happened?'

Rajiid shook his head. 'I don't know.' He looked over to where Bryce was writing furiously in his notebook. 'But I'm not sure I buy Mr Bryce's story of ancient aliens.'

'The Doctor will know.'

'Your friend?'

Ace nodded.

'Well, we'd better get talking to him then.'

Rajiid had turned to get back into his chair when R'tk'tk suddenly surged upwards into the sub, sending water cascading over the floor.

'R'tk'tk! What in God's name...?'

'There's something out there!' The dolphin was almost screaming. 'I can sense it. All the other fish, they're all gone. Shut the hatch. Get us out of here, Rajiid.'

'R'tk'tk...'

'NOW!'

There was stunned silence in the sub for a second, then Greg gave a cry from the control cabin. 'Rajiid, you'd better get up here.'

The Indian darted forward to stand behind Greg. 'Ace, get that hatch closed.'

Ace struggled with the heavy hatch, slipping on the wet floor. 'Bryce, give me a hand here.'

The hatch slammed down and she and Bryce heaved on the locking handles. R'tk'tk lay panting on the floor. Ace could hear Rajiid's voice: 'I don't believe it! Go active on the sonar.'

Ping.

The noise echoed around the sub like a gunshot.

'Is that one creature?'

'Rajiid, what the hell is going on?' Ace could hear the panic in her own voice. The Alpha Centaurians began to chatter nervously to each other. Ace couldn't hear herself think.

'Will you two shut up!?'

Ping.

She crossed to the cabin. The two pilots were staring at a dot on the screen.

'Look at the speed it's moving.' Greg was shaking his head in disbelief.

'It's more than one signal.'

'Rajiid...' Ace shook him. 'Talk to me.'

Ping.

'Two thousand metres and closing.'

'Rajiid, will you get us the hell out of here!' R'tk'tk's translators screamed at the back of Ace's head.

Rajiid slipped into his chair and the motors whined into life.

Ping.

'One hundred and fifty metres and closing.'

'Everyone, strap in. Someone get a harness on R'tk'tk.'

Ace stumbled backwards as the sub lurched forward.

Ping.

'One hundred metres and closing.'

Ace struggled to strap herself in. Holly Relf started to scream again.

Ping.

'Fifty metres.'

'Dear God they're everywhere!'

Ping.

'Ten metres!'

Ping.

'Holy...'

Ping ping pingpingping...

Ace caught a sudden glimpse of claws scything through the water, then the sub lurched and all she could hear was screaming.

Part Two

'Swim,' said the momma fishy, 'swim if you can...'

Chapter Seven

Ace's world had become a kaleidoscope of noise and terror. The sub spiralled towards the seabed, throwing its occupants around like dice in a cup. She tumbled backwards as the sub lurched to one side. She could hear harsh shrieks and scrapings, and the water outside the windows boiled and heaved. The little craft pitched again and she was flung against the hull, her face pressed up against one of the windows.

She gave a gasp of pure horror as one of the things that was attacking them loomed up through the gloom. The creature was huge, its skin plated and ribbed, spines and bristles cresting over its head and down its back. Its eyes blazing with malevolence, it leered at her through the window. The mouth was a vast distended maw. Ace was close enough to see down the gaping throat. She felt sick.

The monster seemed enraged by the sight of her. Its claws raked out, slamming against the hull. Water from a dozen tiny punctures suddenly sprayed across the deck. Ace gasped as the freezing water hit her.

'Rajiid!' she screamed at the struggling pilot. 'We're leaking!' She braced herself against a bulkhead and desperately tried to staunch the flow of water with her hands. There was another rending shriek as the creatures tore at the skin of the submarine, their claws skittering across the metal.

Rajiid was suddenly at her side, an aerosol can in one hand. He pulled her hands out of the way and directed the nozzle at the hull. A thin spray of foam spattered over the metal. Within seconds, it was solid.

There was a cry from Bryce as the floor at his feet buckled and bulged. He curled into a ball, whimpering as more and more of the creatures pressed against the windows raging at their prey.

There was a harsh crack and a spider web of lines raced across one of the windows. Ace snatched the aerosol from Rajiid's hand. She hurled herself forward and squirted foam over the windows, shutting out the creatures.

Holly continued to scream, her eyes wild and staring. Ace caught hold of her arm, spun her round and punched her, hard. Holly dropped like a stone. Cradling her fist, Ace yelled over to Rajiid, 'You've got to get us out of here!'

The Indian scrambled forward to where Greg was struggling with the controls. 'Can we blow the tanks?' The Australian shook his head.

'Not a chance. All our external lines are damaged. They've not punctured anything yet, but it's only a matter of time.'

The sub lurched again and the control column leapt out of his hands.

Rajiid grasped the controls and put the sub into a dive. Greg looked at him in disbelief. 'What the hell are you doing?'

'Heading for the cave. Get over to the blood tank, Greg.'

'What?'

'For God's sake, don't argue! I've got an idea. When I tell you, release all the valves.'

Greg staggered back into the body of the sub, struggling up the wet floor. There was a harsh clang as the creatures slammed into the hull again. He braced himself against a small control panel, staring down at Rajiid in the cabin.

Ace struggled to his side.

'What's the idea?'

Greg shook his head, his face ashen. 'Rajiid's heading for a Ramora cave.'

Ace frowned

'A giant eel.' Greg explained. 'It's part of our tourist package. We release a small amount of fish blood into the water to tempt the thing out. Tourists take pictures... they love it.' He laughed humourlessly. 'They'd certainly get some pictures on this trip.'

The engines whined in protest as Rajiid levelled out and swung the little craft into a tight turn.

'Stand by, Greg!'

'We're too close!'

'*They're* too close!'

Ace pressed herself against one of the windows. The black maw of a cave entrance loomed from a coral mound. The sub slowed and suddenly the creatures were over them again. The hull buckled above Ace's head and freezing water cascaded over her.

'Now! Now! Now!'

Rajiid's voice rang around the reeling sub and Ace saw a cloud of blackness billowing into the water like octopus ink. With a screech of engines the sub lurched forward and Ace caught a glimpse of something huge and sinewy darting out of the cave.

The eel caught the underside of the sub and there was a scream from Bryce as the hull ruptured again. Ace struggled to keep herself braced into the window, her muscles screaming at her to relax. Icy water continued to pour over her. She could hear Greg struggling to stem the flow but she couldn't take her eyes off the battle unfolding in the water.

The Ramora eel was huge, a tube-train-sized mass of fin and muscle sent into a thrashing frenzy by the blood. The creatures tore at its flesh, ignoring the sub, concentrating on this softer prey. The eel snapped at its attackers and Ace saw its powerful jaws crush one of the creatures to a bloody pulp. Two more raced to the attack but the eel arched its body and they were dashed against the coral and crushed under the Ramora's huge bulk. Then a cloud of blood obscured the view, and Ace felt the sub accelerate towards the surface.

The *Zodiac* sped away from the *Hyperion Dawn*. The Doctor stared grimly ahead – that softly shifting mirror beneath them covered something lethal.

MacKenzie had been reluctant to go any further after what they'd seen at the platform and the Doctor had had to invoke the full authority of InterOceanic. It had worked like a charm.

'Nearly there, Doctor,' the professor said. 'There are a least a dozen sites of various kinds on the ocean floor. Maybe more. We hope to investigate them all in due course, if our budget will stretch to it. Seabed archaeology is expensive. Still, one step at a time, eh?'

'What? Oh, yes, yes...'

The Doctor barely heard MacKenzie's words. He was still thinking about the *Hyperion Dawn*.

'Still, if InterOceanic were to become involved...'

'For God's sake, MacKenzie, give the man a chance,' Q'ilp cut in. 'You've only just met him.'

'Ah, indeed,' said MacKenzie, '*mea culpa*. As I said, one step at a time.'

The *Zodiac* slowed, circled and came to a halt. A large marker buoy surrounded by bright floats bobbed in the wake of the vessel. Q'ilp wriggled from his metal walking frame and disappeared into the water.

'See you down there,' he said, and vanished beneath its surface.

The submersible's pilot punched a button and a transparent hatch slid over the deck. Air began to bubble up around the *Zodiac* and the water closed silently over it.

The craft slipped through the quiet green of the water. The Doctor could see lights glimmering on the seabed.

'This is a temple complex,' said MacKenzie. 'We've set up a dome over the remains... expelled the bulk of the water.'

The submersible settled alongside a docking port and there was a soft thump as clamps engaged. MacKenzie ducked into the bow and hauled open an airlock.

'Bit of a tight squeeze I'm afraid, Doctor.'

He disappeared inside the hatch. The Doctor stepped gingerly into the bow and peered down after him. A long plastic shaft with steps set into its side vanished into the gloom. MacKenzie was disappearing down it. The Doctor followed.

The shaft was narrow – a difficult climb for someone of MacKenzie's age, the Doctor thought – but well worth the effort.

'Well, Doctor, what do you think?' the professor asked. 'Impressive, is it not?'

The Doctor gazed around him. Ruined walls flanked wide avenues, roofless halls stood silent and elegant in decay. Algae and other plant life held sway over all. The translucent hull of the archaeologists' dome covered the whole massive ruin, glowing dully with liquid, undersea light.

Still pools of seawater dotted the uneven floor. Q'ilp suddenly surfaced in one of them.

'Tunnels,' he said. 'Useful for me. That clever Dick never gave a moment's thought to how I would get into the dome when he was designing it.'

MacKenzie ignored his cetacean colleague.

'Magnificent, isn't it?' he enthused. He appeared to have completely forgotten the destruction of the cable-laying platform. He was like a child in his favourite toy shop. 'They were quite a civilisation,' he said. 'We still know very little about them. Progress has been woefully slow, I'm sorry to say. Funding again, you see. This is a new colony, and I'm afraid archaeology isn't high on their list of priorities. They are far more concerned with tourism.' He spat out the word. 'The lure of the offworld dollar. Pleasure trips around the quaint ruins...'

'Exactly how much do you know about this civilisation?' the Doctor asked.

'Well, as I was telling you, we have made some progress.' MacKenzie warmed instantly to his theme. He led the Doctor into the remains of a building. 'These mosaics, you see...' he gushed. 'These murals...'

Several large sections of the walls and floor had been painstakingly cleared of sea-growth. The Doctor peered at the ancient stones.

'These hieroglyphs...'

'Yes,' said MacKenzie. 'Very mysterious. Tricky things...'

'The pictures are clear enough...' said the Doctor. 'Some kind of pictorial chronicle. An historical record of the race who built all this.'

'Yes, indeed,' said MacKenzie. 'That's what we think.'

'An aquatic species, as one would expect on a world that's 98 per cent ocean. Humanoid... interesting.'

'This shows them constructing their settlements,' enthused MacKenzie. 'Not their great cities. Not yet. The cities come later.'

He bustled across the room to another faded vista. The Doctor followed. 'And here we see what I believe to be their apogee.'

'Space flight,' said the Doctor. 'Weapons...'

'Oh, they were undoubtedly warlike,' said MacKenzie, 'but what civilisation has not been born out of conflict? Look at the Earth.'

'A somewhat narrow view of history,' said the Doctor.

'Well, perhaps,' said MacKenzie. 'I have in fact written several papers on the subject... In any event, you must admit this was quite a civilisation.'

'But what happened to it?' the Doctor asked. 'What became of them?'

'Ah,' said MacKenzie wistfully. 'A catastrophe, I believe. Come with me.'

The Doctor followed him through a low, cracked arch. A narrow tunnel stretched ahead of them.

'Be careful,' said MacKenzie, snapping on a powerful torch.

The floor of the tunnel was largely gone. A deep, water-filled crack ran its full length, leaving only a narrow, uneven ledge, tight against one wall. The Doctor and MacKenzie had to crouch and hug the wall as they picked their way along the tunnel. Q'ilp swam effortlessly along the deep gash.

'Now take a look at these murals,' MacKenzie said.

'Hmm... Considerably cruder,' the Doctor mused.

'And yet undoubtedly later,' said MacKenzie. 'And look at the images.'

'I know,' said the Doctor. 'War. Destruction. Carnage.'

'Interesting, isn't it? The earlier scenes show military parades, demonstrations of firepower, triumphs, prisoners – but no actual war.'

'Which implies that their victories were achieved far away,' the Doctor cut in. 'Far from the public consciousness. Whereas here...'

'Distressing, isn't it?'

The Doctor ran his fingers lightly over the wall. 'What do you make of these, Professor?'

A new species had appeared in the pictures.

'Savage blighters, aren't they?' MacKenzie said. 'Of course, if we look at ancient Earth history we find similar, mythical figures. The Titans...'

'Legends, you think?'

'Oh, I think so, Doctor.' MacKenzie laughed.

'Have you ever heard of the Krill?' the Doctor asked sharply.

'The Krill... exactly!' MacKenzie exclaimed. 'The little authentic information we have on the Krill – and believe me, it is little – seems to conform to classic mythology patterns on a hundred worlds. The book of Revelations, for example. The Norse tales of Ragnarok...'

The Doctor shuddered at the word.

'And yet Ragnarok and Revelations were visions of a future apocalypse. We're looking at the remains of an extinct society, Professor. It would appear that they had their Ragnarok right here.'

MacKenzie sniffed. 'I would expect this society became extinct by more... natural means. It happens. Societies wither and die. The Egyptians, the Romans... Who would have thought the people who built the pyramids or the Colosseum would ever fade into obscurity and extinction, but fade they did.'

'I recently met a travel writer who held a different view,' said the Doctor. 'I got the impression he had amassed quite a body of tales. He seemed to regard himself as something of an expert.'

MacKenzie groaned. 'Bryce,' he said. 'The man's a sensationalist. He has no qualifications whatever in this field. His Krill stories... well, he made most of them up, if you ask me. He's a charlatan and a nuisance.'

'I wonder...' the Doctor mused. 'Professor, you say this was a temple... What do you know about their religion? What rites were practised here?'

'Well, to be perfectly frank with you, Doctor, our research is still inconclusive at the moment...'

'You call that being perfectly frank?' Q'ilp cut in from below them. 'Be honest, MacKenzie – you haven't got a clue. There are no altars, no religious symbols, nothing.'

'And yet this was a temple, I'm certain,' the professor snapped. 'I'd stake my reputation on it.'

The dolphin emitted a curious, high, snuffling squeak. It sounded to the Doctor as if it was laughing.

'I think you're right,' said the Doctor. 'In a manner of speaking. But where indeed is the altar? Where is the inner sanctum? The holy of holies.'

'You sound as if you have the answer,' MacKenzie said pettishly.

'No,' said the Doctor. 'I don't. I wish I did, but I don't.'

The tunnel ended abruptly in a blank wall. The Doctor edged along the narrow crumbling ledge and studied the wall closely.

'Strange...' he mused. 'Why should they build a tunnel to nowhere?'

'Presumably the temple complex was unfinished,' said MacKenzie.

'Perhaps...' said the Doctor. 'But why would they cover the walls with hieroglyphs and friezes if they were still excavating?'

'Careful, Doctor,' Q'ilp warned. 'The ledge is crumbling. The seabed's unstable around here. This damned place is falling apart.'

'You know,' said the Doctor, 'I think I might have a crack at translating these hieroglyphs.'

MacKenzie scoffed. 'They've quite foxed me,' he said. 'And my colleagues.'

The Doctor didn't reply. His face was pressed close to the wall.

'Pass me the torch, Professor,' he said.

He snatched the proffered torch from MacKenzie.

'Doctor...!' Q'ilp suddenly chirruped. 'Get back! The ledge...'

He didn't finish his sentence. The Doctor suddenly felt the ground beneath his feet slipping into the trench below. He scrabbled at the wall, but his free hand could find no purchase. With a short cry, he fell, plunging into the cold water.

'Doctor...!' Q'ilp shrieked.

The Doctor felt himself being sucked down. The current was strong. The light of his torch was twisted, half-swallowed by the dark waters. Crumbling cliffs of tile and stone rose dimly around him, shedding slow-falling boulders. He couldn't breathe...

The trench closed about him as he was pulled deeper. His hands and feet scrabbled against its rough, sharp surface. His torch's failing light came to rest on something odd – something which shouldn't be there. Surely it was...

He sensed movement in the water above him and saw Q'ilp swimming towards him, diving down through the dark canyon. The dolphin's mouth closed around the tail of his jacket, and began to pull him upwards. His head broke the surface and he gasped for breath.

'Quickly,' he spluttered. 'There's a...'

'Doctor, I really am most dreadfully sorry!' MacKenzie danced on the ledge in agitation. The Doctor scrambled up beside him.

'Thank you, Q'ilp,' the Doctor said.

'This has never happened before on one of my digs,' MacKenzie fussed. 'I hope you won't think too ill of our efforts. The good will of InterOceanic is...'

'Professor, there's a body down there,' the Doctor said sharply. 'It doesn't look human. Q'ilp, please could you go down and take a look?'

'It's pretty rough down there,' the dolphin said slowly. 'Unstable. There are rocks tumbling everywhere.'

'Nonsense, Q'ilp, nonsense,' MacKenzie blustered. 'Anything for our friends at InterOceanic.'

Q'ilp spat a thin, contemptuous jet of water from his snout and dived below the surface. The Doctor peered down into the trench, ignoring MacKenzie's fevered apologies. He could see the dark shape of the dolphin receding beneath the water, then gradually coming closer again. Q'ilp broke the surface raggedly, struggling with a colossal burden. It was a figure, humanoid but huge and thickset, motionless, its diving suit ragged and torn. Dead weight.

The Doctor struggled to drag the figure on to the ledge.

'Don't just stand there, MacKenzie,' he snapped. 'Help me.'

Gingerly the archaeologist extended a hand and tugged feebly at the figure. When at last it was on the ledge the Doctor removed a tubular breathing apparatus from its head. Its skin was thick and hide-like, a dull grey-green colour with pronounced, bony ridges. Its body was squat and muscular, and easily seven feet tall.

'Ugly blighter,' said MacKenzie. 'I suppose you're going to try and tell me this is a Krill.'

'Krill? Hardly, Professor. For one thing, according to these murals the Krill were aquatic. This thing's wearing some kind of submarine breathing apparatus. And besides, it is certainly not a native of this world. Look at its physiognomy. The bone structure implies it evolved on a planet of far higher gravity than this.'

'So what do you think it was doing here?'

'The same as us, I imagine,' said the Doctor. 'Exploring. Looking for something.'

'Doctor,' Q'ilp butted in, 'do you hear that? No – you wouldn't, of course. Too high. It started when I pulled him out of the crevice. I think it's a signal. It's coming from his suit.'

'Let's get him out of here,' said the Doctor. 'I'd like to examine him.'

'Of course, of course,' said MacKenzie. 'You can use my laboratory. All of the institute's facilities are at your disposal, Doctor.'

'You'll never get him up the access shaft,' said Q'ilp. 'I'd better take him through the airlock.'

All the way back on the *Zodiac* the Doctor dripped and dried, and MacKenzie talked.

'It's most gratifying that InterOceanic are taking an interest in my work,' he oozed. 'If necessary I could provide a full report of the progress we have made. If there was any prospect of additional funding...'

The Doctor was barely listening. He watched the island chain coming slowly closer. Something appeared to be happening west of the harbour – a dense crowd was gathered on the beach. As the *Zodiac* slowed in the shallow water the Doctor strained to see what it was all about. A submarine appeared to have run aground on the beach; its nose was partly buried in the sand and it was practically on its side. People milled around it, jostling to see it. A team of paramedics was pushing through the crowd with a loaded hover-stretcher, making for a waiting ambulance. Two Alpha Centaurians were waving about in absolute hysterics. One of the paramedics was trying to calm them. The Doctor could see Edwin Bryce standing on the edge of the crowd looking pale and shaken, taking a deep draught from a metal flask. As he watched him, Bryce turned round and strode off.

85

The Doctor jumped from the *Zodiac* into the shallow water and ran up the beach, with an increasing sense of alarm. The sub had clearly crashed on to the beach at speed.

'Doctor!'

Ace was pushing through the crowd towards him.

'Ace,' the Doctor called, 'what happened?'

'I'm not sure,' Ace said. 'These... things attacked the sub.'

The Doctor moved past her towards the stricken vessel. He ran his hands along the deep, ragged grooves that scarred and pierced its metal hull from one end to the other. The same pattern as the marks on the *Hyperion Dawn*.

'What happened?' he asked again.

'They came through the water... started cutting through the hull. Rajiid saved us.'

'Rajiid?'

'Pleased to meet you.'

The Doctor looked at the handsome young Indian who was standing behind Ace. He smiled slightly at his companion. 'Been making friends, Ace?'

Ace grinned sheepishly at him. 'Rajiid's the pilot of the sub.'

'*Was* the pilot of the sub,' Rajiid corrected her. He looked across at where Greg was inspecting the damage. 'There's not much to pilot any more.'

'Tell me, Rajiid,' said the Doctor, 'have you any idea what happened out there?'

Rajiid shrugged. 'We were attacked. Nothing I've ever seen before. You'd best talk to R'tk'tk.'

'What? Who's taking my name in vain?' The voice was chirruping and irritable. A dolphin was barging its way through the crowd on one of those spider-like transporters.

'Rajiid,' the dolphin grumbled, 'tell me the sub was properly insured. Tell me we're not as far up the creek as I think we are.'

The Doctor doffed his hat. 'I'm very pleased to meet you, R'tk'tk,' he said.

'Mm,' the dolphin grunted. 'Rajiid...'

'I would appreciate a quick word,' the Doctor cut in.

'Look, Mister,' the dolphin chirruped, 'I don't know if you're aware of it, but our livelihood has just gone down the pan. I don't have time for chitchat.'

'Neither do I,' said the Doctor with sudden authority. 'Something attacked you out there, and I want to know what. This has implications far beyond your livelihood. I believe the whole colony could be on the edge of extinction.'

R'tk'tk swallowed hard. 'I don't know what attacked us,' he said. 'All I know is they were humanoid in shape, and moved faster through the water than anything I've ever seen – far faster than I could ever swim. They were naked, and unarmed as far as I could see.'

'How many of them?'

'Three, maybe four. Not that much bigger than a man. And they did all this... I've never seen anything like it.'

'I say, Doctor, what happened here?'

Professor MacKenzie was bustling towards them through the thinning crowd, Q'ilp close behind him. The two dolphins, Q'ilp and R'tk'tk, faced each other, the spider-legs of their walkers tapping in a manner that suggested agitation to the Doctor.

'This your sub?' Q'ilp asked curtly. R'tk'tk nodded.

'And were you driving?'

R'tk'tk chittered angrily. 'We were attacked,' he said bluntly. 'It was probably something out of that hole you're digging under the sea.'

The Doctor could sense the other dolphin bristling. Q'ilp let out a series of high-pitched whistles. R'tk'tk responded in kind.

'Let's not quarrel,' the Doctor said hastily, although he feared R'tk'tk was right. The dig...

'My, my,' said MacKenzie, examining the beached, battered sub, 'what on Earth could have done this?'

The Doctor ignored him. 'Ace, who was on the hover-stretcher?'

'Survivor from some ship,' said Ace. 'We found her in the water in an escape pod. She looked in a bad way. When we found her she was just screaming...'

'So Ace thoughtfully punched her,' Rajiid cut in, smiling wryly. 'Holly Relf, she's an engineer, part of the cable-laying operation. Works for InterOceanic.'

'One of your colleagues, Doctor,' said MacKenzie. 'Oh dear, oh dear. Do be sure to convey my respects...'

'What?' snapped the Doctor irritably. 'Oh, yes, Professor, of course. May I have the use of your laboratory?'

'Of course,' MacKenzie effused. '*Anything* for...'

The harsh sound of a siren cut across the hubbub of crowd and sea. Two gaudy police vehicles glided to a halt and uniformed men tumbled out. Phillip Garrett stepped from the back of one of the transports. He crossed the beach and stared at the crippled submarine.

'Who's in charge of this vessel?'

Rajiid stepped forward. 'I am,' he said. 'Rajiid Woozeer.' He hooked a thumb back at the others. 'That's Greg Mallory; R'tk'tk I think you know.'

'You'll have to make a statement.' Garrett didn't take his eyes from the scarred hull of the vessel. He motioned to the policemen. 'Take him in.'

Ace shot an anxious glance at the Doctor.

'Excuse me,' the Doctor said, 'that seems a little harsh.'

Garrett looked him carefully up and down. 'I don't see that this is any concern of InterOceanic,' he said. 'Bring the pilots and impound the sub. Clear these people away.'

Rajiid, Greg and R'tk'tk were bundled into one of the police vehicles. Ace made to follow, but was thrust roughly back into the crowd. The Doctor found himself being herded away from the wreck with the rest of the onlookers.

'Does the chief engineer usually come on police call-outs?' the Doctor whispered to Q'ilp.

88

'No,' Q'ilp replied, 'but Garrett's a strange one. Very cosy with the colony co-ordinator, Brenda Mulholland. He's got his hands in everywhere.'

'Doctor,' Ace cried. 'What about Rajiid...?'

The Doctor shot her an angry glance. 'I think we have more important things to worry about than your friend talking to the police, Ace. Far more important things.'

Chapter Eight

'Tough... hide like a rhinoceros. Breastbone like titanium. I can barely cut through.'

The alien body from the undersea ruin lay naked on a slab in MacKenzie's laboratory in the research wing of the colony's main admin building. Its diving suit lay on an adjacent bench. Ace sat on a stool in the corner, trying to ignore the smell of formaldehyde that hung about the corpse.

The Doctor seemed to be making slow progress with a laser-cutter, gradually opening the creature up. MacKenzie hovered behind him, picking idly at the diving suit. He lifted a small, flat punch-pad from the belt and began jabbing at it.

'Please don't touch anything,' the Doctor said sharply. Stung, MacKenzie put the pad down. The Doctor immediately snatched it and dropped it into a pocket of his linen jacket.

'Just trying to help, Doctor,' MacKenzie said.

'Yes, of course,' said the Doctor in a more conciliatory tone. 'Tell me, what do you make of the diving suit, Professor?'

'I don't really know, Doctor. Not my field, I'm afraid.'

'Look at the insignia,' said the Doctor absent-mindedly. 'Warlike, wouldn't you say?'

'Well yes, I suppose...'

'The weapon, too. Very nasty. Not the sort of thing you'd normally take on an archaeological expedition.'

'No, indeed,' said MacKenzie.

'Did you notice he was holding the gun when Q'ilp brought him up? Doesn't that strike you as odd?'

'Yes. Well, that is... I'm not sure I follow you, Doctor.'

'He was expecting to find something nasty down there, Professor... Aha!'

The breastbone finally gave way. An acrid swill of blood, tissue and sea water spilled out over the creature's body.

'Massive internal disruption,' said the Doctor. 'Something made soup out of this poor chap's internal organs. Professor MacKenzie, is there any way of sealing off the dig?'

'Sealing... What do you mean, Doctor?'

'It's a perfectly straightforward question,' the Doctor barked. 'Your work must be suspended. I don't want anyone going near that temple.'

'But you don't think...'

'I do think, Professor. And until I'm sure it's safe I don't want anyone going out there. Do you understand?'

'Well naturally, if that's the view of InterOceanic...' MacKenzie tried hard not to look bothered. 'Although I really must contest your conclusions.'

The Doctor took a deep breath.

'Professor,' he said smoothly, 'I might as well reveal to you that InterOceanic are looking hard at putting together a funding package for the splendid work you're doing out there, but you must understand that we could not possibly afford to be associated with anything which might prove harmful to the inhabitants of this planet. Now, until I have looked into this matter more fully, I really must insist that you suspend operations. If you're interested in our money, that is...'

'Of course, of course...' said MacKenzie hastily. 'I... should like something in writing, though. My superiors, you understand.'

'I'll see that you get it,' said the Doctor. He delved back into the huge alien corpse on the slab. 'So much to do,' he muttered.

In the pocket of his jacket the alien data-pad gave a soft bleep.

'General!'

Mottrack swung round in his command chair.

'Well?'

'Contact from Coralee, sir. Weak signal. Standard field operative com signal. It's an old code, sir.'

Mottrack lumbered over to the communications array. His eyes lit up with excitement.

'Vreik's signal! Can you establish a two-way link?'

The officer stabbed at the control. 'No, sir. It's just an automatic signal. No operator online at the other end.'

Mottrack straightened, rubbing at his chin.

'Pull us out of the asteroid field. Contact our scout. Tell him we are on our way.'

Ace and the Doctor wandered out of MacKenzie's laboratory. The Doctor had completed the autopsy of the alien and now his attention was focused on the alien data-pad. Ace couldn't get a peep out of him.

Something seemed to be happening on the other side of the paved square. A big, official-looking transport glided to a halt outside the tall admin building and a woman got out.

'Doctor...'

The Doctor watched her vanish into the medical centre.

'Brenda Mulholland,' he said. 'Excellent. Ace, I think it's time to visit the poor woman you found in the escape pod. We can kill two birds with one stone.'

Holly Relf was still in a coma. The colony co-ordinator was standing at the foot of the bed looking pale and grim when the Doctor and Ace entered the room.

The Doctor cleared his throat.

'Is this your friend?'

Brenda nodded. She looked at Ace. 'You found her?'

'Yeah.'

'Thank you.'

She turned back to the bed. Holly was pale and unmoving, the auto-doc clicking quietly above her. 'Holly's a friend of mine,' said Brenda Mulholland quietly. 'Been working the ocean colonies for years. How could she have ended up like this? I've just been to examine the platform she was working on. It's been...'

'Ripped apart,' said the Doctor. 'I know – I saw it, Miss Mulholland.'

'What could have done that?'

'I'm not sure yet,' said the Doctor, 'but I should warn you, if my worst theory is correct – and they usually are – we're all in danger.'

'Danger...' Phillip Garrett marched into the room and leaned over the bed. 'How is she, Brenda?'

'No change,' said the woman sombrely.

'I know you.' The man was looking Ace. 'You were on the beach.'

'Mr Garrett, this is my... assistant – Ace,' said the Doctor.

Ace gave him her most insincere smile. 'Are you still holding my friends?'

'For the moment, yes.' Garrett's face was without humour. 'I may want to talk to you later, as well.'

He turned to Brenda.

'I've put a security sub out on patrol. If there's something dangerous out there...'

Brenda Mulholland stared hard at Garrett for a moment. 'Good,' she said after a tense pause. 'I should have done it myself.'

'Ace,' said the Doctor, 'we should be going.' He doffed his hat. 'So nice to have met you again, Miss Mulholland. Mr Garrett.'

'Doctor.' The big man moved between the Time Lord and the door. 'I built this colony, practically from scratch. If there's some danger here, I want to know about it.'

'A young woman is in a coma,' said the Doctor firmly, 'the cable-laying platform on which she was working has been destroyed, and a submarine full of people nearly met the same fate. And whatever is out there could do it again. I'd say that constituted a degree of danger, wouldn't you?'

'It's all right, Garrett,' said Brenda Mulholland smoothly. 'I'll handle this.'

The man smiled grimly. 'It's your call, Brenda. Keep me posted.' He turned to the Doctor. 'I'm sure we'll be talking again,' he said, turned on his heel and marched out of the room.

'You mustn't mind Garrett,' Brenda Mulholland said. 'As he said, the colony here is his baby. But if you do know what's going on here...'

'I know very little at the moment,' the Doctor said. 'But I'll find out more.' He smiled at her. 'Don't worry, Miss Mulholland, I'll keep you posted. Come on, Ace.'

Half an hour later the Doctor and Ace were once again sitting in the bar of their hotel. The Doctor's fingers danced across a little electronic notepad. He tutted in frustration.

'Code-locked,' he said. 'It was on the dead alien's diving suit.'

Ace was restless. She sipped her drink and watched the carefree ebb and flow of people. As usual she and the Doctor were up to their necks in something they didn't understand while everyone else relaxed, chatted, enjoyed themselves. Why could life never be that simple for them?

Rajiid and the others had been released without charge, and he and R'tk'tk had gone off to file an insurance claim. With the vessel in custody he didn't hold out much hope of success.

MacKenzie had dogged them all afternoon, dropping heavy hints about funding. Ace was glad to get away from the confusion of people.

The Doctor let out a long sigh. 'People like MacKenzie wear me out,' he said.

'What's all this InterOceanic stuff?' Ace asked.

'A useful lie, Ace,' said the Doctor. 'MacKenzie's a very stupid man. He has little knowledge and no imagination. I'm more concerned about Mr Garrett and Miss Mulholland. One of them is bound to run a check on my credentials. Garrett, I shouldn't wonder. We've got to move quickly.'

'Doctor, do you know what's going on here?'

'Not really, Ace. And I don't think it's going to be very easy finding out. The authorities here know something's up.'

'So what do we do now?'

'Well, as official channels seem to be closed to us, we'll just have to work our way around the problem. I need more background. More history. Now, I'm not well up on the history of this part of the galaxy, but I know a man who is.'

'MacKenzie? But you said...'

'Bryce. He collects folklore. Did you notice how he suddenly disappeared from the beach? That was odd... You'd think that after what happened on the sub he would have wanted to talk about it.'

'You think he knows something?'

'Or suspects something. Either way, I think he's frightened.' The Doctor pulled his watch from his pocket and glared at it. 'I'd have expected him to be here by now... Ah!'

Bryce had just walked in. He sat at his usual table and ordered a drink from a waiter.

'Shall we?' said the Doctor, rising from his seat and picking his way across the crowded room. Ace followed.

'Mr Bryce,' said the Doctor. 'May we join you?'

'Please,' said Bryce. He sounded anything but welcoming.

'That was quite a business on the sub,' the Doctor said.

Bryce took a gulp of his drink and said nothing.

'What do you know about the Krill, Mr Bryce?' the Doctor suddenly asked.

Bryce shrugged. 'Not much,' he said. 'A few stories...'

'You gave me the impression you'd assembled quite a collection of tales,' the Doctor said.

Bryce shrugged again.

'Why did you leave the beach in such a hurry?' the Doctor pressed.

'Things to do, that's all,' said Bryce.

'You looked as if you had something on your mind.'

'I did,' said Bryce. 'Now, if you'll excuse me, Doctor...'

He downed his drink and rose to his feet.

'Not staying for another?' the Doctor said with forced cheeriness.

Bryce didn't answer. He slapped a coin on the bar and walked towards the door.

'Follow him,' the Doctor said bluntly to Ace. 'Don't let him see you.'

'I was supposed to meet Rajiid here,' Ace protested.

The Doctor stared her full in the face. 'I'm sorry, Ace,' he said, 'but I rather think what's happening here has to take precedence over your social life. The entire colony's in danger. We'll meet back at Professor MacKenzie's laboratory.' He slipped a small plastic card from his pocket and handed it to her. 'This will get you in.'

'What are you going to do?' Ace asked sulkily.

'I'm going to find Q'ilp,' the Doctor replied. 'Get him to take me back to the dig, so I can have a look round without MacKenzie interfering.'

'But it'll be dark soon,' protested Ace.

'The nights are short here,' said the Doctor. 'Anyway, two suns. We've a few hours yet.' He rose to his feet. 'And besides, I've been linked with MacKenzie. I suspect that by tomorrow the dig will be under police guard. I've got to get there before them.' He tapped his lips, deep in thought. 'I'm sure the key to this whole thing is out there.'

'Still nothing, Sarge.'

'Keep looking, Norris.'

The police submarine D-19 moved, sleek and near-silent, through the calm ocean, its conning tower cutting the surface like a shark's fin. Police Sergeant Frank Sands could sense the tension in his crew. Call-outs were rare on Coralee.

'Looking for what, Sarge?'

'Beaker' Norris was always asking stupid questions.

'Anything unusual,' Sands improvised. They hadn't told him anything. He didn't know why they were out there. He didn't like it.

'Makes a change from running in drunks,' said Archie Bell, the navigator. 'Nothing unusual about them.'

'What d'you reckon, Sarge?' Norris piped up again. 'Some dolphin done a bank job?'

'Just keep scanning, Norris,' Sands said evenly.

'Sarge...' Annie Clark, communications officer, stuck her head around the low door. 'New orders from Central. They're sending them straight to Navigation.'

On cue the crew felt the vessel list slightly as it changed direction.

'I wish they wouldn't do that,' said Bell. 'Navs is a skilled job. I'm damned if I'll lose it to a machine.'

'All right, Bell,' said Sands.

He reached for his computer terminal. He also wished Central wouldn't go straight to Navigation. Orders should come through him, as a matter of common sense and courtesy. Central only did this when they wanted to avoid awkward questions. When they had something to hide.

'We're accelerating,' said Bell.

A low, even pulsing sound filled the sub. Sands swore under his breath.

He opened a channel on the internal communicator and cleared his throat.

'OK, you can all hear that,' he said loudly. 'Everybody to their posts. We've gone to battle stations.'

He just wished he knew why.

The suns were low in the perfect sky by the time the Doctor and Q'ilp left the harbour aboard the *Zodiac*. The dolphin was uneasy.

'More'n my job's worth, this,' it muttered as it piloted the little craft. 'MacKenzie'll have my skin on his office wall.'

'InterOceanic will smooth everything out,' said the Doctor.

The dolphin swept a mechanical tentacle across the submersible's steering column. The engine died and the vessel glided to a halt.

'Come off it,' Q'ilp snapped. 'You might fool MacKenzie with that bullshit, but not me. You're nothing to do with InterOceanic. I used to work for them. I know how they operate.'

The Doctor sighed. 'I'm afraid you're right,' he said. 'I apologise for the deception. But something's very wrong. I... have a nose for these things.'

'I'm a dolphin,' said Q'ilp drily, twitching his long snout. 'No nose jokes, please.'

The Doctor smiled grimly. 'No offence intended,' he said. 'There's something very old and very dangerous down there. That alien was looking for it, and it killed him.'

'So what makes you think it won't kill us?'

The Doctor didn't reply.

'I see,' said Q'ilp.

'Please help me,' the Doctor said quietly.

Q'ilp sighed. 'I'm no archaeologist,' he said. 'I'm just MacKenzie's runabout. I'm employed for my knowledge of the sea. I heard what R'tk'tk described, and if he's right I say if, because I wouldn't trust him as far as I could walk without this thing – if he's right, then there's something out there which could wipe my people out.'

'Not just your people,' the Doctor cut in.

'I've watched MacKenzie blundering about down there, and if these... things... have anything to do with the dig then he's the last man I want to see in charge. He knew the right people to please – that's how he got his position – but I wouldn't put him in charge of a souvenir shop. If my instincts are right about you, you're different. You look like a clown, but...'

'That's a lot of ifs,' the Doctor said quietly.

'Don't remind me,' said Q'ilp.

He engaged the engine, and the submersible sped across the water.

'There's a diving suit in the locker,' he said. 'It might be a bit big, but I'd recommend you put it on. After what happened last time...'

It was getting dark; everyone around Ace was having fun, while she was hiding behind a rose bush. She wished she was somewhere else. She'd followed Bryce around three bars, each smaller and seedier than the one before. She'd lurked in corners, ignoring the comments and wolf whistles of the patrons, and watched Bryce getting more and more drunk. Eventually she'd tracked him to this narrow street of low, cheap prefabs, where he'd waited for ten minutes outside a shabby door before being let in.

She waited a few minutes, then eased the door open and slipped into a dimly lit, smoky corridor with doors leading off on either side.

'Yes, dearie?' A voice like sandpaper made her stop. The nearest door had swung open and she turned to see a fat, four-armed woman – one of those Dreekans – peering suspiciously at her. The woman was plastered in lipstick and blusher. She wore a shabby kimono and about a ton of cheap jewellery.

Ace looked at her, open-mouthed.

'Not got much to say for yourself, have you?' the Dreekan woman rasped, lighting a cigarette. 'Still, that's maybe not such a bad thing.' She reached out a hand and pinched Ace's arm. Ace winced.

'Plenty of meat on you,' the woman said. 'Good. Most of our gentlemen like that. You get two credits a night, plus room and board. That's if you work out. For the first week it's just room and board. What's your name?'

'Uh... Ace,' said Ace.

'Mmm,' said the Dreekan woman. 'Don't think much of that. You can be Dolores. We lost a Dolores recently.'

'That man who just came in here...' said Ace.

'Mr Jones, what about him?'

'His name's not Jones. His name's...'

The woman shot out a hand and clamped it across Ace's mouth.

'They never use real names – you should know that. If you happen to know them – it's a small world after all – you keep your mouth shut. Understand?'

Ace kept her mouth shut and wondered what to do next.

There was a heavy thumping at the front door.

'Filth!' the woman hissed, waving her four arms around in panic.

The door burst open and two policemen entered.

'Now hold on,' the woman blustered. 'Don't I pay you enough to...?'

'Relax, Rosie,' one of the policemen said. 'We're not here for you. Where's Bryce?'

'Who?'

'The man who just came in here. Where is he?'

'First door on the left,' Rosie said. 'But for God's sake, keep the noise down. If my other punters see you two...'

'Yeah, yeah,' the policeman sneered, and kicked the door open. There was a high-pitched scream from inside, and Ace could hear Edwin Bryce's voice raised in bluster and protest.

'Shut it, Bryce,' the policeman said. 'Someone wants to see you.'

'Now!?' Bryce spluttered.

'Now,' the policeman spat. 'Get dressed.'

Rosie stubbed out her cigarette, and immediately lit another one. 'Bloody cops,' she said. 'Interfering in everyone's business.'

There was a scuffling sound, and Bryce walked out, adjusting his tie, flanked by two policemen. Ace lowered her head and hoped he hadn't seen her.

'Cheers, Rosie,' one of the policemen said. 'Panic over.'

'Where will they take him?' Ace asked Rosie.

'I don't know!' Rosie snapped. 'What am I, psychic? Now, do you want a job or not?'

The pale light of the Doctor's helmet-mounted torch struggled to pierce the murky waters of the undersea ruin. He tried to control his unwieldy, oversized diving suit as he followed Q'ilp, kicking and flapping awkwardly along the waterfilled tunnels that ran in honeycombs beneath the ruined pavements and avenues.

'You all right in there?' Q'ilp chirruped through the Doctor's helmet-communicator.

'I think so,' said the Doctor. 'Where are we?'

'We're close to where we found the body. It's just ahead. The entrance is above us.'

The Doctor's light bounced feebly off the walls of a long, narrow trench.

'Up we go,' said Q'ilp.

The Doctor kicked hard and propelled himself uncertainly to the surface, where he bobbed looking about him at the low tunnel and the narrow, precarious ledge that ran along its edge and ended in a blank wall.

He scrambled awkwardly on to the ledge. The diving suit flapped, huge and ungainly, about his hands and feet.

'Careful, Doctor,' said Q'ilp. 'Remember what happened last time. The place is falling to pieces.'

'I know,' said the Doctor. He began probing the blank wall with his gloved fingers. 'It's difficult to do anything in this suit. I can hardly see.'

He lifted the diver's helmet from his head and peeled the gloves from his hands.

An image of the alien soldier loomed in his mind. Massive internal disruption. He had got this far, but then what? The Doctor ran his hands gingerly down the wall. Just above waist height he encountered the faintest of vibrations. He pressed, lightly at first, then harder.

'Nothing,' he said bitterly.

No. The vibration had increased – ever so slightly, ever so briefly, but it had definitely increased.

'Hang on...' he said.

It happened again.

'What is it, Doctor?' Q'ilp chirruped.

It happened a third time, more strongly.

'It's a sonic lock,' said the Doctor. 'The right frequency will trigger it. Shame I haven't got my sonic screwdriver...'

'You don't need your sonic doodah,' said Q'ilp. 'You've got me.'

The Doctor rubbed his hands together in glee. 'I have indeed,' he said. He tapped his lips thoughtfully. 'But that still leaves us with a problem... Defences.'

'Defences?'

'Let's not forget what happened to our alien friend. Hmm... let's see...'

The Doctor picked up his diving helmet and reached inside it. Carefully he removed the little communication unit and placed it at the foot of the stone door.

'Now,' he said, 'let's get out of this tunnel.'

He edged back along the ledge. Q'ilp swam alongside him.

When they were safely round the corner, the Doctor said 'All right, Q'ilp, let's see what you can do.'

The dolphin began to whistle, to sing into his communicator, low at first, then rising in pitch. The Doctor peered round the corner. In the distance the stone slab began to tremble, he was sure.

'Higher,' said the Doctor. He could see a crack appearing along the edge of the slab.

Quite suddenly the slab whipped back, revealing a square hole of darkness.

Something was happening. The air in the tunnel began to shimmer, to shine. The Doctor threw himself backwards. There was a deafening CRACK...

And then silence.

The Doctor inched forward into the tunnel.

'It appears to be safe now,' he said.

'What was it?' Q'ilp asked as they cautiously approached the doorway.

'There,' said the Doctor.

A disrupter nozzle, not particularly large or dangerous looking, but devastatingly destructive, was set into the stonework.

'They really didn't want visitors here,' the Doctor said. 'A quite dreadful weapon.'

'But why?' Q'ilp asked. 'I thought this was supposed to be a temple. Why would they set a booby trap in a temple?'

The Doctor nodded through the door.

The chamber beyond was small and simple, with none of the ornamentation of the rest of the temple. In its centre a tall, elegant plinth stood on a raised dais. On the plinth was an object – a vertical-standing cylinder, transparent, with a ring of dull green rods inside and a series of metal protuberances, etched with patterns and alien script, outside. Light from the surface filtered down through an array of crystals set into the ceiling so that the cylinder was lit as though in a spotlight.

'It was defending that,' said the Doctor.

'What is it?' Q'ilp asked.

'The holy of holies,' said the Doctor. 'The true Cross.'

'Isn't that a carrying strap on its side?' Q'ilp chirruped, peering into the chamber.

The Doctor stepped inside the chamber and cautiously approached the totem.

'Ah...' he said.'I see.Yes, yes, it all fits.'

'What all fits?' asked Q'ilp, a little irritably.

'The murals show that the race who built this gloried in war. Their holy symbol, it seems, is a weapon. Some kind of biogenetic weapon...'

'What kind of screwed-up people worship a weapon?' the dolphin whistled.

'You recall Earth history?'

'Human history?' Q'ilp queried.

'Eh, yes... quite,' said the Doctor. 'The Crusades. A very unfortunate time. The swords of the crusaders were sacred to them, shaped like the cross, and treated with equal veneration. Curiously, their Muslim enemies' swords were crescent-shaped...'

'Doctor,' Q'ilp cut in, 'I hate to interrupt, but I think something's happening.Vibrations...'

The Doctor paused, listening...

The faintest rumble, the faintest of vibrations beneath his feet.

'Good grief,' he whispered. 'The sonic disruption... We've got to get out of here!'

The floor was definitely shaking now. A thin shower of dust fell on to the Doctor. He lifted the weapon from the plinth and began edging his way back along the ledge. He stopped to pick up his diving helmet and gloves, and put them on.

'Come on!' he shouted as he lowered the helmet over his face. 'I think the whole place is about to cave in!'

He jumped into the water next to Q'ilp. The dolphin circled him twice, then vanished beneath the surface. Clumsily the Doctor tried to follow. He could dimly see Q'ilp's tail cutting through the water in front of him. The dolphin dived into a narrow tunnel; the Doctor struggled to follow him. The heavy, awkward weapon made movement even more difficult. He didn't dare let the dolphin out of his sight – he'd never find his way out of these tunnels.

'Q'ilp!' the Doctor called. 'Slow down...'

Only then did he remember that his helmet communicator was lying at the foot of the hidden door above. He was cut off.

Stones and rocks were falling into the water, plunging around him. He flailed and tumbled in their wake. They began to hit him. He could no longer see Q'ilp. He felt his diving suit tear under the impact of the avalanche and begin to fill with water. The seeping cold shocked him. His mind raced – the helmet would fill in moments. He hugged the weapon to his chest and steadied his breathing. His breaths became slow and shallow... Slower...

The water inched up his chin, over his mouth and nose, his eyes...

The green world swam before his eyes and turned inky black.

Chapter Nine

Ace was in a bad mood. She'd missed her date with Rajiid, lost Bryce and been taken for a prostitute. Now, for want of anything better to do, she picked her way along the warm, dark streets to the main admin building. She swiped the plastic card the Doctor had given her across the main door and it slid silently open for her. A security guard nodded as she passed him.

She entered the lift and ascended to the third level, then tried to find MacKenzie's laboratory. The building was empty, the corridors unlit. She located the lab and groped for the light switch. Where the hell was it? As her eyes became used to the ring-lit darkness she peered about the room. It was a mess. Benches and cupboards were overturned. She felt her way to the big table on which the alien body had lain.

Something was wrong. The body was gone.

Ace froze. She wasn't alone in the room – she could sense it. She began to grope her way towards the door. Somewhere she could hear breathing. It sounded like an animal.

It was coming from the door.

She edged backwards. She could hear heavy, shuffling footsteps coming towards her in the darkness. There was a musky, animal smell.

She peered round, desperate to find another means of escape. She tried to dredge a picture of the laboratory from her memory.

There was a long window dividing it from the next lab. Ace groped for one of the tall metal stools that were scattered about the room. She tested its weight in her hand. She sprang forward, swung the stool over her head and hurled it at the glass. The window shattered into tiny fragments.

The thing in the darkness snarled and lurched forward. Ace

dived over a bench and hurled herself at the window. She vaulted the ledge and landed like a cat in the next room.

The thing roared and lumbered after her, smashing everything in its path. Ace found the door and tugged on it.

It was locked.

She rattled the handle frantically, uselessly. The thing was in the room with her now, bearing down on her. She could feel its ragged breath from half-way across the room.

She ran across to a window and hurled it open.

'Oi!' she yelled into the darkness. 'I could use a hand here!'

There was a walkway outside the window. A good old-fashioned fire escape. She clambered through the window and dropped on to it, breaking immediately into a run. She could feel the vibrations as the creature lumbered after her and began to follow her as she raced along the walkway looking for a ladder.

There was no way down. The ladders were all retracted behind transparent casings. She tugged vainly at one. She couldn't spend all night running around the walkway. She glanced back over her shoulder. She could see a silhouette in the ring-light. The thing was huge.

She began tugging and pushing at windows as she passed them. All were locked.

No – one was open. She heaved herself through it. She was in a storeroom – for chemicals, judging by the vats lining the rows of shelves that divided the room into half a dozen aisles. She found her way to the door. Once more, it was locked.

The thing clambered into the room after her. It lumbered along the rows, sniffing.

It had her scent.

Suddenly it surged forward, running, snarling, straight at Ace. She ran backwards and darted into a neighbouring aisle. The thing followed her, elbowing the shelves, upsetting vats which fell and smashed on the tiled floor.

She began to get an idea.

Even in the darkness she could see which vats contained hazardous materials – the warning stickers glowed in the dark.

She edged her way as quietly as she could into the next aisle and positioned herself next to the lethal liquids. She lifted a jeroboam down to the floor and stuck her head through the gap it left in the shelf. In the next aisle the creature stood, its back to her, sniffing the air.

'Oi, gruesome!' she yelled.

The thing spun round and sprang forward, roaring. Ace pushed with all her strength at the tall shelves. With agonising slowness they toppled forward, crashing down on the creature. Its arms flailed, smashing open the deadly vessels that fell with the shelves.

Chemicals hissed and slewed over the creature. It let out a bellow of pain and staggered backwards. It let out one final, savage roar, then lurched away into the darkness. Ace heard the door to the room splintering as it was torn from its hinges. And then nothing.

She remained motionless for long minutes, her heart pounding. At last she crept towards the door.

There was something in front of her. She yelled and leapt backwards.

The room was suddenly flooded with harsh light. Garrett was standing in the doorway.

'What are you doing here?' he asked.

'That... thing...' said Ace. 'Did you see it?'

'I saw nothing,' said Garrett. 'I heard a commotion coming from in here... And I found you.'

'There's... something in here with us,' said Ace. 'It tried to kill me.'

'Very inventive,' said Garrett. He was pale, stiff and sweating profusely.

'Are you all right?' Ace asked. 'You look terrible.'

'I'm tired, and I've got a bad back. It's the middle of the night. And now I'm faced with a case of breaking and entering and vandalism.'

He slammed his palm against the wall. 'I don't need this.'

'Didn't you hear what I told you?' Ace shouted. 'We've got to see the co-ordinator. We've got to tell her...'

'Oh, don't worry,' said Garrett. 'That's exactly where we're going.'

Brenda Mulholland listened impassively to Ace's story. Garrett scoffed throughout.

'All right, Phillip,' Brenda said at length, 'what's your version?'

'I really am sorry to have bothered you with this,' said Garrett. 'I should probably just have called the police, but given her companion's connection with InterOceanic...'

'Yes, very sensitive, Phillip. Very diplomatic. Get on with it.'

'It's simple,' Garrett smirked. 'She climbed on to the fire escape and got into the building. Then when she was inside, she went on a rampage. Did a lot of damage...'

'Did you see the door to that storeroom?' Ace was angry. 'It was smashed to pieces! D'you think I did that?'

'...and then made up this cock-and-bull story to cover herself,' Garrett concluded.

'I'm not sure,' Brenda mused. 'You remember the girl – the maintenance engineer – who swore she'd seen a monster in the service tunnels?'

'Oh Brenda, come on...' Garrett protested.

'I've seen it myself, remember, Phillip,' she snapped. 'I'm increasing security all around the square. As of now. And get to bed, Phillip – you look terrible.'

With a stiff smile Garrett left the room.

'And you, young woman, make yourself scarce.'

'No problem,' said Ace surlily, turning to go.

'How is the Doctor?' Brenda asked suddenly.

'Busy,' said Ace. 'He'll be in touch when he needs something – don't worry.'

The Doctor awoke to feel the sun on his face and the bobbing deck of the *Zodiac* beneath his back. He drew in a long, slow breath and slowly opened his eyes.

'My God!' Q'ilp yelled, scuttling across the deck on his robot spider-legs. 'I thought you were dead!'

'Respiratory bypass system,' the Doctor whispered. His chest and throat felt bruised and sore. 'Useful in a tight squeeze. What happened down there?'

'You blacked out,' said Q'ilp. 'I had to pull you up. Getting to be a habit.'

'Thank you again,' the Doctor said. 'I wouldn't have lasted long down there.' His mind raced back to the temple. 'The weapon,' he rasped. 'What happened to the weapon?'

Q'ilp extended a metal tentacle and slid the bulky cylinder across the deck.

'I had to go back for it,' said Q'ilp. 'Tricky business. 'D'you know how difficult it was getting you and that thing up on to the boat?'

The Doctor stooped over the ancient weapon and began examining it intently. 'Who knows?' he mused. 'You might have saved the entire colony.'

'Commander, we are receiving a communication from the target planet.'

Bisoncawl marched forward. Bavril leapt aside to avoid him.

'There's a lot of interference,' the communications operator said timidly. Scratcher. Bavril's mate, and the unluckiest man on the ship. Communications operators always got it in the neck.

'Bisoncawl,' the commander growled into the communicator.

'I've located Vreik,' the communicator hissed. 'He's dead. Some humans discovered his body.'

'Did he find the weapon?' Mottrack pushed his number two roughly to one side.

'It wasn't recovered with him,' the voice on the communicator said. 'General, the Doctor – the offworld investigator whose presence I reported – he found Vreik. He's asking a lot of questions. He says he's from InterOceanic, but I don't believe him. He might know more than he's letting on.'

'Then deal with him,' Mottrack barked.

'He's suspicious,' the voice crackled. 'And he's making the authorities suspicious. I'm in danger of being exposed.'

'Then you must conclude your preparations without delay,' said Mottrack. 'When can we proceed?'

His question was met with a staccato burst of static.

'What's happened?' Mottrack growled.

'Interference, General. There's nothing I can do about it. You'll just have to be patient.'

Bavril winced at Scratcher's words. Mottrack let out a low hiss. His hand went to his gun.

'No,' said Mottrack.

Scratcher paled.

'No, take him below.'

'No!' Scratcher shouted. A Cythosi guard gripped him by the shoulders and lifted him bodily from his seat. 'No!'

Bavril took a step forward, then stopped. Bisoncawl was staring at him, his eyes burning out a warning. There was nothing he could do but watch as Scratcher was hauled away.

Mottrack tickled the struggling man roughly under the chin.

'Soon...' he purred.

There was a familiar rattling, clicking sound behind Bavril. He turned as their cetacean guest scuttled past. 'Another morsel for the captain's table?'

'What? Ah, Blu'ip,' Mottrack grunted.

'What's happening?' the dolphin asked.

'We can wait no longer,' said Mottrack. 'Set maximum drive for Coralee.'

Ace must have walked the beach for about two hours. She watched one of Coralee's suns rise over sea while the other was still an orange glow. She'd gone back to the hotel but had been unable to sleep. Where the hell was the Doctor?

'I had a hunch I'd find you here.'

Ace spun around, poised to run. Rajiid was smiling at her.

'Sorry I blew you out earlier,' said Ace. 'Stuff I had to do for the Doctor.'

'It's OK,' said Rajiid. 'I wasn't in much of a party mood anyway.'

'I know what you mean,' said Ace. 'We came here for a holiday.' She sniffed, derisively. 'Fat chance...'

She was suddenly aware of soft footfalls running along the sand behind them. She and Rajiid turned at the same time.

'Troy,' she said in surprise. The boy from the beach.

The lad appeared agitated. In the distance behind him, where the sand gave way to low cliffs, a group of his contemporaries was huddled around something. Troy beckoned urgently to Ace.

'OK, OK,' said Ace. 'We're coming. What is it?'

'In the old shuttle wreck,' Troy said. 'I'll show you.'

They followed him at a trot along the beach. A crowd of kids was gathered around a cluster of rusted metal that stuck out from the sand like the ribcage of a metal animal. As the three of them approached Ace could see the shape of a small shuttlecraft, long since gutted. The kids were sticking their heads into it and jabbering loudly to each other.

'There's something in there,' said Troy. 'A dead thing. No one'll go in.'

Ace peered into the tangle of the wreck. Thick cables and rusted beams formed an artificial cavern.

'Let me,' said Rajiid, squeezing past Ace and into the wreck. Ace squeezed through behind him.

'It's over by the far wall,' Troy called from outside.

Ace could see it. One of the creatures that had attacked them in the sub.

It lay, motionless, on its back, eyes wide and staring. She could study it closely now. It was humanoid – vaguely. Two arms, two

113

legs... But its head was fiercely alien. Rows of razor-teeth lined its open mouth. Its skin was a pale bluish-grey and glistened wetly, putting Ace in mind of the scales of a fish.

A fish that had been gutted. There were deep, long gashes along its front and sides. One of its legs was virtually severed at the knee.

Rajiid let out a low whistle.

'Look at the claws.' He pointed at the creature's outstretched hands. The shell-like talons glinted like cold steel.

'No wonder they nearly tore us apart,' said Rajiid. 'I've never seen anything like this on Coralee... Not anywhere. What the hell happened to it?'

Ace shook her head. 'Beats me. The eel? Could the body have floated here?'

'It's possible.' Rajiid looked at her. 'What should we do with it?'

'I don't know,' said Ace. Not take it back to MacKenzie's lab, that was for sure.

'Maybe we should tell the police,' said Rajiid without much enthusiasm.

'No,' said Ace. That was the last thing the Doctor would want. 'But we need to get it somewhere safe.'

Somewhere the police wouldn't find it.

'I've got a workshop close to the harbour,' said Rajiid, as if reading her thoughts. 'If you don't want anyone finding it...'

It took them the best part of an hour to drag the body across the beach with the help of the kids. They bribed the gang with a handful of change that Rajiid had in his pocket, and Ace promised to take them rock climbing. They lashed the body to a metal plate from the shuttle wreck and hauled it like a sledge to the prefabricated metal shed where Rajiid evidently did all his own repairs on the sub. Greg was there working. Bits of machinery lay everywhere. A spare sub engine hung from a heavy block and tackle. Greg cleared a space on his long workbench, and the three of them heaved the body on to it.

'There's something weird about this thing,' said Rajiid, peeling back a flap of torn skin on the creature's chest. 'Its insides... No proper organs, no proper muscles...'

'What?'

'I was a medical student for a bit,' said Rajiid sheepishly. 'Never got very far. Long story...'

'So what are you saying?' urged Ace.

'Nothing's differentiated,' said Rajiid. 'No specialised organs. Everything looks practically the same.'

'I don't understand,' said Ace.

'Neither do I,' said Greg, prodding the thing's chest with his fingers.

His expression suddenly froze. His eyes widened.

'I'll tell you something else, Ace...' He pulled his hand back and moved away from the body. 'I think it's still alive.'

Ace didn't have time to reply. The body twitched, danced on the table. Before they could move it lashed out, its heavy clawed arm catching Greg across the face and sending him spinning across the workshop. In seconds the creature was on its feet in front of them. It let out a curious, queasy mewing sound. A *vicious* sound...

'What now?' whispered Ace. The thing was looking at her with bright, primitive eyes.

'Don't move,' said Rajiid quietly.

Sod that. Ace dived forward and rolled behind a metal cupboard – just in time. The thing sprang for her, its powerful legs thrusting it forward, its lethal claws raking the air in front of her face.

Rajiid was moving too. He sprang over the workbench, knocking a pile of equipment to the floor, and joined her.

'It seems slow,' whispered Ace. 'Sluggish.'

'Probably because half its guts are hanging out,' said Rajiid. He was rummaging among the debris he'd knocked from the bench. He fished out a small buoy and scrabbled at its base.

In a cacophony of sound the buoy screeched into life, strobing blue light across the workshop.

The creature cocked its head in curiosity. The lights seemed to fascinate it. It had them trapped – it seemed in no hurry to deal with them.

'That wall locker above your head,' said Rajiid. 'There's an antique gun in there.'

Ace pulled the little door open and felt the cold metal of a pistol barrel. A 47 magnum, loaded. She passed it to Rajiid.

'It's years since I used this,' he said. 'Cover your ears.'

He aimed the gun and squeezed the trigger. He emptied the magazine into the creature's torso. It staggered under the impact, and let out a roar of pure fury. Ace could see the holes torn by the bullets. The creature continued to advance.

'Any ideas?' said Rajiid.

The thing sprang again but Ace was prepared. She braced herself against the wall and kicked out with all her strength against the metal cupboard. It tipped forward and crashed on to the creature which roared again, its claws flashing and grating against the cupboard's sides.

Ace watched in horror. The thing's claws were tearing through the metal walls as if they were made of paper. The huge cupboard was being torn to ribbons.

Ace glanced over at Greg, slumped against the wall of the workshop. His face was a deathly white, his arm twisted under him at an impossible angle.

'We've got to get over to Greg,' she whispered. 'We'll have to distract it.'

'Got it!' said Rajiid. He pulled an old box from a shelf and ripped it open. He took out what looked to Ace like a big firework.

'Flares,' said Rajiid. 'This is a time of distress, isn't it? Cover your eyes.'

116

He pulled a loop on the back of the tube. There was a fizzing, and a blinding flash. The creature screamed and clutched its eyes. The flare had hit it square in the face.

'Now!' Rajiid shouted.

They tried to dart around the blinded, flailing monster. With a hiss of fury it sprang into their path.

'It can still see us,' said Rajiid. 'Or hear us...'

The monster staggered around the workshop, tearing wildly at the smoking skin of its face.

It was directly under the block and tackle. Directly under the engine.

Ace threw herself forward, her foot slamming into the winch control.

With a deafening clang of chains the huge sub engine dropped on to the monster, catching it across the shoulder blades. The creature folded almost in half with a horrible whistling rattle.

Ace crossed to it and kicked it. It seemed dead, but she had thought that before..

She joined Rajiid, who was crouching next to Greg.

'Is he all right?'

Rajiid nodded. 'I think so. Some superficial bleeding... and I think his arm's broken. We'd better get him to the medi-centre.'

There was a groaning, grinding sound behind them. Ace spun round – to her horror the huge engine was moving... Slowly it upended itself and crashed on to its side. The creature, crushed and broken, somehow regained its feet and stood regarding her balefully.

'Move back,' said Rajiid quietly. 'It's on its last legs, must be. Maybe...'

With a hiss, the creature lurched forward, its claws scything the air. Ace staggered backwards.

'We've got to get past it,' Ace whispered. 'Get to the door.'

As she spoke the metal door clanged open.

'Ace! Get down!'

Police, armoured and carrying heavy guns, were flooding into the little workshop. The Doctor swept in on the tide, carrying something huge and cylindrical in his arms.

'Get down!' he shouted again. 'All of you!'

The police surrounded the creature and immediately began firing their guns into it. It jerked and twitched and howled, then fell back to the floor.

'Stop firing!' the Doctor shouted over the din.

The barrage continued. Bullets ripped at the creature's flesh. Meat exploded from it in lumps. It was barely recognisable by the time the Doctor persuaded them to stop.

He surveyed the broken body sadly. 'So this is a Krill,' he said.

'Nobody move!' a police officer barked. He turned to the Doctor. 'Thank you, sir,' he said. 'Now, the weapon, please.'

'What? This?' The Doctor clutched the cylinder to his chest. 'I can assure you, officer, this isn't a weapon. It's a religious artefact.'

The officer held out a broad, sinewy hand.

'I can smell weapons, sir,' he said with a steely smile. 'I'm going to have to impound it. It's not registered. We don't allow unregistered weapons on Coralee.'

The Doctor sighed, and handed the weapon over. He turned to Ace and smiled.

'I'm afraid I had to bring the Seventh Cavalry,' he said. 'I had no choice.'

Chapter Ten

'From what I can make of this mess, your observations were quite right, Rajiid,' said the Doctor. 'Almost no specialisation of body functions at all. Ingenious.'

'What are you saying, Doctor?' asked Brenda Mulholland.

They were crowded into the lab next to MacKenzie's laboratory – the Doctor, Ace, Rajiid, Brenda and Garrett, along with MacKenzie himself. The Krill lay dead on a bench; the Doctor stood over it, knife in hand.

'I mean that this creature can withstand enormous amounts of damage to almost any part of its body,' he said. 'When one part is damaged, the others simply take over its functions. Ace was lucky. She hit a very vital area, and that and the damage it had already received were finally too much for it. It must have been repairing itself all the time it was on the beach. I wonder how long it was there... And more to the point, what damaged it in the first place.'

'When I was out swimming,' said Ace, 'when we first arrived, there was this dirty great speedboat. It ran over something in the water – gave the boat a hell of a jolt.' She swallowed hard. 'I was swimming out there.'

'I'll close the beaches,' said Brenda. She pulled hard on her cigarette. 'The tourists will love that...'

'Yes, yes,' said the Doctor wearily. In a way he was grateful for the intrusion of the authorities. He had a sense that things were starting to run out of his control.

The police had been waiting for the submersible when it had put into port. MacKenzie had reported it missing. The Doctor was being escorted back to the hotel in a police transport when the signal from Rajiid's emergency buoy had come through on the vehicle's communicator. Now he had the feeling he was under arrest.

'What else can you tell us about this creature, Doctor?' Garrett asked.

'Not a great deal,' said the Doctor. 'It's genetically engineered, of course. It's a weapon.'

His gaze flashed between Brenda Mulholland, tense and chain-smoking, and Garrett, whose pale, craggy face glistened with sweat.

'A living weapon, created by the people who once inhabited the planet.'

'Doctor,' Brenda asked, 'how many of these things do you think are out there?'

The Doctor shrugged. 'Impossible to say. I don't know nearly enough about them.'

'Doctor...'

Something was happening to the Krill. It was changing. Its skin was thickening. It was becoming coated in some kind of hard, shiny casing.

'Incredible,' said the Doctor. 'Even now there are residual signs of life... Good grief! I understand. When its life is almost extinguished it can return to its larval state. Presumably to heal itself. It's glanding some substance which re-creates its cocoon. It can return to its gestation – the egg stage – and start again.'

He reached into the creature, pulling at strange, unfamiliar organs. The black mucus of the shell was beginning to harden.

With a sharp twist of his hand the Doctor pulled a thick twitching bundle of fibrous tissue from the creature's ribcage. The knife flashed and the tissue was severed from the spine. At once the black slime lost its form and slid down on to the floor of the lab.

'That ought to take care of it,' he said, lowering the knife. 'I'm sorry about the mess.'

He crossed the lab to the sink and washed his hands.

'There's nothing more I can do here,' he said. 'I need to think. Good day.'

He squashed his hat on to his head, then raised it to the assembled company.

'You can't just leave,' Garrett protested, placing himself between the Doctor and the door. 'You're the only one who knows anything about what's happening here.'

Ace tensed.

'Oh, I'll be in touch, of course,' said the Doctor. 'I'll keep you up to date with any developments. Through the proper channels, of course.'

'That's me,' said Brenda.

'Quite,' said the Doctor, smiling broadly at her. 'Get out of the way, please, Mr Garrett.'

'You don't trust him, do you, Doctor?' said Ace. 'Neither do I.'

The Doctor was striding across the square, scowling furiously. Ace trotted alongside him. Rajiid brought up the rear.

'He's terribly interested in administrative matters, for an engineer,' said the Doctor. 'No, I don't trust him. But unfortunately he has the weapon, and now he has the Krill.'

'That big cylinder thing? The police took it,' said Ace.

'I think it amounts to the same thing,' the Doctor replied. 'That policeman wouldn't recognise a million-year-old biogenic weapon if it was fired at his mother. He knew what he was looking for. He was tipped off.'

'By Garrett.'

'Indeed. As for our other dead alien, heaven only knows where he's got to. If I had a suspicious mind, I would suspect that Garrett has him, too, though I can't think why.'

He stopped, and let out a heavy breath.

'Garrett holds all the aces at the moment.' He smiled tenderly at his companion. 'Except one. Tell me, Ace, did you have any luck with our friend Edwin Bryce?'

'I lost him,' Ace replied bitterly. 'I followed him to a brothel, and the police raided the place. They took him away. They said someone wanted to talk to him.'

'Garrett,' said the Doctor.

'What about Brenda?' Ace asked.

'Whatever Garrett's up to, he's acting without the knowledge of Miss Mulholland,' said the Doctor. 'He has no official civic authority. Miss Mulholland's the colony co-ordinator. I imagine if she was involved with Garrett we'd be in police custody by now. Helping them with their inquiries.'

'So what do we do now?'

The Doctor pulled the alien data-pad from his pocket.

'We still have this,' he said.

'Yeah, but that's locked.'

'Yes, and the key eludes me. And then there's Edwin Bryce.' He scanned the bright metal-and-stone holidayscape. 'I'm going to find him. There can't be that many bars on Coralee. Wait for me at the hotel.' Smiling, he tousled her hair. 'This hasn't turned out to be much of a holiday, has it?' he said apologetically.

Ace grinned. 'It's wicked, Professor,' she said.

The Doctor turned in the direction of the Castaway Bar. He feared he had a long night ahead of him.

The Doctor lurked unsuccessfully in six bars that night. From the Castaway he moved on to the Sailor's Rest – the bars on these holiday worlds were monotonously themed – and then to Bernie's Inn, Christopher Columbus's, Molly Malone's and the Happy Alcoholic. His stomach was awash with exotic fruit juices served in strangely shaped glasses, garlanded with bright, exotic foliage and consumed through labyrinthine straws.

In every bar he positioned himself with a view of the door and waited, looking for Bryce, passing the time by punching endless combinations on the alien data-pad.

He decided to go downmarket. He finished the last of his

kwanga juice and stepped into the street. He could hear music and the babble of voices coming from a prefabricated shack under some trees. A crooked sign outside it just said 'Exotic Dancers'. A choking *mélange* of alien tobacco smells hung in a cloud around the low door. Stooping and removing his hat, the Doctor went inside.

It was dark. The only light came from a tiny stage on which an overweight woman in a dirty, too-tight bunny costume wiggled without enthusiasm in time to a fluting, fluttering soundtrack. The uneven floor was crowded with tables; the tables were crowded with mostly middle-aged men.

'Welcome to Next Door to Paradise,' growled a huge Dreekan waiter carrying two trays of drinks. He wrapped his two spare arms, knotty with muscle and dark with obscene tattoos, around the Doctor and began running his huge hands roughly up and down the Time Lord's clothing.

'Weapons check,' he said. 'What's this?'

He pulled the data-pad from the Doctor's pocket.

'Uh, nothing, really. Not a weapon, I can assure you.'

With a grunt the Dreekan handed the device back.

'Now, what can I get you?'

'Uh, nothing, thank you.'

'You got to have something,' the waiter growled. 'You're in here now.'

'Kwanga juice,' the Doctor sighed. He was peering about the gloomy shack, trying to penetrate the veil of smoke.

The waiter snorted and pushed him in the direction of a table.

'There,' he grunted.

'No... I'm meeting a friend here,' said the Doctor. 'There.'

Bryce was sitting at a tiny corner-table, hunched over a line of empty glasses, staring down into them. The Doctor edged his way between the tables and sat down opposite him.

'Mr Bryce,' he said.

Edwin Bryce looked drunkenly up at him.

'Folk tales...' he slurred.

'I beg your pardon.'

'Noth... Nothing but folk tales. Swear to God. I told the police all this yesterday.'

'I'm not the police, Mr Bryce,' said the Doctor gently. 'Why don't you tell me?'

Bryce suddenly gripped the Doctor's sleeve. He was trembling. He was clearly petrified.

'Tell me it's not true,' he whispered. 'The Krill. They're just legends, aren't they?'

'What do you know about the Krill, Mr Bryce?'

Bryce shook his head and shuddered. The Doctor put a hand on his shoulder, and looked deep into Bryce's eyes. He tried to look into the man's mind, but all he could sense was fear and confusion and the jumbled emotions of too much booze.

'I'll be honest with you,' the Doctor said. 'The Krill exist. We've found one, and seen evidence of more. The colony is in danger. We need to know as much about these things as we can.'

'I told Garrett everything,' Bryce pleaded.

'Tell me,' said the Doctor soothingly.

Bryce reached out and grabbed a drink from the Dreekan's tray as the waiter swept past. He downed it in a single gulp.

'There are lots of stories,' said Bryce. 'According to the legends, the ancient masters of Coralee loosed the Krill on their enemies They sent the eggs into space... bombarded their enemies' worlds with them. The Krill laid waste to every world where they set foot. They were like a virus, destroying everything they came into contact with. They were indestructible.'

'Nothing is indestructible,' said the Doctor. 'Well... practically nothing.'

'Even their eggs could survive anything.' Bryce went on. 'They used to drift in the bitter cold of space for years, apparently. Atmospheric burn-up. Intense radiation. According to some tales, they fed on radiation.'

'Fed on radiation...' The Doctor chewed his lips in thought.

Bryce paused for another drink.

'And then what?' the Doctor asked.

'The Krill came home,' said Bryce. 'Home to Coralee. They did here what they did everywhere else. The masters of Coralee devised a weapon to combat them, so the story goes, but they were too late. The Krill destroyed everything on the planet – turned it into a blasted wilderness for millennia – and died out themselves.'

He lurched towards the Doctor, knocking glasses to the floor, gripping the Time Lord's coat and staring imploringly into his eyes.

'They died out, Doctor! They died out!' he cried.

The Doctor smiled softly at him. 'I'm very sorry, Mr Bryce,' he said.

Bryce dropped back into his chair. The Doctor said nothing, just tapped idly at the controls on the data-pad. Suddenly the bar was filled with a loud, painful bleeping. Bryce jumped like a startled rabbit. The big Dreekan waiter stomped over to their table.

'What's going on?' he demanded. 'Shut it up or get out!'

'I can't shut it up,' the Doctor shouted over the din.

'I can,' the waiter said.

He raised an arm and brought his fist thumping down on to the table, crashing down on the pad. The alarm stopped instantly.

The Doctor sprang to his feet. 'You imbecile!' he shouted. 'Do you have any idea what you've just done?'

The waiter looked him up and down. He snarled contemptuously and flexed his fingers together, cracking the knuckles in a fierce staccato.

'Well, Blu'ip, you're going home. How does it feel?'

Bisoncawl and the cetacean were drinking in the first officer's quarters. Bavril was waiting on them, lurking in a corner and trying to be invisible.

'That sink-hole isn't my home,' the dolphin spat. 'Not any more. I hope the Krill tear the planet in two.'

'But what about your own species?' asked Bisoncawl. 'Are there not thousands of cetaceans on Coralee?'

'Cowards and traitors,' snarled Blu'ip. 'They deserve to die. Boy!'

Bavril scuttled across the room.

'Same again,' Blu'ip drawled languidly. 'And don't drown it in soda this time. Or I'll get the commander here to eat you.'

Bavril felt himself tensing. He tried to look calm.

'You don't approve of our eating habits, do you?' Bisoncawl asked the dolphin.

'I don't disapprove,' Blu'ip replied. 'I'm hardly what you'd call vegetarian myself. I just worry that by the time our mission's complete there won't be enough crew left to pilot the ship. You'll have eaten them all.'

'The good ones will be preserved,' said Bisoncawl, looking at Bavril. 'Survival is their reward for loyal service.'

Until the next voyage, Bavril thought. Or the next...

'Yes but... that fellow Mottrack pulled from the deck – he was a communications operator. That's a skilled job. Lose any more like that and...'

'His name is Scratcher,' Bavril said suddenly, without thinking. 'He's my friend.'

Bisoncawl stared coldly at him.

'Be careful, functionary,' he said. 'You want to live, don't you?'

'While my friends die around me,' Bavril said in barely a whisper.

'Speak up, boy,' Blu'ip said.

'Wh... While my friends die around me,' Bavril quavered.

Bisoncawl rose slowly to his feet. He swung a mighty arm in the air and brought it scything down at Bavril. It hit his shoulder with a crunch, and jolted him across the room. Bisoncawl stomped towards him.

'Don't damage him,' Blu'ip purred. 'He's a pretty thing...'

The dolphin extended a mechanical tentacle and stroked Bavril's cheek.

'Get out of the way,' said Bisoncawl.

He aimed a kick at Bavril's prostrate body and propelled it towards the far wall.

'Get up,' he said. Bavril staggered to his feet.

'Never again speak like this. In front of me or anyone else. Now get out.'

Bavril limped to the door and used its frame to haul himself from the room. He slumped against the wall outside. He heard the clink of glasses within.

'To Coralee,' said Blu'ip. 'May she burn in hell.'

'You forget,' said Bisoncawl, 'you'll be going back a hero. We'll all be heroes. We'll be the saviours of the colony!'

The gruff, snorting laughter of the Cythosi mingled with the high-pitched chirruping of the dolphin. Bavril limped away, cradling his bruised body with his arms.

'... And don't come back!'

The door slammed behind the unwilling drinking companions. The Doctor dusted himself down.

'I've been thrown out of better bars than that,' Bryce slurred.

The Doctor peered at the pad. The screen was suddenly awash with data. He scratched his head, and smiled.

'I do believe our friend in there has cracked it,' he said. 'Now we're getting somewhere.'

He settled down on a low wall, Bryce slumped next to him, his head weaving. He pulled his flask from his pocket and took a swig.

'Krill.' He laughed. 'And I thought I was safe on good old Coralee.'

The Doctor didn't look up, absorbed in the data on the screen.

'In my youth I was a war correspondent,' said Bryce. 'I covered the frontier campaigns. Several of the big campaigns too.' A nostalgic smile flickered over his face. 'Even saw some Daleks once.' The smile faded again. 'We set down on a planet near the end of it all, an outpost – deep-space mining colony. The place had been gutted, blown wide open.'

'Daleks?' The Doctor looked up.

Bryce nodded, and swallowed hard.

'Never seen anything like it. They weren't part of the war. Not even from that system. They arrived and massacred everyone. Women, children.'

Bryce stared at the night sky. 'Have you ever been in a war, Doctor? I mean, really in it? People being maimed and killed all around you?'

'Once or twice,' said the Doctor absently, scrutinising the data.

Bryce grabbed his arm.

'Then you know...' he said. 'I couldn't go through that again. Not here. I came here to escape all that.'

The Doctor smiled kindly at him.

'Who knows?' he said. 'It might not come to that.'

'Doctor, you don't understand,' said Bryce. 'The stories – the legends –they all say one thing. The Krill are the embodiment of mindless, destructive fury, Doctor. They are rage. Pure rage.'

Chapter Eleven

Bavril slunk down the quiet corridor. He'd never been down to these decks before. If he was found he'd be killed – or kept here. He shuddered at the thought.

A service robot scuttled out of a low hatch. Bavril froze – the things sensed movement, and Mottrack had set them all to automatic defence mode. They were lethal.

He waited until the robot had scampered away, then moved slowly forward. The silence was gradually giving way to the distant sound of activity. A strange, sweet smell permeated the corridors. It made Bavril feel slightly sick.

He came to a corner, and peered round it. A fat Cythosi was lumbering away from him down a wide corridor. The Cythosi stopped at some large metal shapes hanging in long rows from the ceiling. Bavril's eyes widened. They were cages.

'And how are my little sweetmeats today?' the Cythosi growled. He drew in a deep breath. 'Breathe, little ones,' he said. 'Breathe in the perfumed air. It's good for you.'

He lumbered off, and disappeared through a distant doorway.

Bavril sidled forward along the corridor towards the hanging cages. He felt a wave of desperate, impotent anger rising in him. Each cage held one of his people. The disappeared. Taken below.

Most were slumped, insensible, on the barred floors of their cages. Some moved, slowly and slightly, with varying degrees of lethargy. Some appeared to notice him.

'Pssst... Bavril...'

Bavril spun round.

'Scratcher!' he whispered.

Scratcher was peering at him from behind a set of bars.

'What are you doing here?' Scratcher whispered. 'You know what'll happen to you if...'

'I know,' said Bavril. He tugged at the lock on the cage.

'Don't bother,' said Scratcher. 'I've tried. Go.'

'I'm not leaving you here,' said Bavril quietly.

'For God's sake, Bavril, there's nothing you can do! I'm already cooked and served.' Scratcher smiled weakly.

There was a noise from down the corridor. Two Cythosi arguing loudly.

'I'm coming back for you,' Bavril hissed, and crept back the way he'd come, blinking to clear his eyes of tears.

In the shadows the dolphin Blu'ip watched with satisfaction. Humans were so predictable. He waited until the functionary had crept away and then scuttled forward. He stood, eyeing the rows of hanging cages with malicious glee.

The atmosphere in the colony remained unchanged. From where Ace and Rajiid were sitting in the hotel restaurant they could hear the brisk announcements of the police driving up and down the long beach, clearing the sands of holidaymakers. There was some grumbling – most people assumed that one of Coralee's rare but tempestuous storms was blowing in – but no panic. Holidaymakers cursed their bad luck, but Ace had heard nobody coming even close to the truth. She sighed. They'd find out soon enough.

She tried to put it out of her mind. She'd eaten ferociously, finishing her meal in minutes, much to Rajiid's amusement.

'You're a strange girl, Ace,' Rajiid said. 'You say you're from Earth.'

Ace nodded, swallowing the last mouthfuls. 'Perivale.'

Rajiid shook his head. 'Never heard of it,' he said.

'It's in London,' said Ace.

Rajiid laughed. 'Don't try it on,' he said.

'I'm not,' said Ace.

'Oh, so you come from a city that hasn't existed for five hundred years. OK...' the young sub pilot grinned, '...you want to be a woman of mystery, that's fine. So tell me about the Doctor. What's he – your boyfriend?'

Ace laughed. 'He's... just the Doctor,' she said.

'OK, no more questions,' Rajiid smiled.

'What about you?' asked Ace.

Rajiid shrugged. 'Not much to know. I'm an underwater tour-bus diver. Or I was until yesterday.'

'What about this medical student stuff?'

'Yeah, I did that for a bit,' said Rajiid.

'Why d'you give it up?'

Rajiid shrugged. 'Too much pain, too much suffering. Too much death. It was depressing.'

'So you came here.'

'Rajiid smiled grimly. 'Yeah,' he said. 'According to the brochures, there was no pain here. No death.'

He stared out at the promenade. The police still patrolled the beaches; people still strolled up and down in the sun, rolled in and out of the bars, gambled and drank and laughed.

'Look at them,' Rajiid said. 'They say everyone who comes here is running away from something. "Escape to Coralee" the posters say. We're all in for a shock.'

A wind was starting to blow up.

'It looks like there's going to be a storm,' said Rajiid. 'Let's go inside, shall we?'

'We seem to be stopping, Sarge,' Corporal Bell said.

'Where are we?' Frank Sands asked.

'About eight miles out from the Western Rim. There's nothing out here, Sarge.'

'Are you getting anything, Norris?'

'Nothing, Sarge. Archie's right – there are just tiddlers and rocks down here.'

'Go to visual,' said Sands. 'Constable Clark, are you getting through to control yet?'

'No, sir,' Annie Clark replied. 'It's almost as if the channels are being jammed.'

'Keep trying,' said Sands.

'We've stopped, Sarge,' Bell said.

The engines died. The sudden quiet in the cramped command chamber of police sub D-19, a mile below the surface of the ocean, was ominous. Sands could tell they all sensed it.

He turned his attention to the murky blue water-world that rippled across the sub's view-screen. Norris was right: just a broad bed of rocky undulations – an undersea plateau. Nothing out of the ordinary.

'Magnify the image,' he said.

The rocks leapt forward on the screen.

'What are those?' Sands asked. 'Coral?'

The rocks were densely, darkly clustered with black, ovoid shapes, smooth and shiny, about the size of a man Sands guessed.

'It's not like any coral I've ever seen,' said Norris.

'What's black and egg shaped...?' Sands mused.

'Is this a joke?' Norris asked.

'What?'

'Nothing, Sarge,' Norris said quickly. 'The only thing I can think of is eggs. Big, black eggs.'

'Eggs...' said Sands, puzzled.

'Sarge...' Annie Clark's voice came through the bulkhead door, breathy and nervous. 'I... I think our communications channels are being blocked.'

'What!?' Sands strode through the door, his mind racing.

'And there's something else. I've traced the sub control signal – and it's not coming from Central. It's not the authorised signal – the code's completely different.'

'Do you know what you're saying, Constable?' Sands asked sternly.

'Someone else has control of the sub.' She whispered the words.

'Sergeant Sands...' Bill Hanlon's voice crackled through the intercom from the engine room. He sounded anxious. 'We've got a big problem down here. The reactor's gone berserk!'

'What do you mean, man?' Sands fought to contain the panic in his own voice.

'It's running hotter and hotter,' Hanlon babbled. 'The controls aren't responding. It's as if it's got a mind of its own.'

'Or someone else is controlling it,' Sands muttered. 'All right, Hanlon, initiate emergency shutdown procedure.'

'I've tried!' Hanlon cried. 'It didn't do any good! It's getting critical, Sarge!'

'All right,' Sands barked. 'Constable Clark... put out a general mayday to all vessels. Tell them we have a meltdown on our hands. Give our position and tell them to get the hell away. Norris, Bell, abandon ship. You too, Hanlon.'

'You what, Sarge?'

'Just do it, Hanlon. Get to the escape pods.'

'I've sent the mayday, Sarge,' Annie Clark said.

'Good,' said Sands. 'Now let's get out of here.'

He waited for her to follow the others towards the rear of the sub. Casting a final look around his ship, he dived through the hatch after her. Norris and Bell were already cocooning themselves in their escape pods.

Hanlon appeared in the hatchway.

'It's no good, Sarge,' he said. 'When the reactor blows it'll kill everything within a mile of the ship. We'll never get away in time.'

'Just climb into your pod, son,' Sands said evenly. 'You know the drill.'

He caught Annie Clark's eyes, saw the fear in them. She knew as well as he did that they weren't going to make it.

'Goodbye, Sarge,' she said quietly.

'Annie,' he whispered, squeezing her arm gently. 'Look lively,' he said. 'You don't want to listen to Hanlon. You know what he's like. Voice of doom.'

He watched as Constable Annie Clark climbed into her escape pod and sealed it shut. The others were launching themselves into the ocean. Annie soon followed.

He straightened his uniform and looked around the sub's aft hold for the last time. The air was suddenly, painfully hot. He could hear a whining, screaming, rending sound coming from the guts of the craft.

For the briefest fraction of a second he was aware of a blinding, excoriating light, a furnace heat, a sound like the universe ripping in two; and in that sound he thought he could hear the voice of his father, twenty years dead, calling him, laughing.

'Are you insane, Bavril?'

'It's Scratcher down there,' said Bavril flatly. 'Scratcher.'

'I know,' said Huttle quietly. 'But what you're talking about is mad! Even suppose you do rescue him – what are you going to do with him then?'

Others in the crowded barracks grunted their agreement.

'I don't know,' said Bavril. 'Hide him... You know the Cythosi – they can barely tell us apart. Look, all I want from you is a cutting tool. Just for a short time. You know I don't have access to that sort of equipment.'

'Forget it,' said Huttle.

'I'll get it for you.'

The voice rang out from the back of the long room.

Bavril saw Peck pushing his way towards him. He'd hoped it wouldn't come to this, but had suspected Peck would be the only one to support him.

'I'm a level two engine-room functionary. I can get you something that'll do the job. I'm about to go on shift.'

Bavril sighed.

'Thank you, Peck,' he said. 'But please – be discreet.'

* * *

Edwin Bryce was almost sober by the time he reached the central admin block.

'Let me in,' he said to the security officer on the main door. 'I'm here to see Chief Engineer Garrett.'

The guard looked him disdainfully up and down. Bryce knew he didn't present an edifying picture – he hadn't washed, shaved or changed his clothes since yesterday. He stank of booze. He'd spilled a quantity of the stuff over himself in the course of the day.

'Name,' the guard said.

'Bryce. Edwin Bryce.'

'I've read a couple of your books, sir,' the guard said slowly. 'Didn't think much of them.'

'Just tell Garrett I'm here, will you?' Bryce snarled.

The guard triggered his intercom. 'Mr Garrett,' he said wearily, 'there's a person to see you. Name of Bryce.'

His face registered mild surprise.

'You're to go up,' he said. 'Mr Garrett's office is on the fifth floor.'

Bryce was scarcely aware of walking past the guard and into the lift. He alighted on the fifth floor and picked his way along the corridor of offices. Garrett's was at the far end. He knocked tremulously at the door.

No answer. He knocked harder. He could hear sounds of movement from inside. 'Mr Garrett...' he called out timorously.

He opened the door and stepped inside. The blinds were drawn – the office was in semi-darkness. There was a smell in the room – a rank, sickening smell. Rancid meat.

'I came, just as you said, if the Doctor contacted me...' Bryce coughed. The smell was choking. 'Well, I've just left him.'

'What did he say?'

Bryce jumped out of his skin. Garrett's voice, harsh and breathless, came through an open door in the far wall. The room beyond was dark. Bryce could hear a low, ragged, rhythmic sound coming from it. It sounded almost like... something breathing.

'He... He asked a lot about the Krill,' Bryce stammered.' I... might have told him a little too much...'

Something lying in shadow in the far corner of the room caught Bryce's eye. He stepped closer – and froze in horror. He felt his blood chill.

It was a body. That creature from the dig. Dead. Dead, and... His stomach lurched. He vomited. The corpse's flesh hung from it in ribbons. The thing was half-eaten.

'It doesn't matter,' Garrett growled. 'It's too late for anybody to stop it now.'

Bryce spun around. Garrett was standing in the darkness behind him. His breathing sounded like a broken bellows. There was something about his face...

'What's wrong, Bryce?'

Bryce didn't reply. His throat had dried and closed.

'You look frightened,' Garrett said, taking a step closer. His face seemed to... shimmer... blur and melt...

It wasn't Garrett at all – it was...

Bryce felt a hand shoot out and grab him by the throat. He staggered backwards, screaming.

'I seem to have eaten something that disagrees with me.' Garrett gave a high, giggly laugh. 'They say that you are what you eat. Perhaps I should change my diet.'

A huge arm flashed down and knocked the scream from Bryce. Barely conscious, he was aware of a pair of ferocious jaws opening about his face, and then pain...

Central admin was buzzing with people when the Doctor arrived. Officials were arguing in the foyer. Civilians were clustered around, shouting at them.

'My kids were out there!' one was shouting. 'A day cruise. The *Adair*.'

'We are still trying to establish which vessels are in the area,' an official said, his voice trained to instil calm. It wasn't working.

The Doctor slipped easily into the mêlée, and out the other side. He was in the lift before anyone challenged him.

Things seemed just as bad on the third floor. He could hear raised voices coming from the co-ordinator's office – Brenda Mulholland's, hard and throaty; others the Doctor didn't recognise.

He stepped inside. The room fell silent. Brenda Mulholland was flanked by half a dozen suited or uniformed officials, all standing around the big map of the planet, all staring at him with a mixture of apprehension and expectation on their faces. To his relief, Garrett was absent.

'Doctor...' Brenda Mulholland said.

'Miss Mulholland, I need to speak to you in private. It's important.'

She hesitated for a split second, then nodded. 'Give me a few minutes, gentlemen,' she said. Her companions filed out of the room.

'I need the weapon,' the Doctor said in a low voice. 'The biogenic weapon I found at Professor MacKenzie's dig. The police impounded it – which, as we both know, means Garrett's got it. I don't think I can stop what's happening. It's the only weapon which will be effective against the Krill. I need to examine it. You must get it from Garrett.'

'We've been trying to contact Garrett,' Brenda said. 'We can't find him. He's picked a hell of a time to do a disappearing act... Doctor, I'm glad you're here. A police submarine's been lost at sea.'

'The Krill?' the Doctor asked.

'We don't know,' Brenda said. 'All we know is the reactor went critical. It blew itself apart.'

'It was a nuclear sub?' the Doctor was aghast.

'Of course.' Brenda sounded confused. 'What else?'

The Doctor shook his head in irritation. 'Sometimes I forget what century I'm in,' he said. 'Can you show me where it happened?'

Brenda tapped the map. 'Off the Western Rim Islands,' she said.

The Doctor whipped the data-pad from his pocket and scrutinised the screen.

'This is bad,' he said. 'Very bad. What defences do you have here, Miss Mulholland?'

'We have an automated defence network. Not very powerful. We don't really need it, but it's a standard precaution. It's never been used...'

'Anything else?'

'Only the police. Forty or so. Half a dozen vehicles, one remaining sub. Hand weapons...'

'You must have storm shutters,' the Doctor said, 'from what I've heard about the weather on Coralee.'

'They were Garrett's greatest achievement,' Brenda said.

'Raise them,' the Doctor snapped. 'Get everybody off the streets. We have to seal this place.'

'What's happening, Doctor?' She lit a cigarette.

The Doctor thrust the pad under her nose.

'This is a map of sorts,' he said. 'I believe it shows the nesting grounds of the Krill. And look here.'

'That's exactly where the sub blew up,' Brenda said. 'What does that mean?'

'I talked to Edwin Bryce earlier today,' said the Doctor. 'He's studied the Krill legends. One of the things he told me was that they thrive on radiation.'

He paused, scrutinising Brenda. She looked impatient.

'Think of a seed, Miss Mulholland. Lying dormant, waiting for that first drop of moisture, that first drop of nourishment that will cause it to shoot, cause it to crack open and begin to grow.'

'What are you saying, Doctor?'

'The Krill were an unstoppable and almost uncontrollable weapon. The people who created them probably kept them dormant until they were needed, then fired the eggs into their enemy's territory and followed up with a nuclear bombardment. I believe the Krill are born out of nuclear fusion.'

'Oh God...'

'You remember the cable-laying platform – the *Hyperion Dawn*? When I examined it I found a radioactive element attached to its hull. Now this. Someone's deliberately trying to revive the Krill, Miss Mulholland.'

Brenda Mulholland hit the intercom on her desk. 'Operations?' she said. 'This is the co-ordinator. Raise the storm shutters. And activate the defence grid at maximum strength.'

'How is the colony powered?' the Doctor asked.

'A single reactor... here.' She pointed to an outlying island.

The Doctor thrust the data-pad under her nose again.

'Look,' he said. 'The densest nest clusters are around this island. Miss Mulholland, you built the thing right on top of them.'

'Garrett sited the reactor,' Brenda said slowly.

'Does it have storm defences?' the Doctor snapped.

'Yes, of course...'

'Raise them. The last thing we can afford is for anything to happen to that reactor.'

She took a deep drag on her cigarette. 'This weapon you say Garrett's got – the weapon from the dig – will it stop them?'

'I'm afraid it's not as simple as that,' the Doctor replied. 'As far as I have been able to see, it operates by sending out a massive charged biogenic pulse. It will travel around the planet in minutes.'

'And kill the Krill...'

'I imagine that was its intention. How do you stop the unstoppable?' His face furrowed into a frown. 'Unfortunately, we don't have any idea how it will affect the other species on the planet. I believe it was developed to stop the Krill, which means that potentially it's a more lethal weapon than the Krill themselves.'

Brenda nodded thoughtfully, and opened her door.

'Come in, gentlemen,' she said. The officials filed in again.

'I'm instituting a state of emergency,' she announced. 'I'm imposing an immediate curfew. I want everybody off the streets. I want all police on duty, armed and standing by.'

'Co-ordinator, will you tell us what's going on?' one of the men piped up.

'We've got a hostile invasion on our hands,' Brenda Mulholland said. 'Come back here in an hour; I'll brief you more fully then. But first I want this place sealed tight. Nothing is to get in from outside.'

'Co-ordinator, there are ships out there,' another man said.

Brenda looked searchingly at the Doctor. Her face was grave.

'You heard me,' she said. 'Put out a call to all shipping. Tell them to prepare for attack from the sea. Tell them to defend themselves as best they can.'

Her voice was hoarse.

'Move!' she barked.

The men scurried through the door.

'Where is Garrett's office?' the Doctor asked.

'Operations wing. Fifth floor. But he hasn't been answering his intercom.'

'I have to find him,' said the Doctor.

He turned to go. Brenda stopped him.

'I've put a lot of faith in you, Doctor. Is it justified?'

He fixed her with a piercing stare. 'I don't know, Miss Mulholland. It seems the Krill are pure rage. Pure aggression. There is nothing for me to reason with, nothing that I can appeal to. By now there must be millions of them out there, and I don't know how to stop them.'

Chapter Twelve

For the second time Bavril crept along the forbidden kitchen corridors of the Cythosi ship. Peck had successfully slipped him the laser-cutter, which he now clutched like a gun. He found his way to the cages.

Scratcher, like the others, was slumped in his cage.

'Wake up!' Bavril hissed. 'I told you I'd get you out.'

He switched on the laser-cutter and began burning through the cage's lock.

'Bavril...?'

Scratcher seemed to be drifting in and out of consciousness.

'Tired...' said Scratcher. 'Hard to concentrate... Bavril, listen to me.'

Scratcher clawed his way across the cage towards him. 'I'm losing movement in my arms and legs. Soon... I'll be like them. The Cythosi... pump something into the air down here. They say it flavours the meat before cooking. It's poison to us... paralyses us... It's in my system...'

'I'm getting you out of here,' said Bavril.

The lock suddenly shattered and the cage bottom swung downwards, dropping Scratcher to the floor with a thud. He lay, motionless.

There was a scuttling behind Bavril.

'Naughty, naughty,' said a high, chirruping voice.

Bavril spun round. The dolphin Blu'ip was looking at him, tapping a single metal tentacle on the ground.

'Little boys aren't allowed to raid the larder between meals. You'll just have to wait until supper time.'

'What the hell do you want!?' Bavril spat.

'I've been watching you,' said the dolphin. 'I know all about your little conspiracy.'

'Are you going to report me?' Bavril asked tensely.

'I don't know...' said Blu'ip. 'I'm still thinking about it. You... the human who stole the cutter for you, the rest of the men who were privy to your little discussion. Your friend here... not that it will make much difference to him. I could report you all. But then I got to thinking...'

He scuttled forward. Bavril backed away.

'... it's been a long voyage, and Cythosi don't make the best of companions. I find myself longing for a little... civilised company.'

He stretched out a tentacle and stroked Bavril's cheek. Bavril shuddered at the cold touch.

'You hate humans,' he said.

'Even so,' clicked Blu'ip, 'they are not entirely without their attractions.'

He shot a tentacle around Bavril's waist, and pulled him forward.

'Get off me!' Bavril shouted.

'My, you put up a struggle,' said the dolphin.

Bavril punched at the dolphin. Tentacles effortlessly blocked his blows.

Behind the dolphin he could see Scratcher clawing his way across the floor towards them.

Almost without knowing he was doing it, Bavril triggered the laser-cutter and swung it at the underplate of Blu'ip's exoskeleton. There was a flash and the dolphin scuttled backwards, squeaking and whistling in fury.

'You dare cross me?' he clicked.

He shot out a tentacle and pressed the release button on a wall hatch. A service robot scuttled from the hatch. Bavril froze instantly. So did Blu'ip.

Scratcher kept crawling forward.

The little robot whirred and spun, caught Scratcher in its sights and sprang forward.

'No!' Bavril called. He ran forward. Blu'ip stuck out a tentacle and Bavril sprawled to the ground.

The machine was on Scratcher. Its tiny rotating blades were cutting him to ribbons. Bavril groaned in horror. Scratcher made no sound.

The robot, gory from its kill, spun round.

There was a loud click, and the dolphin's metal chest-unit slid open. Twin gun-barrels peeped out.

Blu'ip began to fire round after round into the little machine. The robot danced about the floor under the impact of the bullets, sparking and twisting until it was just a piece of tangled metal and circuits. Still the dolphin fired.

Bavril lurched to his feet and began to run. The sound of machine-gun fire echoed after him.

Ace and Rajiid lay sprawled across her gigantic bed. The sheets lay in a tangled heap on the floor. Ace gazed up at the white ceiling, her mind a galaxy away from their problems.

The noise from the streets seemed to have increased. Footsteps, raised voices, the incessant, calm, feminine tones of the public address system. Ace strained to make out the words.

'BY ORDER OF THE COLONY CO-ORDINATOR, A CURFEW IS NOW IN FORCE. PLEASE RETURN TO YOUR HOMES OR HOTELS WITHOUT DELAY. ALL BUSINESSES ARE TO CLOSE IMMEDIATELY. PLEASE VACATE THE STREETS NOW. THE CENTRAL ADMINISTRATION OFFICE APOLOGISES FOR ANY INCONVENIENCE CAUSED. BY ORDER OF THE COLONY CO-ORDINATOR...'

The crackle of police megaphones mingled with the gently booming voice. Tersely barked orders cut across institutional calm.

Ace sat up. 'Something's happening,' she said.

Rajiid turned over with a groan and buried his face in a pillow.

'Does this normally happen here?' Ace asked.

Rajiid shook his head.

'Never,' he said. He thought for a moment, then grinned. 'Still... you heard the announcement. Looks like we won't be going anywhere for a while.'

There was a new sound – a deep, throbbing hum that seemed to shake the floor. The streets were suddenly silent. The vibration filled the room.

It was getting dark outside. The room was suddenly bathed in gloom.

Rajiid sprang to his feet. 'They're raising the storm shutters,' he said.

Ace was suddenly anxious.

'I'm going to find the Doctor,' she said.

'How?' asked Rajiid. 'He went looking for Bryce, remember? He could be anywhere.'

'I don't know,' said Ace, 'but I'm going to try.'

The room was suddenly filled with harsh electric light. The twilit streets were drenched in it. Ace crossed to the window and peered out. Where the sand had basked, fringed by trees, and beyond that the sea had stretched to the horizon, there was now only a towering expanse of metal, shining dully in the artificial lighting. The storm shutters were still rising out of the ground, inclining inwards as they formed a perimeter wall around the colony. They towered over the island's trees and buildings. Out at sea a shimmering line of energy sliced across the harbour. A flicker of energy began to arc from the tips of the shutters, veiling the sky with a glittering force field.

Its shadow passed across the twin suns, and it was night.

The door to Garrett's office was open. There was a smell of rank decay coming from within. The Doctor entered cautiously. The room was dark.

He groped his way to the window and opened the blinds. Electric light cut through the slatted darkness.

He turned. Next to him, sprawled dead on a table, was the alien body from the dig. Or what was left of it. Meat hung from the torso in strips. The Doctor examined the great gouges. They were fringed with ragged toothmarks.

There was movement to his left. He sprang back from the corpse as something toppled past him and landed heavily on the floor. It was Edwin Bryce; he was stiff and dead. The Doctor stooped to examine the body. An expression of pure terror was etched into Bryce's face. The flesh on one of his cheeks was gone. The head was half-severed from the trunk.

The body was still warm. The Doctor's gaze flashed quickly about the shadows. He'd have to be quick – whatever had done this to Bryce might still be here.

He began rapidly to search the room. No sign of the weapon. He opened a door at the far side of the room and peered through it.

A control panel covered one wall. The Doctor brushed the controls with his fingers. Remote engine and navigation controls for a D-class submarine. A long-range communicator.

There was a crash from the other room. A smell assaulted his nostrils. Something was in there. The Doctor could hear its harsh, animal breathing.

He stepped back through the door.

'Ah,' he said. 'Our mysterious colony monster. How do you do?'

Brenda Mulholland stood at one of the observation ports in the perimeter wall, her entourage surrounding her. The sea was choppy, the weather was turning against them. That was all they needed.

Police Chief Bodle was talking rapidly into an intercom. He fell suddenly silent.

'I see,' he said gravely. 'Co-ordinator, an SOS has been received from the *Island Queen*. She's a pleasure cruiser. She's being attacked. These things – these... Krill – are swarming all over the ship. They're literally tearing it to pieces.'

Brenda closed her eyes. She shouldn't have to take these sorts of decisions. She was chief rep on a holiday world, for God's sake.

'There's a queue of ships outside the harbour,' said Judd, the harbour master. 'They're demanding to be let in. There's mass panic breaking out on board.'

Brenda peered at the harbour mouth. Ships jostled for position outside the repulsor field. 'The shutters stay closed,' she said hollowly.

Something was happening in the sea. The waters were starting to seethe and bubble. They boiled with fury.

'Sweet Mary...' whispered the harbour master. 'I've never...'

The sea boiled over. It exploded upwards at the metal wall. Krill – hundreds, thousands of them – were hurling themselves from the water, flying towards them. The automatic laser defences kicked in. Sights swivelled, guns aligned, vicious bolts of blue lightning exploded against the frantic horde.

The Krill were clanging deafeningly off the wall. It sounded like the mother of all hailstorms. Many fell back into the sea, their talons raking the huge metal shutters. Others managed to pierce the metal with their razor claws, to hang on. They began ripping at the wall, tearing vicious slivers from its outer shell. The lasers targeted them and fired, time and time again. It was enough in most cases to blow the creatures from their handholds, back into the sea, or on to the rocks below. It didn't stop them. They just picked themselves up and began to climb, relentlessly sinking their claws into the sheer metal wall and dragging themselves upwards.

Still more Krill surged out of the sea, flying upwards in jets of spume, crashing on to the wall.

'There are too many of them!' Walter Creegan, Garrett's assistant, cried. 'The defences can't cope!'

He was right. The Krill were overwhelming the guns.

There was a sound of rending metal. It sounded like

screaming. It was coming from everywhere. Slowly the Krill were ripping their way into the colony.

'Will the wall hold?' Brenda barked.

'Well I... We have to consider...'

'*Will it hold them, Creegan?*'

'It might. The storm shutters weren't designed to take this sort of punishment.' He stifled a sob. 'I wish Garrett was here,' he whispered.

'So do I,' Brenda said stonily. 'There are some questions I want to ask him.'

The creature was advancing slowly on the Doctor. The Doctor was backing slowly away. Predator and prey, they circled the room.

'Really,' the Doctor babbled, 'do you think this is any time to be thinking about lunch?'

The alien continued to advance. The Doctor tried to make out its shape through the gloom. It was much bigger than a human, that was for sure.

'Is this what you did to your friend Garrett? Ate him when he ceased to be of use to you – or when you were feeling a little peckish?'

The alien snarled and swatted a chair across the room.

'Yes, good idea,' said the Doctor. 'Let's sit down and talk. You're an intelligent fellow – I really think you'd regret killing me.'

The Doctor was being driven into a corner.

'Listen to me,' he demanded. 'Have you any idea what you've started out there? The forces you have unleashed might well overwhelm us all. You know what they did to the race who created them.'

The creature paused for a moment. In the gloom the Doctor could see the outline of the thing's head. He stared down at the dead creature on the bench. The same species...

The thing sprang forward, its hands clutching at the Doctor's neck. The Doctor threw himself to the floor and crossed the room on all fours. He crawled beneath the table.

The monster seemed disorientated. The Doctor stood up on the other side of the table.

'What is this?' he demanded. 'Some kind of field experiment? Revive the Krill, test their battle effectiveness against the colony, then press them into service? You've let the genie out of the bottle. And ancient weapon or no ancient weapon, you're not going to be able to stop it.'

With a snarl, the figure lurched across the room. The Doctor gripped the edge of the table and heaved it into the alien's path. The alien slammed into it and stumbled. The table collapsed under him, and he crashed down, wrestling the corpse to the floor.

The creature froze. It was staring at the rancid body, at the half-eaten meal. The expression on its face was unmistakable – nausea; disgust. With a bellow, it threw itself backwards from the corpse and, staggering to its feet, disappeared through the door.

The Doctor straightened his tie and recovered his hat. The weapon wasn't here. The colony was practically defenceless. He'd failed.

Ace and Rajiid never got beyond the hotel bar. They tried – but every door had an armed police guard who, while remaining very polite, absolutely refused to let anyone leave. They could hear the roar of the pulse lasers outside, and the screeching of the Krill attempting to breach the storm defences. Rajiid was pale and sweating, his head jerking up at every noise. Ace placed a hand on his arm.

'It's OK, the Doctor will do something.'

Rajiid smiled grimly at her. 'Will he? Face it, Ace. He doesn't know how to deal with these things.'

There was a muffled explosion outside and the sound of running feet.

'The police aren't going to keep them out for ever. The Krill will get in eventually. They're bound to.'

'Just shut it, all right?' Ace snapped at him. Rajiid looked at her, surprised, and she shook her head. 'I'm sorry. I don't mean to take it out on you. I'm just not used to sitting back and waiting.'

The confusion of voices was almost deafening. Hotel staff rushed about trying to placate guests. Dolphins scuttled about on their walkers, chirruping angrily, and packed the pool in the middle of the bar shrieking at one another.

'They're an incredibly quarrelsome species,' Rajiid said. 'We learnt to communicate with them – taught them to speak – and you know what we found? They've got nearly three hundred sounds for insulting members of each other's immediate families.'

Alarm was beginning to spread through the bar. Hardly surprising, thought Ace. The holidaymakers were finally realising that all the chaos and commotion meant the colony was under attack.

'Why else would they be doing all this?' someone said. 'There have been storms here before. They've never cleared the streets.'

'Those noises... what is it out there? Why is there shooting?'

Ace got up from the bar and walked out through the restaurant to the balcony. A police sergeant guarding it looked at her, fingers tightening on the trigger of his gun. 'Sorry, Miss, I can't let you out here.'

Ace smiled at him in what she hoped was a reassuring way. 'It's OK. I know about the Krill. You don't have to keep it from me.' He relaxed and smiled back.

Ace stepped on to the balcony. 'How's it going?'

The policeman shrugged. 'They're not in... yet.' The sky was lit up by the flashes from the lasers, the tang of blood drifted on the sea air. Ace crossed to the railing. She could see the harsh line of the repulsor field cutting across the harbour. Beyond that line the sea boiled with Krill. The gunmetal of the storm shutters glinted through the trees. She could see men running to and fro, blazing away at the murderous creatures that struggled to get in.

The streets of the colony were deserted. Everyone was cowering in the hotel or the admin block. A sudden breeze blew through the square, swirling sand about in a small tornado. The entire feel of the colony had changed. It was like a ghost town. Ace shivered.

'Look,' she said, 'you've been told what's going on, yes?'

'Sit down, Miss,' the police sergeant said. 'There's no cause for alarm.'

'You know as well as I do that's not true,' she said. 'I know what's going on here. I've seen what the Krill can do.' Her eyes flashed momentarily across the room. 'Look at this lot, they sense they're being lied to. They're getting scared. You've got to tell them something – not how bad things are, of course – but something.'

The sergeant looked troubled. He unhooked his radio and began talking quietly into it. Ace strained to hear what he was saying.

Signing off, he stepped inside and clapped his hands. The room fell silent.

'Ladies and gentlemen,' he said. 'Once again, I apologise for these precautionary measures. The fact is, the colony is experiencing some difficulty... with the natives. I can assure you there's no need to be alarmed – the colony is sealed tighter than a drum. Nothing can get in or out. Now please continue to enjoy yourselves in a quiet and orderly way. Thank you.'

To Ace's astonishment the tissue of unconvincing lies seemed to have done the trick. *A little local difficulty* – the guests were already timidly laughing about it.

Suddenly determined to do something she crossed the restaurant and began pulling bottles from behind the bar. Rajiid looked at her in astonishment. 'What the hell are you doing?'

'Something useful.' She grinned mirthlessly at him. 'Get me some of those bottles.'

She began pouring spirits into pint glasses, mixing them with the garish swizzle sticks that stood in gaudy bunches on the bar. Rajiid stared at her in amazement.

'Are you planning to drink yourself into oblivion?'

Ace held up one of the glasses. 'I doubt you'd want to drink this by the time I've finished with it.' She rummaged in a cupboard under the bar counter and hauled out cans of polish and oil, lubricants for the service robots, candles, anything she could find. She popped the top of one of the cans and took a sniff. 'Smells promising.' She raked around a bit further. 'Ah!'

With a cry of triumph she held aloft a can of lighter fluid and a box of lighters emblazoned with the hotel crest.

She poured the lighter fuel into a glass then carefully divided the mixture between several bottles, shaking each one vigorously.

'See if you can find me something to use as a wick.' Suddenly galvanised into action, Rajiid grinned and began searching in the cupboards behind the counter. Ace grabbed one of the bottles and wandered through the bar, picking up scraps of paper and towels. She began to tear the towel into strips and stuffed a strip into the neck of the bottle.

'Hey, Rajiid!' a thin voice called from the pool.

'R'tk'tk!' Rajiid shouted.

'Can you get me a walker from the lobby?' the dolphin asked. 'It's like a bloody sardine tin in here.'

'Sure,' said Rajiid. 'Back in a sec.'

Ace wandered over to the poolside, still holding the bottle.

'So you and the boss are getting on OK?' R'tk'tk said to Ace.

Ace blushed. 'S'pose so,' she said.

R'tk'tk smiled showing rows of tiny teeth. 'Good on you. How's Greg?'

'He's going to be fine. They're keeping him in the medical centre overnight.'

'Oh, he'll love that. Always had a thing about women in uniform.'

'Here you go.' Rajiid lowered one of the spidery devices into the pool. R'tk'tk wriggled into it.

'Nearly didn't make it,' the dolphin said, scuttling up on to the poolside. 'I was miles out when I got the signal. Time I got here, they'd already put the damned shutters up. I couldn't get in.'

'What did you do?' Ace asked.

'Thank God for this pool,' R'tk'tk replied. 'I swam in.'

Ace digested his words for a second.

'You mean... you swam in from the sea...?'

'Sure,' the dolphin said. 'Through the dolphin canal. For once I didn't have to pay at the tunnel entrance, too.'

'Get back from the pool,' Ace said quietly. She stepped back. 'Everybody get away from the pool!' she shouted.

'Ace, what's up?' Rajiid asked.

'If he came in from the sea this way, so can they,' Ace whispered. 'So can the Krill.'

There was a sudden squawk from the pool, followed by a shriek. The water began to surge and foam and turn red. The dolphins were screaming now. Some managed to wriggle from the pool, only to be dragged back in, squealing. Blood flew through the air. One dolphin was hurled from the pool and landed with a wet, splattering thud close to Ace and her friends. It lay there, flapping and bleeding. Its stomach had been ripped open.

It took seconds – and for those seconds the people in the bar stood in mute disbelief. Then the dam burst: they began to scream and flood towards the doors, trampling and crushing each other. The police cordon broke before them. They jammed into the doorways, blocking them totally, scrambling and climbing over each other in their doomed attempts to get out.

Ace could only watch in horror.

Behind them the Krill surged from the churning water – dozens of them leaping into the bar, teeth and claws already red, snarling and spitting their fury.

Part Three

*'But, mother, please tell me, what can those things be
That crawl up so stealthily out of the sea?'*

Chapter Thirteen

More and more Krill surged out of the slurry of dolphin guts and water, their claws scraping over the tiles on the side of the pool. Ace could hear their laboured breathing as they adapted to the air. Their gaunt bodies were slick and wet, their vicious jaws worked spasmodically as they lumbered into the bar.

All around people were still scrambling for the exits, screaming. Sensing prey the Krill lashed out, hooked claws tearing into the crowd. Ace saw R'tk'tk swept towards the exit, his walker carried along by the crowd.

'Rajiid!' Ace was screaming. 'Lighter!'

'What?' the Indian shouted.

'Cigarette lighter!'

Rajiid snatched a lighter from the bar and flicked it across the room to Ace. She stumbled backwards, time slowing as she watched the tiny silver shape tumble through the air towards her. More and more Krill began to haul themselves out of the pool, their hissing shrieks reverberating around the room.

Ace caught the lighter and spun round. The flame spluttered into life, glinting on the cold fish-eyes of the advancing monsters. The jaws of the creatures opened wide and they screamed in unison as Ace lit the strip of towel in the bottle and hurled her home-made bomb to the floor.

The glass shattered and a sheet of flame roared across the poolside. Ace launched herself towards the bar, clambering over the overturned tables. Rajiid started throwing more bottles on the flames as she scrambled towards him.

'Come on, Rajiid! Out!'

Ace caught him by the collar and hauled him backwards as a Krill burst through the wall of flame, its slick skin steaming.

They dived for the exit, but the Krill pounced on to the bar counter, its webbed feet sending bottles smashing to the floor. It was cutting off their escape.

Ace ran behind the counter with Rajiid following her. She flung herself at the button on the wall next to it, ducking as the razor claws sliced down and the Krill's fetid breath washed over them. She hit the button, and the security grille slammed down from the ceiling.

Glass showered around them as the creature flailed in fury. It began to tear at the grille, ripping it apart.

Ace looked urgently around. More and more Krill were pouring from the blazing pool.

With a harsh, grating clatter the fire alarms went off, and the bar was suddenly drenched in water as the sprinkler systems kicked in.

Ace looked up in horror. They would put the fire out, and then...

Rajiid was screaming in her ear. Ace frantically looked for some way out. With a hissing shriek the Krill in front of them burst through the remains of the grille and dropped to the floor, towering over them.

Laser fire, harsh and glaring, suddenly tore across the room ripping into the Krill. Ace could see ragged holes opening up in its scaly hide but the monster showed no pain, no discomfort.

It spun round and bellowed its defiance. Ace could see the police sergeant from the balcony silhouetted in the doorway of the restaurant, the pulse laser cradled into his shoulder as he unleashed another barrage of fire into the bar.

With astonishing speed the Krill launched itself forward. The guard barely had time to scream before he was enveloped in a mass of the creatures, their hooked claws flicking blood across the tiled floor.

Ace stared at the wall of fire. It was already beginning to die down, doused by the torrent from above. She flicked wet hair from her eyes and grabbed Rajiid's hand.

'Come on!'

The two of them sprinted for the exit, scrambling over tables and chairs, broken glass crunching underfoot. The heat from the flames was intense and choking smoke was beginning to rise in thick clouds. The high-pitched roars of the Krill mingled with screams of terror and death.

Ace could hear someone screaming at her. Screaming her name. Tables suddenly shattered behind her as a Krill burst through the flames. She felt the rush of air as its claws sliced past her. Her heart was pounding. She could hear Rajiid's breathing as he ran alongside her.

They hurled themselves through the door and collapsed. Ace struggled for breath. Behind her there was a harsh clang as a security door slammed down cutting off the bar.

'Come on, Ace! COME ON!'

Someone was hauling her to her feet.

The Doctor.

She opened her mouth to speak but he pushed her forward. 'Later, Ace. Those doors won't hold them for long.'

As he spoke the security door buckled under a series of terrific blows. Claws punched through the metal. Over the blaring alarms Ace could hear the creatures hissing and screaming.

Holding on to the Doctor's arm she stumbled out of the hotel into the square. Hysterical people were streaming from the hotel. She could see Rajiid being bustled away.

Gunfire and roars rang through the colony. A group of colonists, unfamiliar pulse lasers in their hands, hurried forward, ushered on by a member of the security force. Their guns were trained on the hotel doors. One of them waved the Doctor over. 'This way! Come on, move it.'

The ground suddenly shook with a series of muffled explosions. Ace staggered and caught the Doctor's arm. 'What the hell was that?'

'Hopefully that's Brenda stopping any more Krill getting in.'

'You know about the dolphin tunnels?'

The Doctor nodded. 'It occurred to us all at roughly the same time. That explosion should have blocked off the main entrance.'

Ace smiled grimly. 'So now we just have to deal with the ones that got in...'

On cue the door of the hotel burst open and the Krill spilled out into the square. They clambered over one another, never resting on their powerfully muscled legs, their claws striking sparks from the tarmac. They were identical, each a perfect copy of the next. Each pale bluish head glistened with slime, each pair of yellow eyes was wild and staring.

Ace and the Doctor clamped their hands over their ears as two dozen pulse lasers flared into life, cutting a swathe through the creatures. In seconds the steps were littered with flesh, the thick ichor of Krill blood splattered over the whitewashed walls.

Ace watched in horror as several of the creatures pressed forward, despite gaping ragged wounds. One was missing its arm, its shoulder a mess of ragged tissue. The arm itself thrashed on the floor struggling to reach the soldiers. Ace felt sick. These things *were* unstoppable.

The lasers blazed again, streaks of brilliant light tearing into the screeching pack. Only when the monsters were torn into glistening lumps did they finally stop moving. In the doorway to the hotel, more and more of the creatures were massing. There was a brief lull in the deafening noise then the lasers roared again.

Grasping Ace by the arm the Doctor hurried across the square to the admin block. Suddenly a hotel window burst outwards in a spray of glass and a Krill landed wetly on the flagstones of the square. The Doctor pushed Ace behind him and began backing away. The Krill brought its head up and snarled. Ace could see herself and the Doctor reflected in its cold eyes.

The Krill gathered itself to spring, and was hurled backwards by a hail of gunfire.

'Come on you two! Out of here!'

R'tk'tk clattered past them, nestled in the spindly shape of a mobility unit. Two gun barrels projected from the underside of the machine. As more Krill appeared through the shattered window the dolphin's guns roared again and R'tk'tk pushed forward, cutting a bloody line through the monsters.

The Doctor grasped Ace by the hand and hauled her through the doors of the administration building. In the cool of the interior the noise of gunfire and Krill was muted, almost melodic. Ace finally stopped to catch her breath, aware of how bruised and dirty she was.

The foyer of the building was littered with the wounded, medics flitting from person to person trying to treat the worst of the injuries. She could see Rajiid slumped against a wall. He forced a weak smile to his lips. Ace stared up at the Doctor who was pacing to and fro, gnawing at his knuckles.

'It's bad, isn't it?'

The Doctor nodded.

'Doctor...' Q'ilp scuttled down the stairs in his exoskeleton, clouds of cigar smoke billowing in his wake. 'Brenda wants to see you.'

The Doctor stopped his pacing and stared at the dolphin. As if making a sudden decision he set off up the stairs. 'Come on, Ace,' he said.

Ace struggled to her feet, shrugged apologetically at Rajiid, and set off after him.

She bounded up the stairs two at a time, trying to keep pace with Q'ilp's mechanical monstrosity. The Doctor was way ahead of them and, by the time they arrived at the control centre, was already in deep conversation with Brenda. They were crouched over a bank of consoles, talking in low and worried tones.

Ace pushed her way over to them. All around her technicians listened to reports from the defence perimeter. The crackle of gunfire was harsh and tinny over the speakers. A large screen showed the island chain from the air – a low-orbit satellite scan. Figures and graphs scrolled over the read-out. Ace couldn't see anything to get excited about.

Brenda tapped a control and the image zoomed out.

'This is our problem, Doctor.'

Ace looked at the scanner. A large black swirl dominated the ocean. She felt her heart sink.

'Please tell me that's not what I think it is.'

'A hurricane.' The Doctor's voice was soft and low. 'Bigger than anything you will ever have seen on Earth.' He looked at Brenda, steely-eyed. 'How long until it hits?'

'If it continues on its current course, we should start to feel it in about two hours. We're getting constant data from the NavSats, we should be able to plot it accurately.'

The Doctor straightened up.

'Well, there's no other choice then.'

Ace looked at him, puzzled. 'What's going on, Professor? What choice?'

The room was quiet, all eyes on the little Time Lord. The Doctor took a deep breath.

'The defence grid simply won't be able to hold a combined assault by the hurricane and the Krill. And if the repulsor fields fail, the winds will tear this place apart. Our only chance is the TARDIS.'

Brenda looked puzzled. 'TARDIS?'

'My ship. I should have room to get nearly everybody off the island.'

Brenda laughed. 'The entire island? Really...'

Ace cut across her, looking at the Doctor in disbelief. 'But the TARDIS is out on the beach. How the hell are we meant to reach it?'

The Doctor stared straight into her eyes. 'Only I have to reach it.'

'You're not going out there?'

162

The Doctor said nothing. Ace felt herself flush with anger. 'Don't be stupid, you'll never make it through those creatures.'

'The girl's right.' Brenda frowned at him. 'How the hell do you think you're going to get anywhere near...'

'The coastguard flyer.' The Doctor was pacing around the room. 'Your pilot can hover over the TARDIS and let me down on the winch. I'll only need seconds to open the door.'

'You won't have seconds!' Ace was frantic now. 'You know this isn't going to work, Professor! I can see it in your face.'

'Ace..!'

'No, Doctor.' Brenda shook her head. 'I can't allow it. I'm sorry. Perhaps if you and Phillip...'

'Mr Garrett is going to be no help at all!' snapped the Doctor. The room fell silent.

'What do you mean?' There was panic in Brenda's voice. 'Where is he?'

The Doctor closed his eyes and took a deep breath. 'I'm sorry. I didn't mean to break it to you like this. I don't think that our friend Mr Garrett is quite himself any more.'

'Doctor, will you please stop beating about the bush and tell me what the hell is going on!'

The Doctor held his hands up. 'All right! All right!' He turned away, pulling open the slatted blinds that covered the window and staring out over the battlefield that the sea had become.

'The alien body that was stolen from the morgue is in Mr Garrett's quarters. It has been partially eaten.'

'Eaten?'

'Yes. Eaten. And I believe that if the bite marks are examined they will prove to be human. At least, some of them will.'

There was a stunned silence. 'You're not suggesting that Phillip is responsible for biting chunks off the corpse?' Brenda exploded.

The Doctor took a deep breath. 'Look, I don't have all the answers. Not yet. But I'm sure Phillip Garrett is the root of a good many problems, including your so-called monster.' He paused. 'I also found a transmitter. The same technology as our dead alien was carrying.'

Brenda made to interject again but the Doctor cut across her.

'I think that Garrett is working for a third party and I think it is they who need the weapon. Find Garrett and we find the weapon – and, I think, we find a way of stopping the Krill.'

'And if the Krill have already got Garrett?' asked Ace.

'Then we're all dead unless I can get to the TARDIS,' said the Doctor.

In the service tunnels deep beneath the colony Garrett sat, hunched against a wall, his body shivering, sweat pouring from his skin. His head snapped up at the sound of gunfire and the screams of the Krill.

The Krill. With sudden clarity he knew that he shouldn't be down here. He should be in... the control centre. Yes, the control centre. With... Brenda...

He struggled to his feet, and staggered. Something heavy was slung over his shoulders. A cylinder. It glinted in the cold of the emergency lights. It felt unfamiliar in his hands. The weapon from the dig. Why did he have it?

Garrett's face creased with the concentration of trying to remember what had happened to him. He was so tired. He rubbed at his face with his hands, and stopped at the touch of something unfamiliar against his skin. Slowly he drew his hands away, holding them out in front of him. His skin was shimmering, blurring. The skin seemed to flow, one minute smooth flesh, the next gnarled, reptilian.

'What is happening to me?' he whispered.

He slammed the unfamiliar hands against the wall. His brain was in turmoil. Part of him wanted to scream and run; another part told him that the alien skin was right, proper. It was what he should be.

His head snapped up at the sound of more gunfire. Krill screams reverberated along the corridor, closer now. Garrett began to back away.

He stumbled over something on the floor. Something bulky and cold. He bent down.

A body was slumped on the floor. Tentatively Garrett turned it over. The sightless eyes of a security guard stared up at him, the face bruised and bloody, the head lolling grotesquely on a broken neck. Garrett stared down at the livid marks on the man's neck, and at the twisted claws that his hands had become.

With a sudden flash of clarity he could see himself rushing across the lecture room towards Brenda, see his hands around Bryce's neck. He could see himself killing this man. He had memories of standing under an unfamiliar sky, patches of oily vapour writhing around him, the rasping, breathy war chants of his comrades in arms filling the sky.

With a cry Garrett began to run blindly, in no particular direction. The raging in his brain shut out all rational thought. He crashed off walls, slammed through doors, trying to get away from everything. He wouldn't be responsible for more deaths. Phantom shapes lurked in every corner. Garrett screamed his defiance at them.

Without warning he crashed into something, hard. The blow knocked him to the floor.

Through streaming eyes he could see a cluster of pipes slung low from the ceiling. He struggled upright, clutching his head. He was in the power room, deep under the control centre. All around him machinery hummed and throbbed, water gurgled through pipes and soft lights twinkled from computer terminals.

Garrett hauled himself painfully to a wall. He was calmer now, the noises and lights were somehow soothing. And there was something else, a humming on the edge of his hearing. Rhythmic, like clapping.

He closed his eyes. The noises calmed him. Everything was fine. There was no conflict. The deaths didn't matter. They were necessary, primitives who had got in his way. He stroked the weapon in his arms. He had achieved his objective, but...

He frowned. Something was still not quite as it should be, still unclear. He shouldn't be alone. Surely there should be others.

The clapping was faster now, joined by a low chant, reverberating among the pipes and pillars. His skin shimmering and blurring, Garrett hauled himself to his feet and began to lumber towards the source of the noise.

Low yellow light began to flicker through the machinery, casting huge dancing shadows over the walls. Garrett gripped the weapon, suddenly comfortable with its weight against his chest. He crouched behind a huge pump and gazed into the power room. Gathered around a plasma burner were maybe two dozen Dreekans crouched in a circle. Pipes and conduits coiled up into the dark and in the firelight it looked as if they were surrounded by the ribcage of some enormous beast.

All the Dreekans were bare-chested, their skin slick with sweat and decorated with swirling scarlet patterns. They chanted in low musical tones, hands clapping. One of them circled the fire in a complex dance, his four arms passing a wand in spiralling patterns through the air, his eyes rolled back, his body twitching as if in fever. The chant and the clapping got faster and faster, the dance wilder.

Garrett suddenly stepped from the shadows into the firelight.

One of the Dreekan women screamed.

The chanting stopped. The echoes of the scream reverberated around the cavernous room. The men leapt to their feet and lunged forward, knives clasped in their hands, One of them thrust a plasma torch into Garrett's face and recoiled in horror.

'Treeka'dwra!'

A mutter ran through the crowd.

'Treeka'dwra...'

One by one the Dreekans dropped on to their knees. The rhythmic clapping began again, faster and harder than before; a rhythm driven by religious ecstasy. The man who had been dancing stepped forward and handed Garrett the wand.

'You are Treeka'dwra. The beast that is hidden.' He bowed his head, all four arms open. 'What is your command?'

Garrett turned and stared at a glass surface on one of the pump-control banks. His reflection stared back at him, features blurred and shifting. His human face was fused with something else, something brutal and alien.

Garrett smiled, revealing crooked yellowing teeth.

'I have come to lead you.'

The barracks was crowded once more. It was packed. Word had spread at once among the humans about Bavril's rescue attempt. Some of them were scared; others chattered with nervous excitement.

'Well?' Peck asked impatiently.

'Scratcher's dead,' said Bavril.

'What happened?' Huttle grabbed him by the collar of his drab uniform. 'What happened!?'

'The dolphin saw me. He knows everything.'

Huttle gasped in disbelief. 'What are we going to do?' he cried. 'This is an act of mutiny. Mutiny on a Cythosi ship... They'll kill us all!'

'Then we've no choice,' said Peck.

'What?' Huttle spat.

'They'll be coming for us. We've got to defend ourselves. We've got to fight them.'

'This is your fault, Bavril,' snapped Huttle. 'You think of something.'

'We can hope the dolphin won't say anything. I don't think he'll want to explain to Mottrack what he was doing down there.'

'And that's it?' spat Peck.

'I'm sorry,' said Bavril. 'Truly. I'm sorry.'

He turned to go. He was due to report for duty. If he was wrong about Blu'ip...

'They'll kill you if you go up there,' Peck's voice called. Everyone was watching Bavril intently.

'They'll kill me if I don't,' he said hollowly. 'Failing to report for duty.'

'Bavril...' Peck moved between him and the door.

'Look... what d'you want?' said Bavril.

'I want us to give ourselves a chance.'

'And fight the Cythosi? With what?' Huttle cried, stepping between the two men.

'The ship will soon be quiet,' said Peck. 'Most of the troopers will be down on that planet. And we've got a laser-cutter.'

'So?' Huttle appealed, spreading his hands to the crowd.

'I've seen plans of the ship. If we cut up through the deck of B-barracks we come out in a storage area. If we cut through the ceiling of that, we're in the armoury.'

'You intend cutting through two decks with a hand-laser?'

'It can be done,' said Peck. 'Trust me.'

'Even if it could, those floors are riddled with service ducts. You know the robots are set to kill.'

'Why can't any of you get it into your heads?' Peck suddenly bellowed. 'We're going to die anyway. You know the punishment for mutiny on a Cythosi ship. Have we been beaten down here so long we're prepared to just line up and be shot?'

There were murmurings of agreement from the crowd. But everyone still seemed to be watching Bavril, waiting for what he had to say.

'What?' he demanded. 'I'm not your leader.'

'Then maybe I should be,' said Peck quietly. 'Either *you* finish it, or you help *me* finish it.'

Chapter Fourteen

Ace stepped on to the balcony that ringed Brenda's office. Inside the Doctor was talking to the coastguard pilot, pointing out the position of the TARDIS on the huge map pinned to the wall. Position determined, the Doctor began to struggle into a harness.

Ace turned away. She didn't want to see this. He didn't stand a chance and they both knew it. She stared out at the sea, trying to cut out the noise of gunfire and Krill. Tilting her head back she stared at the rings arcing overhead, partly obscured by the gathering clouds. Their adventures were to come to an end on one of the most beautiful planets that they had ever been to. She slumped over the railing, feeling tears welling in her eyes. Stupid. So stupid.

She was suddenly aware of someone standing alongside her. She turned. The Doctor wasn't looking at her. His steely eyes were fixed on the horizon.

Ace rubbed the tears from her eyes. 'Are you set then?'

The Doctor nodded. 'The pilot is just prepping the ship.' He paused. 'Ace...'

'No, Professor. Remember what we talked about the other night in the restaurant, about how dangerous life can be? I told you then that if I couldn't handle it then I'd let you know. Look out there.' She pointed at the storm wall where the guards were firing again and again at the swarming monsters. 'They don't stand a chance. You've got to do this. You've got to save these people.' She smiled weakly. 'It's all part of the job, right?'

The Doctor smiled and tapped her on the nose. 'Yes, Ace. It's all part of the job.'

Ace took a deep breath. 'Let's get on with it then.'

They barely had time to turn before the blow sent them crashing to the floor.

A Krill hung to the balcony rail, its clawed arm flailing wildly, trying to haul itself up. The Doctor lay dazed. Ace staggered to her feet. As she watched, the slashing claw caught on the Doctor's harness and the creature began to drag him towards the edge of the balcony.

'No!'

Ace lunged forward, catching hold of the Doctor's arms, desperately punching at the release catch on the harness. With a harsh shriek the Krill slipped and the Doctor was torn from Ace's hands and slammed against the railings.

His eyes flickered open.

'Doctor!'

He twisted round and stared straight into the open mouth of the Krill. Its teeth crashed together inches from his face. He gave a cry of pain as the harness cut into him, and the creature tried to haul itself on to the balcony.

Ace ran forward, kicking out at the vile fish-like head. With a metallic wrench, the railing buckled and the Doctor slid further over the edge.

'Ace! Here!'

The Doctor thrust his penknife into her hands. Ace began sawing at the harness straps. The Doctor kicked at the Krill. Its other arm caught on the balcony edge and with a hiss of rage it began to haul itself up.

Bars began to snap out of the railings. The entire structure was folding over like a row of dominoes. The Doctor slid further over the edge, dragging Ace with him. She continued to saw at the straps of his harness, cursing him for owning the bluntest penknife in the galaxy. The Krill scrabbled frantically at the collapsing ironwork and they slid further. The Doctor twisted his head and began to struggle wildly.

'Ace!'

Ace stared up in horror as another Krill hauled itself on to the balcony, towering over them, its razor claws raised high.

A harpoon caught it high in the shoulder, spinning it off balance and sending it tumbling over the edge. It vanished with a screech of pain and rage.

Ace punched the air. 'Yes!'

Brenda nodded grimly at her from the doorway and began to reload the gun.

There was a sudden screech of metal and a cry from the Doctor. The balcony railings collapsed completely and the Doctor vanished over the edge.

'No!' Ace screamed and flung herself forward. She skidded to the edge of the balcony and looked down.

The square was six storeys below them, littered with the bodies of the policemen and colonists who had tried to hold the monsters back. The Krill themselves clung to the walls of the admin block like huge, pale leeches. Hauling themselves upwards, their hissing breath formed nightmarish melodies, their eyes reflected her face.

The Doctor hung in mid-air, his umbrella hooked in the tangle of twisted railings. The Krill was still clinging on to the harness, caught like a fish on an angler's hook. With each jerk of the creature's body the Doctor's face twisted in agony.

With a cold shock of realisation Ace stared down at the knife in her hand. The Doctor couldn't release himself. As she watched he finally managed to wriggle his arm out of the harness. With a tearing snap, the rest of the harness disintegrated and the screeching Krill tumbled to the ground below.

Ace's relief was short-lived. The creatures clinging to the wall below the Doctor began to climb faster. The Doctor tried to pull himself up, but the railings twisted again, dropping him towards the advancing monsters.

He started to swing himself back and forth, pushing out from the wall with his feet, swinging far out over the square, his feet inches from the monsters' outstretched arms. Ace's heart jumped into her mouth as one of them caught his shoe a glancing blow.

The Doctor swung towards the wall again and with the sound of shattering glass he disappeared from view.

'He's in the medical centre.'

Brenda was at Ace's side, the harpoon gun in her arms. As they watched, one of the Krill tried to squeeze its pale bulk through the window that the Doctor had vanished through.

Brenda took careful aim with the gun and a barbed rod of steel tore through the Krill's head, punching it away from the wall and sending it cannoning into the creatures below. They hit the ground with wet thuds and, abandoning the twitching body of their comrade, immediately threw themselves at the wall again, their claws gouging chunks out of the concrete.

Brenda shook her head. 'They don't give up, do they?'

The Doctor shook his head and hauled himself painfully to his feet. Glass crunched underfoot and he was bleeding from several cuts on his palms. He looked up. He was in a ward in the medical bay. Two frightened nurses were staring at him. He picked up his umbrella.

'Good afternoon. I'm the Doctor.'

One of the nurses screamed and pointed at the window behind him.

The Doctor spun in time to see the harpooned Krill vanish from sight with a scream of rage. He peered after it. It wouldn't be long before the monsters reached the window again.

He turned to the nurses. 'I'm afraid I may have brought some unwelcome company with me. It might be a good idea if we weren't at home.'

One of the women shook her head. 'We can't leave.' She pointed to a bed in the corner of the room. The Doctor crossed to it, his face grim.

'Holly Relf.'

All the other beds were empty.

'Thank God we have so few patients,' the nurse said. 'We started an evacuation – got most of the patients down to the basement levels. They're setting up barricades in some of the storm shelters. But then the Krill cut us off. There's nowhere to go – they're everywhere.' She stroked the unconscious woman's forehead. 'Maybe we could make it, but we won't leave the patients.'

They started as the door slid open with a soft hiss. A young policeman, his face bloodied and bruised, appeared in the doorway. 'They're on this level. We've got to leave – now!'

The nurses looked at the Doctor in desperation. 'But we can't...'

The Doctor pushed them forward. 'Get out of here. Leave her to me.'

'But...'

'I'm the Doctor. *Go!*'

The policeman bustled the nurses towards the emergency exit. The Doctor watched them go and pressed his hand against the door panel. The frosted glass slid shut, cutting out the noise of battle. The Doctor turned back into the silent medical bay. The only noise breaking into the quiet was the hum of the auto-doc suspended over the one solitary patient.

He crossed to Holly's bedside. The sleeping woman's breathing was steady and low, her face peaceful. She was completely unaware of the battle for existence raging around her. Not for the first time the Doctor marvelled at how such fragile creatures could have survived so long when the universe continued to throw up enemies that were better armoured than them, more vicious, more ruthless.

Behind him he could hear hissings and scrapings in the corridor. The Krill were gathering.

The Doctor leant forward and placed his hands on either side of Holly's face, holding her head ever so gently. He took a deep breath and pushed her head sharply to the left.

Holly's eyes flickered open. They stared straight up into his. He smiled.

'Hello. I'm the Doctor.'

Holly smiled nervously back. 'Doctor?' She looked around her. 'How did I...?'

'Ssh.' The Doctor put his fingers to his lips. 'Quietly...'

Her brow creased, 'I was at sea, I remember...' She suddenly caught sight of the silhouetted shapes of the Krill outside the door and drew in a breath, about to scream.

The Doctor caught hold of her nose and squeezed it gently, stifling her scream. His steely eyes fixed on hers.

'You have been through more than anyone should have to go through, and I wish I could let your body heal in its own time, but we are in deadly danger and I need your help.'

Holly nodded and the Doctor released her nose.

Tears began to flood into Holly's eyes as her memory began to come back. The Doctor laid a gentle hand on her arm. 'I'm sorry about your friends, but this is not the time to grieve. You've seen the Krill. You've seen what they can do. They are here now, and will be coming through the window any minute. These creatures are overrunning your entire colony and we have to find a way of slowing them down.'

He slipped away from the bed and passed Holly a white lab coat from the back of a chair. 'The Krill aren't aware of us yet, but it's only a matter of moments before they are.'

Holly clambered unsteadily from the bed, pulling on the coat and rubbing the tears from her eyes.

'D'you have a plan?'

The Doctor cocked his head to one side. 'How well do you know this colony?'

Holly looked at him. 'I've been helping to build it for the last four years of my life.'

'Then I have a plan.'

* * *

174

Ace pulled a handful of harpoons from a carefully arranged display on the wall behind Brenda's desk, hefted the gun in her hands and turned to leave the control room.

Brenda caught her arm. 'Where are you going?'

'After the Doctor.'

Brenda shook her head. 'Let the riot teams get him.'

Ace pulled herself free angrily. 'Listen, missus, the Doctor is my responsibility, get it? We're a team.'

Brenda opened her mouth to argue but Ace's expression was stony. She stared down at the determined girl, suddenly seeing herself reflected in the rebellious eyes of this teenager. Loyalty and bravery were all too rare these days. She wondered what she would do in Ace's place. If they were *her* friends out there.

She stepped aside.

'Then take care.'

Ace nodded her thanks and hurried through the control room and out into the corridor. All through the building she could hear screams and gunfire. With a sudden cold chill, she realised that she might not come out of this one. Gripping the harpoon gun tightly she crossed to the stairwell. Below her she could hear the sound of running feet, could almost smell the fear. She edged tentatively down the stairs, her finger twitching on the trigger of the gun.

The Krill appeared when she was only half-way down, its hooked claws tearing a lump from the wall. Ace threw herself into a roll and fired the harpoon gun. The spike tore up through the monster pinning it to the wall.

Ace was back on her feet in moments, bounding back up towards the command level. She could hear claws scrabbling on the stairs behind her.

She launched herself at the top step and rolled into the corridor.

She heard a soft chime as the lift doors slid open ahead of her.

And a Krill stepped out.

* * *

The Doctor watched from the access panel in the wall where he and Holly had tucked themselves, as three Krill padded around the mess of the medical bay. The glass door lay shattered in a million pieces, and spilt liquids ran in rivers around piles of broken equipment.

The Krill lashed out at anything that wasn't fixed down. He watched them with interest, trying to see any glimmer of intelligence that he could work with, anything that might help him try and communicate with them.

One of them picked up a child's teddy bear from one of the beds. The monster brought the toy up to its face, cradling it in its huge claws. It scrutinised it for a moment, as if confused as to what it was, then, with a savage twist of those razor claws, the bear was torn in half and cast to the floor. The Doctor shook his head. These creatures were no product of nature, no result of an evolutionary process. They were engineered. Constructed. Designed to do nothing but kill until there was nothing left to be killed.

He closed his eyes, creating a space in his subconscious, a place into which he would push all the guilt when the time and opportunity came to destroy these monsters. In the quiet and blackness behind his eyes he realised that his mind was already too full of those pockets of guilt.

He opened his eyes again and found himself looking at the disembodied head of the teddy bear, its cheerful face staring up at him. Something innocent destroyed by something evil. So simple. So easy. But to turn the tables...

A snarl from the room brought his attention back to the creatures. With no prey visible in the room they seemed to be losing interest. They began to lumber to the door, lured by the sounds of firing from the upper floor.

The Doctor and Holly waited until they were sure the Krill had left and then pushed at the heavy medical bed. The structure swung away from the wall with a quiet hum and the

Doctor unfolded himself from the access panel. He crept across the shattered room, wincing at each crunch underfoot. He peered out into the corridor. There was no sign of the Krill.

He waved back at Holly who crawled from the access panel and continued her work on the exposed optical cables that ran from wall to medi-bed. She had already dismantled the auto-doc by the time the Krill had started to break their way in.

The Doctor had been trying to concoct some form of repellent from chemicals on the nurses' desk when Holly had pulled the bed back from the wall revealing the access conduit. They had barely made it inside and swung the bed back into place before the Krill smashed through the door.

Now Holly was working like a woman possessed; patching cables across each other, running bypasses, linking everything through a hand-held medical terminal. The Doctor looked at her with concern. Her coma had been a way of dealing with the shock of seeing her crew ripped apart, and bringing her out of it had been a terrible risk; something that he would never have done in ordinary circumstances. Now she was dealing with it by throwing herself at her work as if nothing else mattered, but that could only last so long. She needed friends around her, people who could talk to her, love her. He sighed. All he could do at the moment was keep her busy.

He crossed to her side. 'Any luck?'

She nodded, not looking up from her work. 'I've managed to isolate the security shutters from the fire systems.' She jerked a thumb back at the mess of cables in the alcove. 'There's a common optical link that runs through all essential computer systems, easy to hack into if you know where to look.'

The Doctor grunted. 'Easy to say when you're the one who put in the system in the first place.' His face tensed. 'Does this mean that we can close the security shutters throughout the complex?'

Holly held up the medical pad. 'All from here.'

'Then do it.'

'It won't stop them.'

'No.' The Doctor's face was grim. 'But it might slow them down.'

'If there are people still trapped in the corridors...'

The Doctor stared down at the dismembered teddy bear and opened another space in his subconscious. 'Then it will be quick.'

Ace skidded backwards down the corridor as the Krill bellowed at her. By the time she had reloaded the harpoon gun the creatures would be on her. Right now it was just dead weight and her only chance was to be agile; she knew how fast these things could move. She tossed gun and ammo to one side, the spare harpoons clattering like matchsticks. Balancing on the balls of her feet she tensed herself to run.

With a grinding roar of metal on metal, heavy steel shutters began to slide from the roof, compartmentalising the corridor. She was going to be trapped with the Krill.

Ace hurled herself forward, blood pounding in her ears. The gap between shutter and floor looked far too small, and was getting smaller. She threw herself to the floor and slid across the polished surface.

She crashed into something that knocked the breath from her. Tentatively she opened her eyes. She was in a tangled heap against the wall, the shutter tight against the floor behind her. Skid marks crossed the floor like tramlines, and one of her trainers was crushed under the bulk of the shutter, torn from her foot.

Ace rubbed at her heel, looking at the mangled shoe. She sat for a moment, trying to still her pounding heart. Holding her hands in front of her she tried to stop them shaking.

There was a crash from the shutters. She scrambled to her feet. The heavy metal shook as the Krill threw themselves against it on the other side. Already it was beginning to buckle, huge bulges and cracks appearing even as she watched.

The needle-tip of a claw punched through and began to saw its way down the metal sheet. Another shutter blocked any escape further along the corridor. She punched at the control panel. The computer bleeped cheerily.

'Please insert your security override key.'

Ace cursed and looked for another way out. Nothing. The only break in the blank walls was a cupboard full of fire-fighting equipment.

There was another wrench of tortured metal and the eye of a Krill peered at her through the disintegrating shutter.

The shutter.

The shutters had slid down from above.

Ace looked up. The ceiling was false – plastic panels held in a delicate frame.

She grasped the cupboard and dragged it into the middle of the corridor. The enraged Krill began to push through the hole they had made. Ace scrambled on to the cupboard and punched at the ceiling. The panel swung up with a crash and she clambered up.

The roof space was cramped and tangled with machinery. Ace crawled blindly, the screams of the Krill ringing in her ears. Her head cracked against beams and pipes, sharp edges cut into her hands.

A sudden waft of air washed over her. She stopped. A sliver of light cut through the blackness ahead of her. A way out on to the roof. Ace scrambled forward.

An emergency hatch was set into the concrete. Sobbing with relief, she grasped the handle and twisted it. The mechanism was stiff with disuse and her hands slipped on the grease. She gripped the handle with both hands and put all her weight on it. With agonising slowness it began to move.

There was a hiss from the darkness. Shapes began to flow

from the shadows. Slimy fish-flesh shapes squeezing through the confined space.

Ace screamed with effort and the hatch clicked open.

She hauled herself on to the roof and slammed the heavy emergency hatch shut, lying on top of it, almost crying with relief. The wind tugged at her hair and her eyes streamed in the bright glare of the sunlight.

A shadow suddenly fell across her.

Ace looked up in despair.

Garrett stood silhouetted against the crackling force field that swept across the sky, the cylindrical bulk of the ancient weapon cradled in his arms. He twisted his head down and smiled at her. His face was decorated with livid patterns in red and black.

Ace rubbed at her eyes. Beneath the paint Garrett's features seemed blurred, indistinct. She couldn't seem to focus on them. From behind him dozens of figures began to appear. Dreekans, their faces and skin painted in similar patterns, their eyes glazed and rolling, their hands clapping in complicated rhythms.

Ace could hear the razor claws of the Krill clicking on the hatch, the ragged hiss of their breathing. With a metallic crunch the hatch burst open.

Garrett raised the weapon.

And triggered it.

Aboard the Cythosi ship an alarm screeched across the bridge. Bisoncawl's head snapped up from his controls as troopers snatched off headphones and struggled to shut down overloading systems.

'What is happening!?' roared Mottrack.

Bisoncawl crossed to the sensor array and punched the screen into life. Data flickered across the screen.

'Unknown energy signature, General. Very localised. Very powerful. Nearly overloaded every system on the ship.'

'The Weapon?'

Bisoncawl nodded. 'It would be logical to assume that this is what we have been waiting for, but without confirmation...'

Mottrack's fist slammed down on his console.

'I need no further confirmation! Close down the planet's communication grid. Complete blanket. I want continual sensor sweeps relayed to my command position. Warn off any ships that come near. Those that persist, destroy.'

He snapped on the com system.

'All hands, this is General Mottrack. Prepare to drop to low orbit. All troops to drop ships.' His voice echoed around the cavernous bulk of the battle cruiser. He swung round and pointed at Bisoncawl.

'Take the ship down to strike range, Commander. As soon as it is done, join me in the assault shuttle.'

Hauling himself from his chair, Mottrack lumbered from the bridge.

In the shadows Bavril's heart pounded. The Cythosi were going to be preoccupied. The last thing on their minds would be the functionaries.

For the first time in his life Bavril felt a surge of hope.

The engines on the lumbering battle cruiser flared into life and, like some huge barnacled sea creature, the Cythosi ship began to descend towards the gentle blue globe below it.

Chapter Fifteen

Ace sat in a corner of Brenda's office nursing her throbbing head. Outside she could hear signs that the colony was slowly coming back to life. Damage control teams and medics scurried everywhere like ants. Rajiid crossed to her side, handing her a glass.

'This should help with the head.'

Ace smiled at him. 'Thanks. Where's R'tk'tk?'

'Down at the harbour, seeing if he can help with repairs.'

In front of them the Doctor and Brenda were arguing about what had happened, while MacKenzie and Q'ilp looked on. Ace took a sip of her water, grimacing at the bitter taste. Her head was beginning to clear already, but things were still fuzzy.

She remembered Garrett raising the weapon, remembered looking right down the stump of the barrel. There had been a bright glaring light and then a... sensation, a rush of pins and needles through her body. After that... nausea. She remembered vomiting...

She shook her head. The next thing she remembered was the Doctor shaking her awake, leading her back down the ladder.

Of the Krill there was nothing left except stains on the floors. Everywhere there were small pools of steaming slime that had once been monsters.

Garrett had gone, vanished with his wild-eyed followers. Ace had a vague recollection of his laughing face, bright with patterns and colours.

'Preposterous, Doctor. Absolutely preposterous.'

Brenda was shaking her head. Ace could see that the Doctor was getting angry.

'What other explanation would you have?'

Brenda laughed. 'Phillip transforming into an alien monster? A weapon so discriminating that it chooses its victims?'

'Yes!' The Doctor held up a jar full of the goo that had once been a Krill. 'I told you, it's a biogenic weapon. It's keyed specifically to the Krill's biorhythms... I hope.'

'You hope...'

'You felt what it was like when he triggered the thing. Everybody did. Even I was affected. I hope it was just a mild reaction – otherwise, heaven knows what damage Garrett's done.'

'Definitely Garrett...'

'Yes!'

'Who is no longer entirely human.'

'Yes!'

Brenda snorted and turned away.

The Doctor turned to Ace. 'Tell her, Ace! Tell her what you saw.'

'Professor, I've been through this...'

'Well, tell her again!'

Ace sighed. 'Garrett's face was blurred... shifting, like a mask. It was as if there was something trying to get out.'

'I thought you said his face was painted,' Brenda scoffed.

Ace could feel her own temper rising. 'Now listen, matron, his face was painted as well. Him and those four-armed blokes. The Dreekans.'

The Doctor caught hold of Ace's shoulder and pushed her down on to the sofa again.

'Our Mr Garrett is in possession of the only effective weapon that we have against the Krill, and he is in a desperately unstable state. It is imperative that we locate him as soon as possible. Now does anyone here know what those symbols might mean, or know why he would be in the company of Dreekans?'

Brenda cast a look over the room at MacKenzie. The Doctor nodded and leant across the desk, staring at the archaeologist through a cloud of cigarette smoke. 'What do those symbols mean, Professor?'

'I'm not sure.'

There was the harsh rasp of a match as Q'ilp lit up a cigar.

'Sounds like Dreekan voodoo to me,' clicked the dolphin.

'Voodoo?' Ace was suddenly at the Doctor's side. He waved his hands at her to be quiet.

'They brought it with them to the planet. There's only a small number of them practise it – primitive types mostly, who keep away from the colony – but lately we've had some trouble.'

'Yes,' the Doctor tapped his lips thoughtfully, 'We've seen.'

'What? The graffiti on the fountain!' said Ace. 'I've seen worse. Back in Perivale...'

'Don't underestimate them,' Q'ilp snapped 'Dreekan voodoo is a nasty little religion. The Dreekan economy was nearly wrecked by it. A drug culture encouraged by the cult swept across the planet. At one point there were nearly three billion addicts being treated.'

'But why would they latch on to Garrett?' mused the Doctor.

Q'ilp took a long drag on his cigar and blew a cloud of blue smoke at the ceiling. 'There are legends of a Messiah. A saviour of the people. The Treeka'dwra. From what we can make out it's some kind of animal god.' He managed the dolphin equivalent of a shrug. 'Maybe Garrett fitted the picture.'

'And do you have any idea of where they might have gone?'

MacKenzie stepped forward. 'Q'ilp and I have discovered a number of ritualistic implements over the last few months, plus of course the pictograms that turn up every now and again. We haven't any proof, but we think that there could well be a temple out in the jungle.'

The Doctor rounded on Brenda. 'You must organise a search of the surrounding jungle immediately.'

Brenda looked at him incredulously. 'Doctor, my colony has just been attacked by an unknown form of life, there are dozens

185

– maybe hundreds – dead, my chief engineer is missing, I have over two hundred cetacean life forms trapped in their habitat dome, a major hurricane is about to strike...'

An alarm went off.

'And I rather think that you've just lost your entire communication and data grid,' said the Doctor.

Pandemonium erupted in the control centre. Technicians punched at controls, desperately trying to coax life back into dead read-outs. Brenda stared at the Doctor incredulously for a moment, then launched herself into the mêlée.

'Get the emergency systems online! Now!'

The Dreekan technician held out his hands hopelessly. 'The problem's not internal! We're being jammed by an outside source!'

Ace sidled over to the Doctor's side. 'What's going on now, Professor?'

The Doctor put a finger to his lips and pointed at the ceiling with the tip of his umbrella. The entire building shook with a shattering roar as something black and ugly thundered overhead.

'Dear God!'

Brenda was staring out of the control room window. Ace hurried to her side.

'Wicked!'

The huge shuttlecraft, its hull pitted and barnacled, swung low over the harbour, retros thundering. In a shower of spray it settled on to the waves. Ace clamped her hands over her ears as two more craft roared overhead.

The Doctor joined her at the window, his chin resting on the handle of his umbrella. Ace looked at him, her eyes shining, revelling in the excitement of something new. 'Who are they, Professor?'

The Doctor didn't take his eyes from the sea.

'The answer to a lot of our questions, I think.'

* * *

The Doctor sat on the edge of the fountain watching as Brenda Mulholland and a handful of colony officials pushed their way through the growing crowd that stood nervously in the shadow of one of the alien ships. This one was a slightly different design to the others; smaller, and covered with communication arrays.

A command shuttle probably, mused the Doctor. He frowned. He still hadn't placed the species. He had pored through the notes in his diary, but notes from a thousand planets over nine hundred years, and all in seven different styles of handwriting, made it a less than efficient reference work. He sighed. 'Perhaps I should get myself an electronic organiser,' he murmured.

With a clatter of mechanical legs, and trailing a fine mist of water droplets, Q'ilp crossed the square and settled down beside him.

'Any movement from our new friends yet?'

The Doctor shook his head. 'No. No, they're being decidedly mysterious at the moment.'

The dolphin gave a click of impatience. The shuttlecraft had stopped coming more than twenty minutes ago. Now the sea beyond the harbour wall was black with them. Q'ilp looked around the crowds, mechanical arms unwrapping another cigar.

'Where the hell has MacKenzie got to? I thought the old git would want to be here to do his First Contact bit.'

The Doctor smiled. 'Oh, I sent him to do a little errand for me.'

Ace looked across her hotel room at MacKenzie, who was standing on the balcony, staring down at the alien ship in the courtyard. He was too absorbed in the new arrivals to take any interest in her. Crossing the room she pulled open the wardrobe, hauled out her rucksack and chucked it on to the bed. The Doctor wanted her to go after Garrett, and beach wear was hardly right for traipsing through thick jungle.

She kicked off her remaining trainer and slid out of her shorts. She hauled off her T-shirt and stood in front of the full-length mirror for a moment. The fight with the Krill had given her a few more bruises to add to her collection. She flexed the muscles in her arms. Still... the exercise was giving her a good physique.

She pulled a clean shirt over her head and struggled into a pair of jeans. She reached into the wardrobe for her jacket and her hand brushed against the soft silk of the dress she had worn in the restaurant the night they had arrived. She pulled the dress from its hanger and stood there for a moment, running the material through her fingers. Such a short while ago, but already the memory of that meal was like a distant dream. Ace sighed, hung the dress back in the wardrobe, and took out a pair of boots. Perching on the edge of the bed she began to lace them. She called out to MacKenzie on the balcony. 'Anything exciting happened yet?'

'No, not yet.' He turned and looked at her pleadingly. 'We couldn't stay a little longer, could we?'

Ace shook her head. 'You heard what the Doctor said. We have to get a head start before the aliens try and stop us.'

'Do you really think that they might?'

Ace shrugged. 'Doesn't matter what I think, mate. The Doctor's the boss and he says we've got to get going.' She stood up and stuffed her jacket into her rucksack, looking around the room for anything else that might be useful. Nothing. Like all hotel rooms anywhere it was full of complimentary soap and little else.

'Right, Professor. Let's get going, shall we?'

With a last lingering look at the alien ship, MacKenzie shrugged on his jacket and followed Ace out of the room.

He made for the lift, but Ace caught him by the arm.

'I think we'll take the quiet way out, Prof. Rajiid's meeting us by the fire exit.'

Ace raced down the stairs, followed by the puffing archaeologist. Rajiid was waiting for them at the bottom, clutching two wicked-looking machetes. Ace raised her eyebrows.

Rajiid grinned. 'They belong to my dad.'

Ace took one, testing the weight. 'Remind me to see what other weapons of mass destruction your father has tucked away.'

'I got these too.' Rajiid passed a couple of heavy rubber torches to Ace and MacKenzie.

Ace nodded approvingly. 'Right, let's get going.'

She pushed open the heavy fire door and the three of them stepped out into the backyard of the hotel. The mountain loomed before them, the trees on its summit already beginning to bend under the growing force of the wind.

MacKenzie looked nervously at the ominous sky. 'That hurricane is starting to get terribly close, you know.'

'Then the faster we find Garrett, get that weapon and get back the better.' Ace didn't disguise her impatience. 'Which way do we go, Professor?'

MacKenzie looked at her blankly. 'What?'

'Well, you're the archaeologist. Where do we find this voodoo temple?'

'Oh...' MacKenzie pointed to a tangled path along the edge of the perimeter wall. 'This way.'

Ace rolled her eyes at Rajiid and the two of them set off after the professor.

The colony was quiet. Most of the surviving inhabitants were either wounded or in shock, mourning their dead or watching the alien craft that now floated off the coast. The trio passed through the building work on the edge of the colony – service drones were lashing equipment down, preparing for the coming storm.

As they crossed the colony perimeter, Rajiid stopped.

'Ace, come and look at this.' Ace crossed to his side. A section of the colony's huge perimeter wall lay in the sand, returned to its rest position by huge hydraulic rams. The steel surface of the storm shutters was pitted and scarred. In places the metal was almost torn through. Rajiid looked up in awe.

'Those bastards were nearly in.'

Ace wandered along another section of the wall. 'Same here.' All around on the sand were dark stains where the Krill had been obliterated. She shook her head. 'We'd better hope that there are no more of those things out there.'

MacKenzie looked at her in alarm. 'More Krill? Surely not. Surely Garrett destroyed them all with the weapon.'

Ace shrugged. 'Possibly. But if that's true, why is the Doctor so keen to get it back?' She hauled her rucksack on to her shoulder. 'Come on, Professor. Lead on.'

With a lingering look at the damaged shutters, MacKenzie set off along the path again.

For several minutes they walked along the curve of the bay, the colony becoming a distant white stain among the green. Soon the path itself began to become more indistinct, and the jungle began to thicken. Ace pulled her jacket around her as the wind whipped in off the sea. Rajiid nodded at the sky.

'Much as I hate to agree with him, MacKenzie is right. If we get caught out in the open when that hurricane hits we haven't got a chance.'

Ace nodded. She realised that things were getting desperate or the Doctor would not have sent her into such a potentially hostile situation on her own, but she was secretly pleased. 'Be careful,' he had said. 'Don't take any stupid risks.' But she could tell from the look in his eyes that he knew he could rely on her. The headstrong teenager from Perivale had changed. Was changing. Every day she spent with the Doctor taught her something new.

She wondered if the Doctor's other companions had been changed in the same way. For the first time in ages her thoughts turned to Mel.

Mel. On the surface so vulnerable, so trusting. But

underneath...

She looked over at Rajiid. Another pawn unwittingly drawn into the Doctor's game. There was a brief flush of anger. Once again the Time Lord had arrived and taken control of people's lives. She suddenly checked herself. Rajiid was only part of this because of her. It was only because she'd spotted a pretty face that he was involved at all.

He caught her looking at him. 'What?'

Ace smiled, leant forward and kissed him. 'Nothing. Come on, we'd better get moving.'

The Doctor's head snapped up at the sound of a low hum coming from the shuttlecraft.

'Come on, Q'ilp. I think we're about to meet our guests.'

He pushed through the crowd towards Brenda as a bright line appeared in the underside of the ship. With a mechanical drone, a ramp unfolded from the belly of the shuttlecraft, grinding down on to the flagstones of the square.

A murmur of concern ran around the crowd. The Doctor could see itchy fingers tightening on the triggers of guns. It was a dangerously volatile situation – the Krill attack had put everyone on edge. He pushed through to Brenda's side.

'I hope we're going to be model hosts,' he murmured, nodding at the armed guards.

Brenda nodded back, catching his meaning. She crossed to the security chief and there was a brief discussion. To the Doctor's relief the men lowered their guns.

There were more noises from the ship. A hatch slid open and there was a gasp from Brenda as several huge figures lumbered down the ramp.

'That creature from the dig... They're the same.'

'Yes.' The Doctor nodded. 'Yes, I rather thought that they might be.'

On a slab in the lab the creature had been disturbing enough, but seeing the aliens moving about was terrifying. They were massive, well over seven feet tall, their bulky, rhino-skinned frames clad in glistening battle fatigues. Deep-set eyes, glowering from under heavy brows, swept over the crowd. The Doctor stared at the huge energy weapons slung from their belts. All the guns were holstered, but he could see the tension in the creatures' massive frames.

Six of them formed a cordon at the foot of the ramp. Brenda took a deep breath. 'Well, I suppose I'd better go and introduce myself.'

The Doctor put a gentle hand on her arm.

'Why not wait until there is someone important enough for you to introduce yourself to? Look...'

Two more figures made their way down the ramp. They were just as massive as the others, but their manner was more intelligent and proud. One of them glared around arrogantly.

'Who is in charge here?' The guttural bellow rang around the square. All eyes turned to Brenda Mulholland. With a nervous glance at the Doctor she stepped forward.

'I'm the colony co-ordinator.' She held out her hand. 'Brenda Mulholland.'

The creature took her hand in a massive gauntleted paw.

'General Mottrack, of the Cythosi seventh battalion.' He waved the other figure forward. 'My adjutant, Commander Bisoncawl.'

Brenda stared up defiantly at the two Cythosi. 'And is this an invasion, General?'

Mottrack smiled, revealing ragged yellow teeth. 'Whatever gives you that impression, Miss Mulholland?'

'The complete loss of our communications network, and the number of your ships in our harbour. You're not telling me that this is a social call?'

Mottrack held out his hands apologetically. 'The loss of communications is an unfortunate side effect of our ship's arrival. We picked up your distress call and are here to offer...'

technical assistance. And to collect some property of ours.'

'Property?' The Doctor appeared at Brenda's side. 'What might that be, General?'

Mottrack's smile faded. 'I'm afraid that is a classified military matter, Mr...?'

'Doctor.' The Doctor raised his hat.

'Ah.' Mottrack bared his teeth again. 'The investigator from InterOceanic.'

The Doctor raised an eyebrow. 'I didn't realise I was so well known.'

'We have our sources, Doctor.'

'Gentlemen!' Brenda's voice cut across them. 'In less than two hours a major hurricane is going to hit this island. At the moment we have no way of tracking it and a major hole in our defence grid. So if we can cut the pleasantries...'

Mottrack nodded, curtly. 'Of course. If you will show Commander Bisoncawl where he can set up a command position, I will talk with your chief engineer about the problems with the defence grid.'

Brenda gave the Doctor a sideways glance.

'I'm afraid that our engineer is unavailable, General. The Doctor will give you any information that you require.'

Mottrack's smile vanished completely. 'What do you mean by "unavailable", Co-ordinator?'

'We are currently... unaware of his whereabouts, General.'

'He's having a bit of an identity crisis,' quipped the Doctor. 'Popped off into the jungle for a few days. Soon be back to his old self, I'm sure.'

Mottrack loomed over the little Time Lord, his eyes blazing.

'General.' Bisoncawl was at his commander's shoulder. 'Once our forward command position has been established then perhaps we can... assist in the search for this engineer.'

Mottrack kept his eyes fixed on the Doctor. 'Sound advice, Commander. As always.'

He turned on his heel. 'I will be in the command shuttle. Let me know when you are ready.' The huge bulk of the Cythosi general lumbered back into the hull of the shuttlecraft.

Bisoncawl turned to Brenda. 'If you can show me a site, Miss Mulholland, then I can install my equipment and get my troops to start assisting you with the reconstruction of your defence grid.'

Brenda nodded. 'This way, Commander.'

The Cythosi commander barked a guttural set of orders back into the ship. With a high whine, boxes began to materialise on the shuttle transmat pad. Dozens of armoured troopers clumped down the ramp, each of them hoisting equipment into their arms.

The crowd parted as Brenda Mulholland set off towards the administration block, the Cythosi lumbering in her wake.

The Doctor watched them go, his expression unreadable. Q'ilp clattered to his side, and blew out a cloud of smoke. 'So, Doctor, what do you make of it all? They seem polite enough.'

'Yes, don't they? I think we're in very, very deep trouble.'

Inside the Cythosi shuttlecraft, Mottrack watched the Doctor on a monitor. He punched at a control and the picture zoomed in until the Doctor's face filled the screen.

Mottrack's lips curled back in a snarl as he watched the little man and his dolphin companion walk through the crowds. He ground his claws on the arm of his chair.

'Take care, Doctor,' he muttered. 'You will find that I am not someone who deals well with imbeciles.'

He snapped off the monitor and punched at the communications relay.

'Mottrack to base ship.'

'Yes, General.'

'I want a complete sensor sweep of the planet's surface – spiral pattern, starting at this shuttle. I want location of life forms and any residual traces of that energy signature.'

There was too long a pause from the communicator.

'Well...?' Mottrack's voice had dropped to a low growl. Even over the communicator he could detect his sensor officer's fear.

'We still have only partial sensor systems online, General. The energy wave from the planet...'

'I don't want excuses!' Mottrack's roar echoed around the shuttle. 'I want full sensor data back online within the hour.'

He snapped off the communicator and thrust himself back in his seat, trying to control his rising rage. It was at times like this that he needed a good interrogation session. He cast a glance around the silent control cabin. Technicians busied themselves at their tasks, desperate not to make eye contact with him. Several of the human slaves huddled nervously in a corner.

Mottrack's eyes narrowed. They were expendable, but had none of the fight of a Zithra. They died within minutes of the start of an interrogation, leaving him frustrated and unfulfilled.

'Get out,' Mottrack hissed.

He slumped back in his chair, glowering at the read-outs. The Doctor's face swam into view before his eyes. There was a man who he would look forward to interrogating after all this was over.

A smile crossed the general's face.

Now he had something to look forward to.

Chapter Sixteen

Holly Relf sat in the cool of the boathouse staring at the space where the *Hyperion Dawn* was usually berthed. She was in her usual boiler suit, her tool pouch slung around her waist, ostensibly back on duty with the repair teams, helping to get the colony back together.

The doctors and nurses from the medical centre had complained, of course. There was no way she should be up and about, let alone back at work. But they could find nothing physically wrong with her and had reluctantly agreed that keeping busy was probably the best thing for her.

As she had left the control centre with R'tk'tk, the little man who had helped her – the Doctor – had stopped her. He had looked at her, concern in those mysterious grey eyes, saying nothing. Then he had smiled, thanked her for her help and bustled away with the crowd surrounding Brenda.

Holly shook her head. There was something very strange about that little man, but at the same time she felt more at ease with him than with anyone else she had ever met. When they'd been working so desperately together there had been something between them, as if they'd been relying on each other for years.

That familiarity was comforting now as she looked around at the shattered remnants of her life, and as the full enormity of what the Krill had taken from her began to hit home.

She crossed the boathouse to a set of lockers. The crew lockers from the *Hyperion Dawn*.

Jim. Trevor. Auger. Geeson.

Just names now. Tags on metal cabinets that were all she had left of her friends.

She opened Jim's locker, not quite knowing what she expected to find, or wanted to find. She pulled out his oilskins, unpacked in readiness for the stormy season. A gust of wind rattled the boathouse and sent waves skittering over the surface of the water.

The hurricane was practically on them.

'Holly...'

R'tk'tk was bobbing in the water, regarding her solemnly. Years of dealing with the cetaceans had taught her to recognise the subtlest of expressions on their faces and she could see that the dolphin was concerned.

'I'm OK, R'tk. Everything all right out there?'

'I think you'd better come and look.'

Holly hung the oilskins back in the locker and followed the dolphin out into the harbour.

'Good God!'

'Yup. It's a worry, isn't it?'

She stared out at the dozens of shuttles and transports that dotted the surface of the sea. As she watched another thundered overhead to settle in the bay.

She turned back and looked along the jetty. She could see a crowd in the town centre.

'Rescue ships?'

The dolphin shook his head. 'They're no type I've ever seen. These are out-of-town boys.'

A gust of wind blew spray across the water and Holly began to shrug into her jacket.

'I think I might wander back up to control, find out from Brenda what the hell is going on.'

She set off along the jetty. R'tk'tk watched her go.

'I'll just float around here then,' he chirruped.

Coralee control bustled with activity. Humans, Dreekans and cetaceans vied for position as the Cythosi installed their equipment in the damaged control room.

The Doctor and Q'ilp stood to one side watching the proceedings with interest. The Cythosi commander, Bisoncawl, moved among the chaos like a huge battleship, keeping everything running smoothly. The Doctor eyed him warily. His every instinct screamed that something was not right, but he could find no fault with the work the Cythosi were doing. Everything seemed to indicate that the aliens were genuinely helping to repair the perimeter storm wall, and Bisoncawl's air of quiet authority had already commanded nervous respect from the islanders. Not that any of the humans went that close to him. He was a terrifying figure.

The Doctor tapped his lips with the handle of his umbrella. He looked up to see Holly Relf enter the control room and waved her over. Holly looked at the Cythosi in disbelief. 'What the hell are they?'

'Would you believe good Samaritans?' the Doctor said, his eyes twinkling.

'No!'

'Holly, I'm glad you're here.' Brenda crossed from her office. She squeezed her friend's arm. 'How are you doing?'

Holly shrugged. 'OK. Glad to be busy.'

'Well, we could use some help here. The Cythosi are having trouble patching into our NavSat grid and we need to be able to track that hurricane.'

Q'ilp puffed nervously on his cigar and nodded at the lumbering Cythosi technicians. 'We can trust them?'

Brenda cast a look at the Doctor. 'Our friend here thinks not, but at the moment they've been nothing but perfect guests and have already stepped up the repulsor-field efficiency by 12 per cent.'

Holly raised her eyebrows. 'I'll have to see if I can pick up a few tips. So, Doctor, what's your problem with them?'

A Cythosi pushed past, forcing the Doctor and Brenda to step back. The Doctor sniffed the air.

'That!' he cried in triumph.

Holly's nose wrinkled. 'So they smell a bit on the damp side...'

'Oh my God...' Brenda's eyes opened wide.

The Doctor looked at her expectantly. 'Yes?'

'That smell. It's the same as the creature that attacked me!'

'Exactly.' He lowered his voice. 'The Cythosi have had an operative here all the time. They are responsible for everything that happened here, and they are Mr Garrett's allies.'

'So all this...'

'Is a deception to gain your trust. They are after the weapon, and at the moment they have no idea where it is.'

Q'ilp's face cracked into a toothy smile. 'So MacKenzie and your friend...'

The Doctor put a finger to his lips. 'Ssh.'

The massive figure of Bisoncawl lumbered over. 'General Mottrack would like to see the Doctor in the command shuttle,' he grunted.

The Doctor raised his eyebrows. 'Really?' He pulled his pocket watch out. 'Well, it is nearly tea time. I do hope the general has put the kettle on.' He doffed his hat. 'If you will excuse me, ladies and dolphins?'

He trotted out of the control room, dwarfed by the Cythosi commander. Brenda, Q'ilp and Holly watched him go.

'He's quite mad, isn't he?' said Q'ilp.

Brenda nodded. 'Quite. But he's also the only one with the faintest idea of what is going on.' She clapped Holly on the arm. 'Come on, you. We've got a hurricane to look after.'

Ace stopped and stared back at the beach below her, now a thin strip of yellow bordering the deep blue of the sea. She rubbed her hand across her brow. It had been a hot, exhausting climb, with only the freshening wind to cool them down. Rajiid had been surprised at just how unfit he was. MacKenzie was still several metres down the path, red and panting.

The path had veered off from the far end of the beach, following the banks of a sizeable river that tumbled across the sand from a source high in the mountain. The three of them had set off into the interior of the island with confidence, but the pretty postcard vistas of palms and tropical flowers had soon given way to thicker, less friendly jungle, and before long Ace and Rajiid had been wielding their machetes, trying to make a passable track through the encroaching foliage.

The river, too, had become less inviting. At first Ace had waded through the cool shallows watching the fish pooling at her feet, enjoying the pull of the current against her skin. Now the water was a raging torrent, tumbling over savagely jagged rocks, the spray turning the path into a treacherous slide of mud and wet leaves.

They had just finished an exhausting climb alongside an almost vertical waterfall. Only now that she was at the top, with enough time to catch her breath, did Ace finally have time to realise how breathtakingly beautiful the view was.

Her delighted smile faded as she turned her eyes to the sky. Out on the horizon clouds boiled, a tumbling mass of black and purple, coiling into huge angry shapes. She shivered at the display of malevolent nature, and with a cold chill finally realised how vulnerable their position was. The first fingers of wind tugged at her hair.

Rajiid was suddenly at her side, following her eyes and catching her thought.

'MacKenzie says we're nearly there. The Dreekans chose a high spot so that they would be well protected.' He shrugged. 'There's nowhere on the island much higher than this.'

He cocked his head to one side and looked at her quizzically. 'Once we find Garrett, do you have a plan to get the weapon off him?'

Ace hefted the machete in her hands.

'No. We'll just busk it,' she said.

* * *

The Doctor trotted up the ramp of the Cythosi shuttle, dwarfed by Bisoncawl. It was cool and dark inside the ship and it took several seconds for the Doctor's eyes to become accustomed to the gloom.

The interior was bleak and functional, no concession made to comfort. Equipment was crammed into every available space, control positions and gun emplacements barely big enough to contain the bulk of their Cythosi operators. Patches of oily vapour coiled through the service areas leaving a slick deposit over the walls and ceiling. The smell was musty – like the lion house in a zoo.

A hatch slid open with a hiss and the Doctor followed Bisoncawl into the command area. Mottrack dominated the room, his control chair high above the rest of the crew. Bisoncawl crossed to him and saluted stiffly, waiting for the general to acknowledge him.

The Doctor peered around the control room with interest. Despite himself he was impressed. The Cythosi were advanced in many areas. There were smatterings of technology that he recognised in among the machines that he didn't. The creatures didn't mind taking the lead from other civilisations, it appeared.

Here too, clouds of vapour drifted through the dim light. As one of them came close to the Doctor's face he stuck his head forward and took a tentative sniff.

The vapour caught at the back of his throat and he began to cough violently. Bisoncawl shot him an angry look and the Doctor hauled his handkerchief from his pocket, covering his mouth.

He realised that he was being watched. He turned. The figure was too small to be a Cythosi. To his surprise a human stepped from the shadows. Thin, emaciated; fear looming large in his eyes. He watched the Doctor nervously.

'Good afternoon,' the Doctor smiled.

The figure nearly smiled back but one of the Cythosi

operatives reached out casually and cuffed it savagely with a gauntleted claw.

'Get out of here.'

The human vanished into the bowels of the ship. The operative glowered at the Doctor. The Doctor held his gaze, his face hard.

Perhaps the Cythosi weren't so advanced after all.

'Doctor.' Mottrack's voice rang across the room. 'Will you join me, please?'

The Doctor crossed to the Cythosi general. Mottrack's face split into a smile that had far too many teeth to be friendly. He indicated a chair on the other side of the control dais, and turned to Bisoncawl.

'Thank you, Commander, that will be all,' he said.

Bisoncawl nodded and, with a glance at the Doctor, crossed to his own console. The Doctor struggled into the huge chair, dwarfed by its size, his feet dangling off the floor like a schoolboy's.

Mottrack stabbed at a control and the air around the control dais shimmered and darkened, solidifying to a smoky glass consistency.

'A little privacy, Doctor,' Mottrack purred.

'Very cosy, I'm sure.'

'I thought it was time that you and I had a little chat.'

'Yes.' The Doctor's face flickered into a half smile. He'd rather hoped the general would want to see him. There were gaps that needed filling in.

Mottrack leant back in his chair. 'Can I offer you any refreshment, Doctor?'

The Doctor nodded, and Mottrack pulled a thick bottle from an alcove in his desk.

Two glasses clattered on to the table-top and Mottrack poured a generous measure of viscous liquid into each. The Doctor sniffed at his glass and grimaced. There was a chuckle from the Cythosi.

'Not to your taste, Doctor?' He downed the liquid in a swift gulp.

The Doctor picked up his glass. 'General, I'm not here to pass the time of day with you. You are embarking on a very dangerous course of action. The Krill are the most vicious creatures I have ever encountered and you seem to think that you can use them like some sort of tool.' He swirled the liquid around in his glass, aware of Mottrack's eyes burning into his skull. 'The people on this planet are not part of your plans, General. They only just survived the Krill this time; they might not do so again. However you help, whatever defences you put in place, if the Krill attack again the only chance for any of us is that weapon.'

The Doctor looked up from the glass. 'Leave these people alone, General. Let them have Phillip Garrett back and then leave them alone.'

For a moment it looked as though Mottrack was going to explode. Then, with a barking laugh, he filled his glass again. 'You think you are so clever, don't you, Doctor? Think you have got it all worked out. You haven't the faintest idea of what we are trying to do.' He leaned close, his breath hissing in the Doctor's ears. 'You are an interfering meddler. You will not be permitted to stand in the way of my plans.'

Cythosi and Time Lord glared at one another, then the Doctor raised his glass.

'Cheers.'

He drained the liquid in a single gulp, his eyes streaming as it slid down his throat.

Mottrack bellowed with laughter, and shook his head. 'You are a strange one, Doctor.' He cocked his huge head to one side. 'Not human, I'd wager?'

The Doctor dabbed at his eyes with his handkerchief.

'What have you done with Phillip Garrett, General?' His voice was hoarse. 'The *real* Phillip Garrett.'

'There is no real Garrett, Doctor.'

Mottrack leant back in his seat again, amusement dancing in his eyes. 'Phillip Garrett is a deep-cover operative. His name is Skuarte. He has been living among humans for nearly twenty years – the longest any Cythosi has remained undercover. We developed personal morphing generators a long time ago, Doctor, but this is the most successful operation of that device.'

'So the siting of a colony on this world, having Garrett as chief engineer...'

'Was all planned and executed according to the design of Cythosi High Command.'

Ace crouched down in the long grass staring at the cave mouth. MacKenzie huddled alongside her.

'That will almost certainly be it. Dreekan voodoo ceremonies tend to revolve around fire and darkness, that would be a perfect temple for them.' Ace nodded, her eyes scanning the surrounding jungle. The wind was tearing at the trees now, the noise of rustling foliage making it almost impossible to hear anything.

Rajiid scrambled up the slope towards them.

'I can't see anyone, but there are sounds of movement from inside.'

Ace looked up at the boiling sky overhead as raindrops, fat and heavy, began to splash off the wide leaves around them. With shocking suddenness the sky opened and torrents of water began to fall.

'Come on,' she said. 'If nothing else it will give us somewhere to shelter from this storm.'

The three of them pushed their way through the creaking trees to the cave mouth. Their feet sank into the floor of the jungle as water saturated it. By the time they reached the cave mouth they were soaked through. Ace flicked her wet hair from her eyes and peered into the gloom.

From the depths of the cave she could hear rhythmic drums and the low murmur of voices. She looked expectantly at the professor. MacKenzie's face was pale and clammy.

'Yes, that's it. That's them.' He caught her arm. 'Do we have to go in?'

Ace shook herself free impatiently. 'Wait here if you like. You can let us know if anyone else comes in behind us.'

She stared out at the hammering rain and raging wind. It was a fairly safe bet that no one would. She pitied anyone caught out in the storm.

She snapped on her torch and ran its beam over the walls. It revealed a tunnel covered in swirling patterns, a painted path snaking its way into the heart of the mountain. Water was already beginning to pool in the entrance to the cave, a small river forming at their feet.

Ace reached back and caught hold of Rajiid's hand. 'Ready?'

'As I'll ever be.'

Leaving MacKenzie shivering in the cave mouth, Ace and Rajiid descended into the dark.

A gust of wind slammed against the buildings of the colony, making Holly jump. Rain streamed down walls, sheets of water blew across the near-deserted streets.

Holly struggled across the harbour, her jacket pulled tight against her. She cursed as the wind pushed her sideways, her feet slipping on the wet flagstones.

She could see the glow from her workshop ahead of her. A wave crashed over the jetty. Where were those damn sea defences?

On cue there was a deep throbbing hum and the shimmering line of the repulsor field arced across the harbour. Slowly the huge metal shutters that formed the storm wall slid from the beach once more.

The air overhead shimmered with the effects of the force field and at once the wind lessened and the rain eased off.

Beyond the defences the sea churned and roared.

Holly shivered, watching the Cythosi ships pitch and roll in the ocean. One by one they activated their own defence shields and the bay was filled with shimmering shapes.

She hurried into the workshop. R'tk'tk bobbed in the water.

'About time! I was beginning to think you were going to let us all get swept out to sea.'

Holly grunted and crossed to the heater in one corner. She shrugged out of her soaking jacket. 'It took some time to get the Cythosi equipment patched in. Not all of it was compatible.'

'Cythosi?'

'Our new-found benefactors.' Holly struggled into a thick pullover. 'Big, ugly bastards, but clever technicians.' She looked grim. 'They got our sensor grid back on line. That's one hell of a storm out there. We only just got the shutters running in time.'

R'tk'tk squeaked worriedly. 'Any news on Rajiid and Ace?'

'They're still out there, somewhere. The Doctor wants to try and keep them a secret from our guests.'

'He doesn't trust the Cythosi?'

Holly shook her head. 'No, and I don't think they trust him. The Doctor has just been called for an audience with their great white chief.'

Ace's eyes had gradually adjusted to the dark, so when the glow filled the tunnel it seemed as if it were almost as light as day. She ran her hands over the faintly luminous walls. Natural phosphorescence. The Doctor would have liked this.

Rajiid crept close behind her. She could feel the warmth of his body pressing against her through her damp clothes.

'Here. There's no time for that sort of thing,' she whispered.

'It's perfect. Low lights, soft music,' he nodded towards the distant sound of drums. 'They're playing our song.'

Squeezing his hand, Ace adjusted her grip on her machete and crept forward.

The tunnel began to widen out into a natural cavern. The throbbing, insistent beat of the drums was all around them now. Ace and Rajiid ducked back as wild flickering shadows danced over the walls. Motioning to Rajiid to stay put, Ace dropped on to her belly and began to edge forward.

About thirty Dreekans were gathered in the centre of the cave, all of them bare chested, all of them slick with sweat. The floor of the cave was marked out with a trail of wet sand – huge, sweeping, swirling patterns on the rocky floor. A fire blazed in the centre of the cavern, sending clouds of sweet-smelling smoke into the air. Dancers swirled through the smoke, breathing deeply.

Ace cursed. There was no sign of Garrett.

The cave was irregular, the far wall deep in shadow. Ace tried to see if there was any other exit, any other chamber where he might be lurking. It was difficult to see, difficult to concentrate. She could feel her head swimming. The smoke...

Water trickled from the ceiling. Ace slid her head under it, trying to clear some of the fuzziness. Cracks of light broke the dark of the distant rock roof; water was beginning to stream down from outside. The floor was already ankle deep in it.

She was about to call back to Rajiid when she saw a figure loom in the tunnel mouth, and her heart sank.

MacKenzie staggered from the tunnel into the cave, his jacket torn, his eyes wild.

'MacKenzie!' Ace hissed. 'Get back!'

Rajiid reached out and tried to haul the professor back into the shadows, but Ace knew it was already too late. The drums stopped and cries echoed across the cave. The cultists swarmed forward.

Ace swore and launched herself into the open, catching one of the Dreekans in the small of the back, sending him crashing into the floor.

She grasped MacKenzie by the collar and propelled him

towards the tunnel entrance. Rajiid was on her heels. The tunnel mouth loomed before her, and then something sent her sprawling.

She crashed backwards, the breath punched from her. A huge figure towered over her. It was Garrett, a hideous blend of human and alien, the flesh flowing across his face in waves. Wild eyes stared down at her, and Ace felt herself being hauled upright, many arms tightening around her. She could see MacKenzie and Rajiid held fast by the Dreekans. Garrett pulled the machete from her hand and held it up. He began to pace before them, the blade held aloft.

The Dreekans began to moan softly, swaying. Ace struggled, but the blue flesh of her captors was like steel. She bit and kicked them but their glazed eyes showed no pain.

Garrett suddenly held both arms out, and silence fell over the cave.

He pulled the mighty weapon from his shoulder. 'The sea sent us a saviour from the creatures of the deep,' he intoned, 'and now the land has sent us a fitting tribute.'

He placed the weapon on the ground reverently.

'We must honour the saviour with blood.'

He raised the machete.

'And the Treeka'dwra must spill it.'

Ace closed her eyes as the blade sliced down.

Chapter Seventeen

The Doctor stood with Mottrack in the observation dome at the top of the Cythosi command shuttle, watching the hurricane rage outside the storm shutters.

'Why, General? What was all this for?'

Mottrack was silent for a moment, watching the rain shimmer and boil on the force fields. When he spoke his voice was low and vicious.

'Victory, Doctor. Victory over the Zithra.'

The Doctor sighed. 'Ah. War. Nothing else.'

'There is nothing else!' Mottrack hissed. 'The beings in this galaxy know nothing of conflict. Your petty wars are like children's games beside the battles we have fought.' His voice dropped to a low growl. 'The Zithra came without warning and tore an entire galaxy apart. But we fought them. Strike and counter-strike, battle upon battle. Generation upon generation of watching them decimate our worlds. Holding them at bay – but only holding them, never driving them back. And then the legends reached us. Intelligence reports about a world whose people had developed war into a sublime art, who had developed a creature that was the perfect weapon.'

'The Krill.'

'Yes, Doctor! The Krill!' Mottrack's eyes were shining. 'The Zithra know nothing about this world. Through our operatives we have let these puny humans do all the work for us, our hand unseen. No risks. No possibility of discovery. Generations working towards this moment, when we can harvest our prize and unleash them in their millions upon the worlds that the Zithra have taken from us.'

'And then use the weapon to sterilise those worlds.'

'Exactly. Take back what was stolen from us. Rebuild a galaxy free from the tyranny of the Zithra.'

'But it's gone wrong, hasn't it, General?' said the Doctor, sadly. 'Without the weapon, without the means of destroying the Krill, you can never use those worlds, never regain them.' He stared out of the dome again. 'Garrett... Skuarte is unstable, isn't he? The strain of twenty years undercover.'

Mottrack nodded. 'Our psi-evaluators indicated that schizophrenia was a theoretically possible, if unlikely, side effect.'

The Doctor smiled faintly. 'I rather think your psi-evaluators owe him – them – an apology, don't you?'

Mottrack's face hardened. 'Hear this, Doctor. I will not let the Krill or the weapon fall into the hands of the Zithra. Before that day I will smash this planet from existence.'

The Cythosi turned and lumbered from the observation dome.

The Doctor chewed on his fingernails. Somewhere out in the storm was a creature who didn't know if it was Cythosi or man. A mad thing – and he had sent Ace after it.

Ace sat slumped against the damp wall of the cave staring into the dark, trying to shut out the memories of what had happened. She could still see the huge machete raised before her, still hear the sickening noise it had made as it had sliced into MacKenzie's neck.

The corpse lay slumped on the floor not far from her. Ace turned away, trying not to look at it, but even with her eyes closed she could still see the headless figure, its blood leaking over the wet stone floor; still see the expression of disbelief that had remained on the professor's face even as his head separated from his shoulders.

MacKenzie's death had sent the Dreekans into a whirling frenzy. She and Rajiid had been lifted into the air and daubed with his blood before being paraded around the cave. Garrett had stood staring at the corpse in silence, his eyes blank, as if the murder had somehow been performed by someone else. One of the Dreekans had tried to prise the blade from his grasp, pointing excitedly at Ace and Rajiid. Ace had felt his gaze drift over them and had steeled herself for one final effort, one desperate attempt to fight back.

But Garrett had pushed the man to one side and dragged himself across the cave, slumping on to the stone dais that had been set up as his throne. There he had sat, staring at the blood dripping from the machete blade, while the Dreekans danced and whirled around him.

They had lit more fires, throwing handfuls of dried leaves on to them, filling the cave with pungent, choking smoke. It became like an oven. Ace's head had begun to reel, and everything was dream-like.

Outside the cave the hurricane had built and built. Water streamed from the cave mouth, forming dark pools among the swirling sand patterns. The trickle from the roof had become a torrent, tumbling from high in the smoke-filled cave and vanishing through cracks and fissures into the depths of the planet.

Ace had no idea how long the ritual had gone on. She had become at one with the blur of flames, the roar of water and the beat of drums as she was whirled around and around.

Now everything was quiet, the fires little more than glowing patches on the wet floor. The Dreekans were sleeping in piles, bodies sprawled across the rocks, oblivious to the storm raging outside. She and Rajiid had been bound and dumped in a corner. She had come to a couple of hours ago.

Ace raised her head, searching for Garrett. His throne was empty. Her eyes were still streaming and sore from the smoke.

There was a groan alongside her. Rajiid twitched in his sleep. She managed to lay a hand on his forehead. He was hot. It was impossible to know what had been burnt in the narcotic fires of the Dreekans. Why the hell had she involved him in all this?

She looked up again. Straight into the face of Garrett.

She almost cried out, but he clamped a hand over her mouth. He was staring at her with wild, pleading eyes, his face almost human again.

'Please,' he whispered, 'please don't cry out. I'm going to help.'

He pulled the machete from behind his back. Ace tensed.

Garrett sawed at her bonds and her hands were suddenly free. She scrambled backwards, poised to lash out if he tried anything.

'What the hell is going on, Garrett?' she hissed.

'I don't know what's happening to me.' He held his arms out, staring down at his hands. 'I get so many different voices in my head, telling me so many different things.'

As he leant back into the soft firelight Ace could see the metal cylinder of the weapon slung around his neck.

Garrett suddenly lunged forward, gripping her arms. 'Tell me what's happening to me!'

Ace shook him free. 'I don't know!'

He slumped back on to his haunches. He had dropped the machete. Ace stretched for it. If she could get the weapon from him...

Garrett spun round and saw her outstretched hand. He snatched the blade up, his face wild.

'No! You're just like all of them. Against me!'

'Garrett...' Ace kept her voice calm, hoping he couldn't hear the tremble in it. 'The Doctor can help you. Let me get you to the Doctor.'

'Yes. Yes. The Doctor.' Garrett nodded enthusiastically. 'The man from InterOceanic. He'll know, he'll know.'

Cradling the weapon to his chest, Garrett rose to his feet. 'Back at the colony.' His face clouded again. 'The voices keep telling me about the colony, what I must do.'

214

He began to wander towards the tunnel, cooing to himself.

'Garrett! Garrett, wait.' Cursing, Ace bent to untie Rajiid. She shook him awake. He started, panic in his eyes.

'Wha...? Ace?'

'Yes. It's me. Come on.'

Grasping his hand she hauled him to his feet and the two of them crept into the tunnel. The floor was a small river now, the wet rocks treacherous underfoot.

Dull light seeped from the entrance to the tunnel, blinding after the gloom of the cave. Ace and Rajiid emerged to a jungle that thrashed as though shaken by a giant hand. The hurricane was at its height. Of Garrett there was no sign.

The Doctor looked up in alarm as the shuttlecraft lurched and lifted from the colony square.

'General...?'

A figure appeared in the doorway of the observation gallery. Bisoncawl.

'The General has other business, Doctor, on Coralee. He thought that you might like a closer look at our operations.'

'How very thoughtful of him.' The Doctor's mind whirled. That Mottrack didn't trust him was obvious. But was this just a ploy to get him out of the way? He looked out of the dome, watching the energy waves as the shuttle passed through the force field that arched from the tops of the storm shutters.

Immediately, the little craft lurched as the winds slammed into it. The Doctor watched the racing waves beneath them. He was aware of Bisoncawl's eyes on his back. How far would the General go to ensure success?

Holly Relf watched as the shuttlecraft vanished into the driving rain. 'Wonder where they're going,' she murmured.

She turned to R'tk'tk. 'Have you got an energy coder for the screens?'

215

The dolphin bobbed his head up and down. 'All cetaceans with level three clearance and above have got them.'

'How d'you fancy a little jaunt?'

'After the shuttle?'

Holly nodded. 'They're headed due west. No prizes for guessing their destination.'

'The reactor.' R'tk'tk flexed his tail. 'It'll take me a little while to get out there.'

Holly knelt down and slipped a com collar over the dolphin's head. 'Call in if you find anything. And, R'tk... don't take any stupid risks.'

With a splash and a blur of grey hide, the dolphin was gone.

The Cythosi shuttlecraft dropped low over the churning ocean. Out of the driving rain the dim shape of the colony reactor began to take shape, a mass of angular steel on huge legs, towering over the water. Spray crackled off its repulsor fields as huge waves crashed over it. The shuttle made a low circuit, then its nose dipped and the little craft sliced into the water.

The violence of the storm was suddenly gone and the shuttle drifted down past the reactor's huge legs. The Doctor stared out of the observation dome, Bisoncawl at his shoulder. Cythosi in diving gear glided over the coral outcrops, the water turning them into elegant, graceful creatures. The Krill cocoons covered the rocks, the grime of centuries chipped away, uncovered by the alien workers. The skin of the eggs was iridescent, shimmering in the light that filtered down from the surface.

'I should have brought my oil paints.'

The Doctor stared up at the Cythosi commander in surprise. Bisoncawl didn't look away from the window.

'Do you know the work of Turner, Doctor?'

'Yes.' The Doctor nodded. 'Yes I do, I just didn't expect...'

He tailed off.

Bisoncawl looked at him. 'You just didn't expect an alien killer to like art. We're not all like General Mottrack, Doctor.'

The Doctor looked at his feet, embarrassed; a rare occurrence for him. 'Forgive me, Commander. Where did you learn to like Turner?'

'I spent seven months as communications officer on a Terran freighter ferrying Guldarian farming drones to outposts along the Brago Nebula. No military goal, just early deep-cover tests of the new cloaking technology.' Bisoncawl grunted. 'Have you ever done a long-haul cargo flight, Doctor? Months of tedium. I went through every data cube in the library, tried every leisure programme. I developed a taste for painting. It is an... underdeveloped occupation back home.'

He nodded at the workers outside in the water, his mood changing, the moment of intimacy over. 'Look, Doctor. We're about to make a transfer. The first gathering of the harvest.'

The Doctor watched as a gentle flickering light bathed a section of the coral. When it faded the cocoons were gone.

'A matter beam, transporting the eggs directly to holding tanks on the mother ship?'

Now it was Bisoncawl's turn to look surprised. He nodded. 'We have a containment team working on the mother ship and a relay transmitter on the reactor.'

There was a soft tremor as the ship came up hard under the reactor.

'Come, Doctor. I will show you.'

Garrett stood staring up at the storm shutters, watching the water dance and hiss on the energy barrier. Around him the hurricane raged, but he seemed oblivious to it. He had pushed through the jungle as if it wasn't there, in a stumbling run from the mountain, the weapon clutched to his chest. His overpowering urge was to get to the colony. His skin had thickened again, and water ran from the rough hide.

Voices urged him on, each of them screaming at the other.

He was Phillip Garrett.

He was Skuarte.

He was the Treeka'dwra.

He was traitor.

He was destroyer.

He was saviour.

Garrett had bellowed at the storm and plunged onwards. Now he crossed to a hatchway in the cold metal of the colony perimeter and reached for the computer pad set into the wall next to it.

Clumsy clawed hands stabbed at the controls and the hatch slid back.

His head cocked to one side, as if listening, Garrett slipped into the colony and the hatch slammed shut.

The Doctor stepped from the hatchway into the main control centre of the colony reactor and stared around him with interest. Cythosi technicians filled the small control room, making the human-made equipment look tiny. A huge gnarled piece of Cythosi machinery dominated the centre of the room, ugly and crude next to the elegant simplicity of the reactor controls. The Doctor crossed to it.

'The transmat relay?'

Bisoncawl nodded. The Doctor peered closely at it. Like most Cythosi devices it seemed to be an amalgamation of technology from a dozen different worlds, crudely lashed together. He tutted at connections that worked more by luck than judgement – this was the kind of lash-up even he would think twice about. He could see why Mottrack and the other officers still travelled by shuttlecraft – the transmat wasn't the most reliable example of its type.

As he watched, the technicians made a series of adjustments to the controls. With a crackle of power, the machine throbbed into life as more Krill eggs beamed to the mother ship.

* * *

In the cool corridors under Coralee central control, Garrett slid through the shadows, his form ebbing and flowing – human and Cythosi – beneath the painted patterns on his skin, sweat beading his brow as he tried to keep his thoughts focused. In his mind he could see the reactor, see the remote console, and he knew in his heart that that was where he must go.

There was movement ahead of him. A Cythosi trooper, plasma weapon hefted in his huge arms, was patrolling the corridors. Garrett slipped into a pool of shadows, concentrating, willing his form to change.

He felt his skin harden around him, felt his form toughen. Then he stepped out into the light. The Cythosi guard brought the gun up at the unexpected intruder, then relaxed. 'At last. You should have relieved me of duty hours ago.'

Garrett nodded at him and strode forward. When he was alongside the guard he lashed out with huge gnarled hands, clubbing him to the floor.

He pulled the body into an alcove and stripped it of communicator, entry coders, anything of use. He pulled a small device from the guard's tunic. A transmat pad. He smiled. Things were going just as he had hoped.

Satisfied that the guard was safely tucked away in the shadows, he edged forward into the power room.

Warmth flooded through him. This was where he had first felt at peace. In the dark, with the echoing throb of the drums in his ears, he crossed to the console. Yes. This was right. He began scanning over the myriad of controls.

His hands hovered over the reactor console. His brow creased. Jumbled images and thoughts crowded through his brain. He had to complete his mission, but everything was so confusing. Clear in his mind was the order that if anything went wrong, he was to detonate the reactor. Destroy the enemy. And everything *was* wrong. Everyone was the enemy.

Behind him he could hear booted feet, cries of alarm as the

body of the guard was discovered. He knew what it was that he had to do.

The feet came closer. The creatures were close. Yes. The aliens. They were evil. Must be destroyed.

With sudden clarity, Garrett punched at the controls on the board. Read-outs began to fluctuate wildly, lights blinked red in danger areas. Klaxons began to sound, deafening in the surroundings and echoing off the pipes. Garrett raised the plasma gun and fired charge after charge into the console.

There were harsh cries from behind him as troops swarmed into the sub basement. Garrett smiled and triggered the transmat control.

In Coralee control Brenda and Q'ilp looked up in disbelief as emergency klaxons blared across the colony. Human and dolphin stared at each other.

'You've got to be kidding...' said Q'ilp.

Mottrack lumbered to Brenda's side. 'What?'

'That's the reactor!'

She barged through the milling technicians to a control board. 'Good God. They've shut down the coolant flow.' She rounded on the Cythosi general. 'What the hell do you think you're doing, Mottrack?'

Mottrack hissed angrily. 'This is not our doing. I too have men out there.'

The communicator on his belt screeched at him.

'Yes!' The general's face clouded with rage. 'Then find him, now!' He turned back to Brenda. 'Someone has sabotaged your reactor.'

Brenda knew what he was going to tell her. 'Garrett?'

'I believe so. I'm afraid that I am going to return to my shuttle, Co-ordinator. Things are becoming a little...how shall we say...uncomfortable down here. I do hope that the loss of your reactor will not inconvenience you.'

He barked a series of guttural commands at his troops, and

marched from the room.

Bisoncawl's head jerked up as the alarms went off. Emergency lighting bathed the control room in a deep red glow. The Doctor raised his eyebrows quizzically.

'Oh, dear. That doesn't bode well.'

Bisoncawl shot him a venomous look and crossed to his panicking staff who were struggling with the reactor controls.

'What is the reason for these alarms?'

The technician didn't take his eyes from the monitors. His fingers moved clumsily over the keyboard, the human-made instruments looking tiny under his huge hands.

'Coolant flow to the reactor has been shut down, Commander. The systems are going critical.'

'How?' Bisoncawl stared at the Doctor, who smiled innocently back at him. 'How has this been done?'

The technician shook his head. 'The problem isn't at this end, Commander. The coolant has been stopped from a remote terminal at the colony and locked down. There is nothing we can do from this end.'

Bisoncawl was reaching for his communicator when it shrieked into life.

'Bisoncawl.' His face went grim as a voice bellowed at him from the speaker. He nodded. 'Yes, General. I understand.'

The Doctor strained to hear the conversation. His mind was racing. Something was going wrong with the Cythosi plans and he wasn't sure if that was a good thing or not.

As he watched, Bisoncawl snapped the communicator back on to his belt and strode into the centre of the control room, straightening his uniform.

'Your attention please.' His voice drowned the blaring alarms. All eyes turned towards him. 'This establishment has been sabotaged. The reactor is going critical. We are ordered to abandon the site and return to the mother ship. Dive crews will be recalled and all troops will return to their assault shuttles.'

There was a moment of shocked silence when no one moved, then the control room erupted into a frenzy of activity.

Bisoncawl had turned towards the doorway when the Doctor stepped in front of him, his grey eyes blazing. 'Commander, you understand what will happen if this reactor explodes?'

'Yes, Doctor. We will die unless we get out of here.' He tried to step past the Doctor but the little Time Lord stepped into his way again.

'The Krill will be released into the water in vast numbers. The colony will be completely wiped out.'

Something akin to guilt flashed across the Cythosi's face. 'I'm sorry, Doctor, but I have a responsibility for my troopers.'

'But I can stop this!' The Doctor caught him by the arm. Bisoncawl's face darkened and he bared vicious teeth.

'Get out of my way, Doctor.'

'Listen to me!' the Doctor bellowed. 'I can use the transmat to get all the Krill eggs out of here before the reactor goes critical. This disaster doesn't need to happen!'

Bisoncawl shook himself free of the Doctor's grasp. 'The parameters of the device don't allow that kind of bulk beaming, and we don't have time to do it in batches.'

'The parameters can be changed. Do you think that this equipment is complex? It's primitive junk, Bisoncawl. I can make it do whatever I like!'

Time Lord and Cythosi glared at each other. The room went silent, the troops staring in shock at the little humanoid. No one talked to the commander in that way.

Bisoncawl turned to the technicians at the bulky transmat controls. 'Leave that. Get to your ship.'

The troopers lumbered from the control room.

'I will leave you the transmat controls, Doctor,' said Bisoncawl, 'but I will not risk even one of my troopers.'

He crossed the control room and squeezed himself through

the narrow hatch. He didn't turn around. 'Goodbye, Doctor.'

The Doctor stood in the centre of the red-tinged reactor control room, the sounds of the alarms ringing about him. He pulled over a chair so that he could sit between the reactor controls and the transmat unit and waggled his fingers like a concert pianist.

'Now then...'

The Doctor's hands moved in a blur. One hand swiped back and forth over the Cythosi transmat controls and the other danced a complicated jig over the keyboards controlling the reactor, his fingers tapping a complicated tattoo on the keys.

He had turned off the alarms but the background hum of the reactor had now risen to a piercing shriek. The Doctor shut the sound out of his head, concentrating on the tasks in hand. He performed a number of lightning-quick calculations and keyed more commands into the reactor central computer, giving himself a few more seconds' grace.

He couldn't stop the explosion, that had become clear to him, but he was managing to slow things down. A second here, a second there, anything to give him more time with the Cythosi transmat unit.

He decided that his boast to Bisoncawl, that he could make the equipment do whatever he liked, might have been a trifle wild. Cythosi operating systems were complicated with dozens of conflicting programmes forced to work in unison; and he was trying to make this system do something different again.

The reactor's shriek stepped up a pitch and another bank of warning lights blinked into life. The Doctor sighed. There was nothing he could do now, he had extended things as long as he could. Abandoning the reactor controls he turned all his attention to the transmat.

Ace struggled to drag Rajiid to his feet. The wind battered her like a living thing, tearing at her clothes and at her hair, flinging the rain against her so hard that it hurt. Leaves and debris swirled around her, a whirlwind of stinging grit.

'We'll never make it!' Rajiid had to scream in her ear to be heard, the words torn from his mouth and whipped away by the wind.

Ace dragged him towards a huge tree, pulling him to its vague shelter. The two of them cowered against the trunk as the tree groaned under the onslaught of the wind.

Ace cupped her hands over Rajiid's ear. 'We have to get after Garrett, and he's managing to get through this. We can't stay with the Dreekans.'

'I know that, but this storm is going to tear us to pieces. Surely we can try and weather it out and *then* head for the colony?'

Ace shook her head. 'It'll be too late by then. That weapon is the only defence we have against the Krill.'

Their argument was cut short by a crack that rang around the mountainside like thunder, drowning out the sound of the hurricane. A bright white glare – brighter than the two suns – bloomed on the distant horizon, the storm clouds swept aside.

They turned away, shielding their eyes. As the glare faded Ace stared at the mushroom cloud billowing in the distance, then the storm clouds swept in once more.

Part Four

'There are holes in the sky where the rain comes in...'

Chapter Eighteen

The EM pulse hit Coralee central control like a fist. Sparks showered from equipment sending technicians scrambling for cover. There was a low whine as the emergency generators kicked in. Brenda stared in disbelief at the emergency lights winking across the boards. She turned to the window. Before she could say anything the wind punched out the glass.

Holly Relf watched as the mushroom cloud vanished up into the swirl of the storm clouds. Out in the harbour the repulsor field flickered and died and the waves surged in.

A lone Cythosi shuttle, crippled by the burst of electromagnetic radiation, was struck broadside by the sudden wind and sent tumbling towards the water. Its engine pod was torn free on impact and the ship nose-dived, metal plates torn apart as the waves caught it in their grip. From somewhere inside there was the dull thump of an explosion and fire flared from the stricken ship.

Holly's workshop shuddered under the wind and roof panels began to tear themselves loose.

She heard glass shatter and turned in time to see one wall smashed apart by the sea. She scrambled to her feet and was racing for the jetty when the freezing water slammed into her back. She flailed wildly for something to hold on to, her hands raking across the floor as the sea tumbled her over and over.

Something slid through her outstretched fingers and she grasped at it blindly, her eyes streaming and her throat raw from the salt water. The rush of water tugged at her clothes trying to drag her back into the sea. She tucked her head against her chest and hung on for dear life.

The grip of the water began to subside and she scrambled to her feet again. The walls of her workshop were split apart, crushed by the force of the waves. Through the ragged gaps she could see boats piled up in the harbour like kids' toys, rigging lines flailing like whips.

The colony was dark, only the pale glow of the emergency lights piercing the gloom of the storm. Holly could hear the screams and shouts of people caught in the chaos. Burning fuel from the Cythosi shuttle flecked the tops of the waves, the flames fanned by the vicious wind. She could see the storm shutters, dark and useless, towering over the buildings, waves shattering over their tops.

A sheet of corrugated metal, torn from one of the harbour buildings, sliced through the air like a scythe. Holly dived to the ground to avoid it, and watched as it was flicked across the jetty like a playing card, gouging lumps out of the tarmac.

With a splintering crash another wave tore the remains of her workshop apart and Holly curled herself into a ball as the sheet of water crashed down on top of her. She managed to snatch a breath of air and the next thing she knew she was helpless in deep water, virtually blind, terrified.

Her lungs bursting, she tried to establish where the surface was, but the churning water flipped and span her. She could feel blood pounding in her ears and her chest felt as though it was on fire.

With a sudden shock of cold air she was back on the surface, taking in great whooping gulps of air. A smooth grey shape bobbed under her arms. R'tk'tk made a series of clicks and began swimming towards the shore. 'Didn't anyone ever tell you that it's dangerous to go swimming in a hurricane without a dolphin?'

Garrett stood for a long time in the darkness, listening to the Cythosi ship breathing around him. He struggled to make sense

228

of the sounds. Familiar, and yet... utterly alien. He struggled against an onslaught of strange memories.

Skuarte. The name sounded strange to him. A voice was screaming at him. Skuarte was... his Cythosi disguise. His cover. He stared at the transmat pad in his hand. Had he used this, or had he been brought here?

He looked at the huge cylinder he was carrying under his arm. The weapon...

With a roar he hurled the transmat pad aside and lumbered off down the corridor.

Confusion reigned on the Cythosi ship as shuttles docked. Waves of soldiers and technicians, just teleported in, milled about the command deck awaiting orders and arguing.

'Silence!' bellowed Mottrack. 'I want to know what happened down there. Bisoncawl...'

'We're still not certain, General. Sabotage, certainly...'

'The Doctor was out at the reactor with you.'

'He never left my sight,' said Bisoncawl. 'Besides, he knows what a nuclear explosion down there would mean for the colony he's been fighting to save...'

'Enough!' barked Mottrack. 'Then we must assume that the saboteur was Skuarte. For whatever reason, our agent is now working against us.'

'General,' one of the functionaries said timidly, 'something's happening... The teleportation systems are overloading...'

A tremor ran through the ship. The lights dimmed for a moment, and a peculiar hissing, groaning sound filled the room.

Bisoncawl strode across to the functionary and pushed him aside. Bavril followed in Bisoncawl's wake.

'What is happening?' Mottrack demanded.

'There's a massive influx on the teleports... It's the holding tank!' Bisoncawl unholstered his gun. 'Three squad, with me,' he barked.

* * *

Garrett gazed in wonder at the massive, transparent holding tank, thick with an amber liquid that shimmered and groaned with the swirling mass of quantum energy that had appeared within it. Slowly, shapes were beginning to appear in the maelstrom. Shiny, black ovoids. Giant eggs... They seemed familiar to him. Edgily he fingered the weapon.

His uneasy reverie was broken by the sound of heavy footfalls. His eyes flashed about him, and he disappeared at a run into a gloomy corridor.

Through Bisoncawl's twenty-strong squad Bavril could just about make out the weird light dancing in the huge tank, gradually darkening as it gave way to hundreds of black shapes which pushed up the liquid level in the container until it was touching the tank's thick ceiling.

'Surround it,' said Bisoncawl. The troops fanned out on his order.

He raised his communicator. 'The eggs, General,' he said. 'They're in the holding tank, just as planned. I don't know why or how...'

'Commander,' one of the troopers grunted. 'There's something else in there.'

Bavril could see he was right. Something was moving – thrashing around in the viscous liquid.

A human hand slapped against the inside wall of the tank. Two hands. A man's face pressed against the thick, transparent metal.

Bavril recognised him. He had visited Mottrack on the shuttle.

He seemed to be screaming...

'You,' Bisoncawl barked, 'open this thing. Get him out of there!'

A trooper climbed the ladder set into the side of the mighty tank. He triggered a release mechanism, and a panel rose on the lid. He fished inside, gripped the man by his coat, and lifted him high into the air.

The man hung like a rag doll in the Cythosi's hand, dripping thick, yellow goo. It was in his eyes. In his mouth. The guard descended and laid the man at Bisoncawl's feet.

'General, it's the Doctor,' Bisoncawl said into his transmitter. 'He was in the holding tank. In the preserving fluid. He's dead.'

'Trying to save his life,' said Mottrack. 'It was a good attempt.' Then he lost interest. 'Place a guard on the tank and return to the bridge.'

'Sir.' Bisoncawl gestured to his troops, and they filed out. He turned to Bavril.

'Dispose of the body,' he said, and marched away behind his troopers.

Bavril waited until the squad had gone, and then stooped to examine the body.

A whisper, from the shadows. 'Bavril!'

'Peck,' muttered Bavril, as his fellow functionary stepped forward. He was carrying a plasma gun.

'What did you find out?' asked Peck.

'I've seen the planet,' Bavril whispered excitedly. 'It's habitable. There are humans already there. We have a new home, Peck!'

'We have the weapons,' said Peck. 'And the Cythosi still don't seem to be on to us. We're ready to secure the lower decks. Who's he?'

He gestured down at the body at their feet.

'Bisoncawl called him the Doctor,' said Bavril. 'He was with Mottrack on the planet. He's dead.'

'No, he's not,' said Peck.

He was right. The body moved, ever so slowly. It let out a soft groan.

'Unpleasant stuff...' it said.

'It'll evaporate soon enough in the air,' said Peck. He pointed his gun at the figure. 'Get up.'

The man clambered weakly to his feet.

'How do you do?' he said. 'I'm the Doctor.'

Peck ignored the proffered hand.

'I didn't have time to reprogramme the transmitter,' the Doctor said. 'Did you rescue me from in there? If so, thank you.'

'The Cythosi did,' said Bavril.

'Then I owe them my thanks.'

Bavril gestured at the shapes in the tank. 'Did you bring that lot up?' he asked.

'I suppose I must have,' said the Doctor.

He peered into the tank. His face creased with worry. He clambered up the ladder, fiddled with the hatch release and opened the hatch. He stuck his head into the tank.

'I must get to the command deck,' he said, springing back down the ladder. 'I must see General Mottrack at once.'

'Oh no,' said Peck. 'No chance.' He pushed the gun into the Doctor's stomach. 'There's a revolution going on here,' he snarled. 'We're going to have your friend General Mottrack's head on a stick.'

'I can assure you, the general is no friend of mine,' said the Doctor.

'And yet you've just completed his mission for him,' said Bavril. 'You've successfully transported these things aboard.'

'I transported the Krill here to prevent a holocaust on the planet down there,' said the Doctor. 'I had no desire to help Mottrack. This holding tank seemed to offer my only solution. I was wrong.'

'Whatever... you probably heard what I said when you were lying there. You know our plans. We can't...'

'Wait a minute,' Bavril interrupted. 'What d'you mean, you were wrong?'

'The eggs are hatching,' said the Doctor. 'Perhaps the initial radiation leak down there was sufficient to trigger them... perhaps the teleportation process did it. I don't know – but I can assure you they're starting to hatch. I must see General Mottrack.'

Bavril looked painedly at Peck. Peck's features were set.

'Do you know what those things currently hatching can do? Do you know what they're capable of?'

They were interrupted by shooting, somewhere in the distance.

'It's begun!' exclaimed Peck, his eyes shining. He turned away from the Doctor. 'Come on. Bring him, Bavril.'

Bavril tried to look authoritative.

'It's all right,' said the Doctor. 'I'll come.'

Chapter Nineteen

Brenda watched from her shattered office window as the sea smashed into the harbour sector. She could hear screams carried on the wind, smell burning fuel from the mess that had once been a Cythosi shuttle.

For one brief moment she almost gave up, almost surrendered to the despair in her gut. There was nothing she could do, nothing to save the colonisers who had already been through so much.

She swept the thought from her mind as soon as it arrived. She was the co-ordinator of the colony, people relied on her, and she was damned if she was going to sit back and let years of work be taken from her.

Behind her the technical staff were staring open-mouthed at the destruction. Brenda turned and bellowed at them.

'What the hell are you staring at! Get the back-up generators online, and get the coastguard down to the harbour. Full emergency kit and personal tracers. I don't want anyone taking stupid risks. Does anyone know if the medical unit still has power?'

Blank faces looked back at her.

'Well find out! And get some geiger counters up here. The reactor was meant to be at a safe distance away but given that Garrett sited it I want to be sure. Get the medics to break out the anti-radiation gear anyway.'

Around her there was a whirl of activity. Brenda watched as the wind swept papers from her desk and scattered them across the room.

'You rage all you like,' she growled, lighting a cigarette in defiance.

* * *

The first Bisoncawl knew about the functionaries' rising was a hail of gunfire that cut through his men as they prepared to ascend to the command level. It caught them completely by surprise. Four fell instantly.

'Take cover!' Bisoncawl shouted, unholstering his gun. He dived round a corner and through an open door and spun round, ready to shoot. He could see his squad falling beneath the barrage. Two troopers managed to join him. He sealed the door behind them.

'It's the functionaries,' said one of the troopers, his voice registering utter disbelief.

'I know,' said Bisoncawl. He'd expected this to happen one day, on some ship or other. 'We must get to the command deck.'

He opened the door again.

'Come on!'

He lurched into the corridor, laying a blanket of plasma-fire in front of him. The troopers followed. The barrage came again. He saw his two colleagues cut to pieces beside him. He charged forward firing, darting round a corner. Blaster fire burnt him. He threw himself round another corner and down another corridor, running hard.

A door next to him slid open.

'In here,' a voice whispered. The Doctor...

Bisoncawl dived through the door, which slid shut behind him.

'I thought you were dead,' he said.

Ace stumbled through the storm, numb with shock. A nuclear explosion. That could only mean that the Doctor had failed, that the Krill were on their way. As the glow had faded from the sky and the clouds had swept back in she had tried to tell herself that this was all part of the Doctor's plan, that it was some grand scheme of his, but she knew that without the weapon she could do nothing to save all those people. She had failed them all.

Failed the Doctor.

Somehow the determination to make things right, to prove to the Doctor that he *could* rely on her, had forced her onwards even though she knew it was futile.

She had screamed at Rajiid, forced him to follow her into the storm, knowing full well that she had no chance of fighting through the hurricane.

Now Rajiid was leading her by the hand, dragging her through the thrashing waterlogged foliage, trying to find shelter deeper in the jungle. Only their combined weight stopped them being hurled into the air by the ferocity of the wind.

They were following a path that had to have been made by Garrett – a ragged trail, sometimes of slashed branches cut with a machete, sometimes of trees torn up by their roots. Palm leaves whipped at their faces as they struggled on, now ankle deep in mud. Rajiid pushed Ace to one side as a huge branch crashed down in front of them.

She flicked the wet hair out of her eyes and stared back at the mountain, now a dim hazy shape in the rain. It was impossible to say how far they had come – every step was an effort. Water streamed around her legs, bringing a constant avalanche of rocks and twigs. She grasped at Rajiid for support as her feet were whipped from under her for the millionth time.

He looked at her in despair. 'We're going to have to find some shelter soon, Ace, otherwise we're dead.'

Ace nodded her head, weary and defeated. The two of them began to push deeper into the jungle.

Chaos reigned on the lower decks of the Cythosi ship. Securing them had been relatively simple for the rebels. The Cythosi's complete lack of preparation for a rising among the functionaries – an unheard-of occurrence – had made it easy.

The six lift-access points to the lower decks had been taken with virtually no resistance while the bulk of the troops were still teleporting back to the ship. Guards had been posted, and strategic points had been booby-trapped with explosives. The kitchen cages had been opened and the captives released – though most of them were clearly dying. Now the heavily armed functionaries, drunk with the promise of liberty and, in many cases, the heavy Cythosi wines which had been freed from the kitchens, roamed the corridors shouting and singing, shooting randomly at service robots and just about anything else that took their fancy. Some accidentally triggered the explosive traps and blew themselves to pieces. The decks were running with blood and booze and tears of suppressed resentment and anger.

Things were tense in the long barracks which was the centre of the revolution. Nobody quite knew what to do next. Peck was angry.

'What do you mean, you lost him?' he demanded.

'He must have slipped away during the fight,' Bavril pleaded.

'He was the perfect hostage,' Peck grunted. 'The Doctor's obviously been working with Mottrack. He could have been our bargaining chip.'

'He must still be on the lower levels,' said Bavril. 'There's no way he could have got to the lifts.'

'I know,' said Peck. 'Bisoncawl's down here too, somewhere. I want them found!'

'They'll be looking for us, you know.'

'I know,' grunted Bisoncawl, opening a channel on his communicator. 'Bisoncawl to command deck.'

'Bisoncawl! Where are you? What is happening?' General Mottrack's voice growled from the tiny device.

'I'm cut off, on the lower decks,' said Bisoncawl. 'The Doctor is with me. He's alive.'

'General,' the Doctor interrupted. 'We have a big problem. The Krill eggs in the holding tank are starting to hatch.'

'The tank was built in anticipation of a few eggs hatching,' said Bisoncawl, 'but it was not designed to withstand an attack by hundreds of Krill.'

'The tank is constructed of fourteen layers of dryanthrite,' said Mottrack. 'Between each layer is a force field.'

'It won't be enough,' said the Doctor grimly.

'I don't see the problem.' A voice unfamiliar to the Doctor drifted over the communicator. 'The holding tank is right in the middle of the decks now held by the humans...' the voice spat the word '...so we just wait and let the Krill dispose of them.'

'And then what?' snapped the Doctor. 'They will be unstoppable once they break out of that tank.'

Bisoncawl leaned close to the communicator, pushing the Doctor aside. 'We're going to try to reach you,' he said, and closed the channel.

'Who was that?' the Doctor asked Bisoncawl.

'His name is Blu'ip,' Bisoncawl replied. 'He's a cetacean, from Coralee. A criminal – a terrorist, wanted on a dozen frontier worlds, Coralee included. It was he who helped us locate the Krill nesting sites.'

'He would seem to be a dolphin with strong opinions.'

'He hates humans. He blames them for the systematic extermination of cetacean life forms over the centuries.'

'I see,' said the Doctor. 'I look forward to meeting him. Shall we go?'

The Doctor and Bisoncawl moved cautiously along the miles of corridor.

'Keep behind me,' Bisoncawl had said. The Doctor had been happy to comply. The huge alien soldier had already gunned down a drunken huddle of mercenaries who were taking pot shots at a Cythosi flag.

'Was that really necessary?' the Doctor had asked.

'I am a soldier,' Bisoncawl had replied. 'My ship is under attack... and as you have pointed out, the lives of everyone aboard are under threat from the Krill. What would you have me do?'

The Doctor had said nothing.

Now they were approaching one of the lifts. It was at the end of a long corridor and was surrounded by perhaps twenty armed rebels.

'Any suggestions?' the Doctor asked.

'One,' said Bisoncawl. He stepped out into the corridor and fired a low-intensity plasma charge. It dropped a rebel where he stood. The man's startled comrades turned and began returning fire. Bisoncawl leapt back round the corner. The Doctor could hear the running feet of the advancing rebels.

Bisoncawl leapt out again, firing. The Doctor peeped round the corner. Bisoncawl's plasma blasts were ricocheting low off the walls. He didn't seem to be trying to hit the enemy.

The Doctor looked on, puzzled. Bisoncawl was blowing the covers off the service hatches. Suddenly dozens of small robots, each equipped with whirring blades, streamed from every side of the corridor. They immediately began tearing into the flanks of the advancing rebels, who screamed and fell, shooting wildly. The Doctor closed his eyes – the robots' whirring blades and laser-torches were splattering the walls with blood.

An awful silence fell, then Bisoncawl began shooting once again.

He was plastering the corridor with plasma fire, incinerating the service robots.

'Come,' he said to the Doctor. 'The lift.'

Phillip Garrett had watched the carnage with confusion and pain. The vicious struggle of human against Cythosi had seemed to mirror and mock his own feelings.

Now, in the quiet after the shooting, he felt unnaturally calm. His physical form had finally stopped its agonising shifts and ripples. He was stable now. He was human.

He always had been human. He mingled now with his fellow humans, sharing in their triumph, feeling their exhilaration. They clapped him on the shoulders and gave him drinks. Some danced with him.

Finally, he returned to the Krill holding tank. The area was deserted except for a single guard. Garrett smiled as he approached him.

'I've come to relieve you,' he said. 'Go and enjoy yourself.'

The guard grinned and trotted towards the door.

Casually, Garrett raised his gun and put a plasma bolt in the man's back.

He turned and peered into the tank. The eggs were indeed hatching. He looked down at the huge cylinder he still carried. The weapon which gave him power over the Krill.

Everything was in place now. For the first time he understood his life – understood why he, Phillip Garrett, had been made to live among aliens, to live as one of them. A Cythosi.

The Dreekans had seen it first. They had recognised him – they had hailed him as their liberator-god, Treeka'dwra. Had he been on Earth he might have been called Moses, or Jesus or Mohammed. He was here to free his people, and to destroy their oppressors – and he had been given control of the ultimate weapon with which to achieve his sacred goals.

Ace and Rajiid huddled together for warmth, tucked into the curve of a large tree. The wind tore at the branches overhead and raindrops splashed off the leaves around them. Every few minutes the wind would drop and they could exchange brief snatches of conversation, but then the storm would build in a crescendo again and all they could do was tuck their heads down and try to protect themselves from the driving rain.

As the wind died down again Ace cocked her head to one side. Above the wind and hiss of rain she could hear something else. A roar, a vibration, building all the time. She looked at Rajiid in alarm.

Water began to fountain around the roots of the tree, loosening the soil, coating Ace and Rajiid in thick gelatinous mud. There was an ominous crack and the tree shifted. They threw themselves forward as it toppled into the jungle. Seconds later the surge of water hit them.

They tumbled down the hill, carried on a tide of debris. Ace felt a sharp pain as she cannoned off a boulder tumbling into a ravine. Everything span around her, then something cracked into her skull and the world went still and black.

'Commander! What is the situation?'

Bisoncawl saluted his superior.

'The rebels have control of the lower decks. They're disorganised, but heavily armed.'

'What do you estimate are the chances of successfully retaking the decks?'

'General Mottrack...' the Doctor tried to cut in.

'It ought to be possible to take the decks back,' said Bisoncawl, 'but it will not be quick or easy.'

'General, I really think we have more to worry about than a dispute below stairs. The Krill could even now be fully hatched.'

'What do you suggest, Doctor?'

'Teleport the lot into space.'

'Not possible, Doctor. You, I believe, saw to that. The mass transport of the Krill eggs to the ship completely overloaded the teleport systems. It will take days to repair them.'

'Then strengthen the tank's force fields. Divert your external shielding.'

'And leave ourselves defenceless?'

'General, the enemy's in here with us, remember.'

'Do as the Doctor says.' Mottrack was convinced.

'It still might not be enough,' said the Doctor. 'You must stop fighting and evacuate the ship.'

'Impossible,' Mottrack barked. 'The Cythosi do not make peace with insurrectionist scum – nor do they abandon their ships. Evacuation is impossible. The matter transmitters are down, and there are not nearly enough shuttles for the evacuation of Cythosi, let alone humans. Cythosi ships are not built to be abandoned.'

'We must still make peace with the humans,' the Doctor insisted. 'I need to get a look at the holding tank – to find a way to strengthen it.'

A dolphin scuttled forward in a metal walker. 'I say we attack.'

'Ah, you must be Blu'ip,' said the Doctor. 'From what I've heard about you, I'm not surprised you take that view.'

'Think what it would mean if you were to negotiate with these humans,' the dolphin continued. 'Cythosi society is built upon absolute human servitude. This would be the beginning of the end of Cythosi civilisation.'

'Civilisations based on slavery rarely stand the test of time,' said the Doctor acidly. 'Shall I tell you what will happen, General, if we don't sort out some kind of agreement with the humans? If the Krill break out before I get to the tank? They will kill everyone – Cythosi, humans and dolphin alike. Then they will attack the ship itself, which, if it falls from its present orbit, will crash down on to Coralee. The Krill will be released into the oceans, and the energies released by the destruction of a ship this size will almost certainly cause more eggs in the sea to hatch. The colony will be utterly destroyed. General, your war is with the Zithra, not with the people of this planet. Your mission has failed. No one can use the Krill as a weapon. Your only remaining duty is to save your crew, and the people of that planet. They made you welcome... Please, talk to them.'

'General,' a Cythosi trooper stationed at a communications console said suddenly. 'The rebels are trying to contact us.'

'General Mottrack here. Who am I talking to?'

'My name's Peck.'

'Peck, I call upon you and your people to surrender.'

'What? And be executed or eaten by you?' Peck sneered into the captured communicator. 'You're on the menu this time!'

There were cheers all around the barracks. Bavril remained grim.

'Surrender your ship,' Peck demanded, 'or we'll take it from you.'

'Listen!' Another voice. The little man – the Doctor. 'We're all in great danger. The Krill in the holding tank are hatching. You know what that means.'

Bavril stared at Peck, who licked his dry lips.

'You're bluffing,' he said. 'The tank will hold them.'

'For a while, perhaps,' said the Doctor. 'A day, at most, I'd say. Of course, it will be your problem before it's the Cythosi's...'

'I don't think he's bluffing,' said Bavril. 'Perhaps we should listen to him.'

'Shut up, Bavril!' Peck snapped.

There was a hurried muttering on the other end of the transmitter.

'Bavril, is that you?'

Bisoncawl.

'Listen to me, Bavril. We are not trying to dupe you. If you won't do anything else, at least give us access to the tank.'

'Let me come down there,' said the Doctor. 'I'll come alone.'

Mottrack was angry. 'I am in command of this ship. I would counsel you all to remember that.'

He levelled his gun at Bisoncawl. 'I could shoot you on the spot. The next time you undermine my authority, I will.'

'Sir!' barked Bisoncawl.

'Nevertheless,' said Mottrack, 'a temporary cease-fire would seem advisable.'

Blu'ip whistled in irritation.

Mottrack ignored him. 'Very well, go, Doctor,' he said.

Chapter Twenty

The handover was silent and tense. The Doctor stood with Bisoncawl and three guards at one end of a long corridor. He began to walk. In the distance he could see the lift doors. As he walked they began to open. He heard the Cythosi to his rear readying their guns. If the lift was occupied, he'd be caught in the middle of a fire-fight.

But the lift was empty, just as arranged. He broke into a jog, and breathed a sigh of relief as the doors closed around him.

His descent began.

The doors opened on half a dozen armed and angry-looking humans. He recognised one of them.

'Hello,' he said. 'It's Bavril, isn't it?'

The holding tank seethed with Krill. They slashed and tore at its clear walls, which crackled with energy.

'Oh dear,' said the Doctor.

'Is there anything you can do?' Bavril asked.

'I think I should be able to strengthen the shields still further by diverting power from other systems on the ship,' mused the Doctor. 'The walls of the tank should be able to take the extra energy input... That should give us time to repair the teleport system.'

'How long is all this going to take?'

The Doctor turned to address the newcomer. 'Mr Peck... yes. Perhaps a day?'

'In which time the Cythosi can be formulating plans to retake the ship.'

The Doctor sighed. 'That's a chance you're just going to have to take, isn't it?'

'No!'

A new voice boomed from the shadows. A figure stepped forward.

'Garrett,' the Doctor said. 'Or is it Skuarte? I'm not sure at the moment... and I suspect you aren't either.'

Garrett circled them slowly. Under one arm was slung a plasma gun; under the other, the ancient weapon from the temple. The Doctor's heart surged.

'Garrett,' he said evenly. 'The weapon. You've got to give me the weapon.'

'But Doctor,' Garrett beamed, 'it isn't a weapon. It's a religious artefact, remember? I have simply claimed what is mine.'

'Listen, who the hell are you?' snapped Peck, stepping forward.

'The day of liberation is upon you, my child,' Garrett said sweetly. 'I am here to deliver you from bondage.'

He unslung his plasma gun.

'The trumpet has sounded! I am here to set free the purging fires of the Last Judgement!'

Smiling beatifically, Garrett pumped round after round into the giant holding tank. Its walls buckled and gave way.

'Run!' the Doctor shouted. He threw himself at Garrett, desperately grappling for the weapon. With Cythosi strength Garrett threw him across the room.

Krill were surging from the tank, stretching and mewling.

It was strange – the sight of Garrett seemed to make them freeze. They circled him slowly, warily. He raised the ancient weapon above his head, and they shrank back still further.

'Go, my children,' he said. 'Go and do my bidding.'

He brought the weapon down and the Krill scattered across the holding bay. They were at once themselves again, sniffing and seeking prey.

The Doctor scrambled to his feet and ran as hard as he could. He could see Bavril and Peck disappearing down the corridor and caught up with them at the lift.

'Barracks level,' Peck gasped as the doors closed. 'At least they won't know how to use lifts.'

'Don't be so sure,' said the Doctor. 'And Garret seems to be able to drive them. They have some mental reaction to the weapon. Give me your communicator.'

'What for?' asked Peck.

'I need to inform General Mottrack of the situation.'

'Inform the enemy of our position?'

'Don't be stupid, Peck,' Bavril cut in. 'You saw those things.'

'The Krill are the enemy, Peck,' the Doctor snapped. 'Yours and the Cythosi's. And mine. If I can't convince you – not to mention General Mottrack – of that we're all doomed.'

Holly stumbled through the gloom of her apartment, shrugging off wet clothes and hauling dry ones from her cupboards.

R'tk'tk, now cradled in his exoskeleton, lurked in the doorway.

Like all the buildings in the colony, the apartment block was dark. Tourists and home-owners alike were cowering behind locked doors waiting for the hurricane – or worse – to come tapping at their windows.

Holly struggled into a pair of jeans and tugged on a heavy jacket.

'How come you were there for me, R'tk?' she asked. 'I thought you'd gone over to the reactor.'

'Too rough.' chirruped the dolphin. 'I was being tossed around like a dice. Decided to head back. Was almost home when the reactor blew. Finding you was pure luck.'

'Well, thanks. I owe you.' She snapped a torch on and played the beam over the waiting dolphin. 'Right. We'd better get up to control, see what we can do to help.'

The two of them struggled through the lashing rain, trying to keep to the walls and out of the wind. The central square was a mess of broken roof tiles and debris from the jungle. There was even the mast of a sailing vessel in the fountain.

Holly pushed open the sliding doors of the admin block and the two of them pushed inside.

'I guess it's the stairs.'

Holly set off at a trot, R'tk'tk clattering behind her. When they arrived at Brenda's office Holly stared in astonishment at the mess. Papers lay scattered in pools of rainwater, hurricane lamps guttered on top of computer consoles, the huge glass windows were being boarded up. Glass sparkled over everything. Brenda sat perched on her desk, her ashtray full to overflowing.

Relief washed over the older woman's face as Holly peered round her office door.

'Thank God,' said Brenda. 'I thought I'd lost you again. We sent someone down to your workshop, but...'

'It's gone. Yeah, I know. I was a bit close when the storm shutters went,' Holly said. 'I went in, but R'tk got me out.'

There was a surprised click from the other side of the room. 'You went out in that? I'm impressed.'

Q'ilp stood in the shadows, the glow from his cigar like a baleful red eye.

R'tk'tk rounded on him. 'Give me a break, OK? It's been a long day. I haven't seen you out risking your neck.'

'Pack it in, you two!' Brenda caught hold of Holly's arm, pulling her to one side. 'Things are bad up here.'

'So I see. Why aren't the emergency systems online?'

Brenda shook her head. 'We don't know, it looks like they were set to blow with the first surge from the main reactor. Whoever set us up knew exactly what they were doing.'

'And the Krill?'

Brenda shrugged. 'For the moment – not a sign. But that doesn't mean the buggers aren't on their way. We have to get the defences back up.'

Holly nodded. 'Do we have power anywhere?'

'The coastguard have emergency power, and Med-lab is still operational.'

Holly slid out of her jacket.

'Then I'd better get busy.'

'Doctor, what is the situation?' Bisoncawl was on his communicator.

'About as bad as it could be, Commander. Garrett – Skuarte – is aboard ship. He's destroyed the holding tanks. The Krill are free.'

Blu'ip scuttled close to Bisoncawl. 'You can hear their screams,' he chittered with quiet bliss. 'Human screams...'

'Bisoncawl,' said the Doctor urgently. 'We must evacuate these levels. You must let us through.'

'What? Open the doors?' Blu'ip squeaked. 'And let the Krill in here?'

'Your defences won't stop the Krill,' said the Doctor, 'but the people down here are caught like rats in a trap. The Krill are advancing all around.'

'Shame,' chuckled the dolphin.

Bisoncawl snatched the communicator away from him. 'If you utter another sound I'll have you removed from the command deck,' he barked at the dolphin. 'Perhaps I will put you on a shuttle and evacuate you to Coralee.'

The dolphin whistled angrily. Bisoncawl knew that Blu'ip was right and that he couldn't open the doors – but he didn't need that fact to be pointed out to him by a psychopathic dolphin.

'I'm sorry, Doctor,' he said. 'I can't do that.'

The Doctor switched off the communicator.

'What did you expect,' sneered Peck, 'from a Cythosi?'

'From any soldier,' said the Doctor sadly.

They were sitting in a barracks crowded with panicking

people. A little man pushed his way towards them.

'They're everywhere!' he cried. 'They're killing us all! There's no one left!'

'Calm down, Huttle,' snapped Peck. 'I'm thinking.'

'Doctor,' said Bavril quietly, 'what should we do?'

'Get as many of your people together as you can. You need to get to the shuttle bay.'

'That's beyond the command deck,' the new man, Huttle, cried. 'We'd never make it.'

'Take the service ducts,' said the Doctor. 'The Krill won't be able to crawl into them.'

'That's not possible,' said Bavril. 'The service robots are programmed to attack on sight.'

'What would you rather face?' asked the Doctor. 'Your service robots or the Krill? We have to try it. I'll come with you – at least as far as the command deck.'

'What do you plan to do?' Bavril asked.

'I must find Garrett,' said the Doctor. 'He has the only thing that can stop the Krill. I imagine he'll make for the command deck. He's nothing if not an egotist… I imagine he'll want to sit in Mottrack's big chair and lord it over everybody before we die. Now come on – get moving.'

Ace awoke with warm sunlight on her face and cool water trickling over her forehead. Tentatively she forced her eyes open, squinting at the glare. She was lying at the edge of the jungle, half buried in silt and foliage, the river flowing round her. Her head was spinning. She stared up at blue sky. The hurricane was over!

She tried to sit up, the dried mud flaking from her in a brittle crust.

'Rajiid?'

The rush of water had swept tree roots and leaves into a huge pile on the edge of the beach. Ace could see a limb sticking out from a pile of leaves. Her heart caught in her mouth.

She struggled to her feet, wincing at the sharp pain from her shoulder, and hauled herself through the muddy water.

'Rajiid?'

There was a low groan from the pile of foliage. Ace felt her heart begin to settle. He was alive. She began pulling rocks and branches off him. Gently she turned him on to his back. There was a livid purple bruise across his forehead and his arm hung limply at his side. Ace tried to move it and Rajiid gave a cry of pain.

'Well, that's broken, then.'

Rajiid stared up at the mountain they had just rolled down. 'I never did like roller coasters.'

Ace smiled and kissed his cheek, then frowned as a gust of wind tugged at her hair. She looked up across the beach and the smile disappeared. Out at sea a wall of angry grey cloud boiled and writhed, churning the water in its path. She suddenly remembered a science lesson – a video about hurricanes. This was the eye of the storm. The hurricane wasn't over. It was only half over.

Soon the winds would build again, blowing from the other direction as the second half of the storm washed over them. Only, this time, they had no shelter.

'I take it from your expression that things are not good.'

Ace shook her head. 'You don't know the half of it. Come on.'

Gently she manoeuvred Rajiid to his feet, trying to support his arm as best she could.

Around the curve of the beach they could see the colony, dark and grey behind the storm shutters, tiny against the wall of cloud advancing towards them.

'It's a long way, Ace.' Rajiid looked at her with concern. 'I'm only going to slow you down.'

'As if I'm going to let you.'

Ace pulled off her belt and strapped Rajiid's arm tight to his chest, ignoring his yelps of pain. As spots of rain began to speckle the sand, she pushed him forward and the two of them started to run across the beach.

Chapter Twenty-One

When the Krill broke through on to the upper levels of the ship the Cythosi were still struggling to set up defences. The creatures came crawling up the lift shafts, their claws digging at the walls, slicing through the doors. The assault was met by a hastily erected plasma cannon which sent them screaming and burning back down the shaft.

Mottrack was awed. Some Krill had managed to keep their foot- and handholds through the blast. Some even kept coming. The cannon fired again, and again.

A vicious spiked claw lanced through a wall next to Mottrack's head. More claws followed it. He lurched away, spraying the wall with blaster fire. The Krill burst out into the path of his gun.

'Fall back!' Mottrack shouted.

A second cannon was in position, further back up the corridor. As Mottrack's men retreated towards it, the Krill sprang forward, leaping on to them, claws and teeth ripping into them. Some Cythosi tried to fight hand-to-hand with the Krill. One trooper bit the neck of one of the creatures with his great jaws. The Krill didn't seem to feel the bite.

Mottrack gained the relative safety of the cannon. 'Fire!' he said. 'Maximum concentrated burst.'

The cannon sounded. The corridor was filled with a plasma backdraught that burnt Mottrack. He watched his troopers and their Krill attackers burst into flame.

More Krill were advancing, leaping through the flames. The cannon fired. The Krill burnt. More Krill came.

His holy sceptre held before him, Garrett wandered the miles of corridor, watching the carnage he had created. An end to the war between Cythosi and Human. An end to the war in his head. The Krill would destroy one and all. Unity in bloody death.

Most of the humans, it seemed, were already dead. Their cut-to-ribbons corpses littered the corridors. Some Krill, too, had been felled; even now some were cocooning themselves in shiny, black carapaces.

The battle was moving to the higher decks. The creatures had ripped great holes in the ceilings as they advanced upwards. Garrett saw four or five service robots tumble from the holes and attack the marauding Krill. Drills and lasers hacked vainly at the monsters. The Krill tore the robots to pieces.

Garrett followed in their wake, up through the decks. The lifts had been crippled by the Krill onslaught. No matter; he followed his children through the tears they had made in the fabric of the ship.

Sounds of battle were all around him now. He could hear the blood-oaths and orders of the Cythosi, the vicious mewling of Krill at the slaughter. He came upon a group of six Cythosi cornered at the far end of a blind corridor. A spirited junior officer was barking rapid orders. Raising their guns, the men charged in a line towards perhaps a dozen advancing Krill, howling, and blasting them with furious plasma fire. They closed on the monsters. Garrett watched, fascinated. They were engaging in close combat. From the bottom of each Cythosi gun slid a bayonet – a vicious choreography of whirring, spinning blades. The Cythosi stabbed and hacked at the enraged Krill, who slashed viciously with their claws. A Cythosi arm, sliced from the shoulder and sent spinning through the air high over the heads of the Krill, landed at Garrett's feet and lay twitching and spurting blood.

The other Cythosi were breaking through... Garrett's eyes widened as the troopers succeeded in scattering their enemy. He stepped back into a doorway, and the Cythosi charged past him, bellowing in savage exhilaration, the officer still shouting furious orders.

But for the most part the Cythosi were being routed. Command had broken down. Here and there small pockets of troopers rallied and mounted a few hasty skirmishes, but most of them were wandering, wounded, through the corridors, hoping to avoid their mindless executioners.

Garrett thought of Mottrack's empire, crumbling around him, and smiled.

Barely thirty of Bavril's people could be found to follow the Doctor into the service tunnels. The rest were dead, or dying, or scattered beyond reach. The Doctor peered through a service hatch – the tunnels were a metre square and receded into the far metal distance. He could see endless intersections in the side walls, and automatic hatches in the ceilings and floors.

Peck elbowed him rudely out of the way. 'I'll go first,' he said.

'You know what you're undertaking,' said the Doctor. 'You will be more at risk of attack than any of us.'

'Can you find your way to the command deck?' Peck sneered.

'No,' admitted the Doctor.

'I can.' Peck's lips were set. 'You come next, Doctor. Then the rest of you. Bavril, bring up the rear.'

Peck was clambering through the access hatch when the Doctor tapped his plasma gun. 'You can't use that in there,' he said. 'The discharge in such a confined space would kill us all. Haven't you got any small arms?'

Peck shook his head. 'The Cythosi don't really go in for small arms,' he said hoarsely. He paused for a moment, swallowed hard, and slung the gun on his back. He took a laser-cutter from his belt, switched it on and crawled into the gloom.

The Doctor followed him. Huttle crawled behind the Doctor, whimpering. The others followed, one by one, tense, silent.

They crawled in a straight line, no one saying anything, for about ten minutes, then Peck turned to the left. His human train followed. Beyond the walls they could still hear heavy weapons exploding and the cries of combat.

The Doctor's mind was wandering. 'Tunnels,' he muttered, 'always tunnels...'

In front of him, Peck stopped.

'What is it?' whispered the Doctor.

'The passage is blocked,' said Peck.

In the gloom in front of Peck the Doctor could see a tangle of metal and severed cables. Peck was trying to pick his way past the damage; as he did so a severed Cythosi head rolled down the twisted mass of debris and came to rest next to the Doctor's head. Its eyes stared up at him, fierce and dead.

'It's no good,' said Peck. 'We'll have to go another way.'

'Quiet.' The Doctor held up a finger. 'Listen.'

A few seconds passed, punctuated by the cries of the dying and the rattle and hiss of high-energy weapons. 'There's nothing,' Peck said. 'We've got to go back.'

The Doctor reached out and clasped his leg. 'No,' he whispered urgently, then hissed over his shoulder, 'Still! Everyone!'

A high-pitched whispering came from one of the side passages, and for a moment the Doctor entertained the hope that another group of weary refugees was creeping through the ducting towards them. But there was an eerie metallic quality to the sound.

'I hear it,' said Peck.

'Quiet,' the Doctor hissed.

Down the side passage he could see the distant movement of service robots. There was no chance of outrunning them in these passages and he hoped the robots hadn't detected them.

They had. Within a moment the were scuttling towards the stranded convoy, straight towards the Doctor. There was only one thing he could do.

'Peck,' he said quietly, 'could I borrow your laser-cutter?'

He took the cutter from Peck and stationed himself in the side passage, braced for the assault by the little robots. He could hear their lethal tools extending from their casings, powering up.

All of a sudden the wall between the Doctor and the robots bulged, buckled. The lethal arc of a Krill's claw sliced through the metal. A Krill arm burst through the wall.

The little robots turned as one, their sensors bleeping and flickering. They closed on the Krill arm, drills and lasers engaging with its armoured flesh.

The Doctor moved hastily back into the main passageway, mopping his brow with a large paisley handkerchief. 'Peck – we've got to get through, somehow,' he said. 'Put that blockage between them and us.'

'Tricky,' said Peck. 'Too many exposed cables.'

'We've got to try,' said the Doctor. 'Here.'

He thrust the laser-cutter towards Peck, who took it with a doubting smile. 'OK,' he said. 'Here goes.' He moved slowly forward. 'I'll have to cut this strut.'

'Quickly,' said the Doctor. The Krill was inside the tunnel, up to its waist now. Robots milled around it and it slashed at them with fury.

Peck's legs disappeared into the mass of metal that twisted across the shattered tunnel. The Doctor crawled quickly after him. Peck was right – the debris was a jungle of deadly, severed cables, inches from their bodies, and unstable metal spurs and splinters that creaked and groaned and threatened to collapse beneath their weight.

The Doctor hauled himself out on the other side of the blockage with a sigh of relief.

'Come on,' he called back into the ragged hole that Peck had made in the barrier. 'Be careful – don't touch any of the cables.'

With agonising slowness the column ahead of Bavril moved forward, snaking its way through the metal. Down a side passage he saw a Krill tearing service robots apart as if they were made of cardboard.

He clutched at his plasma gun, knowing he couldn't use it in the tunnel. It was the only weapon he had. He was at the back of the column. If the robots – or the Krill – came after them...

The harsh sound of ripping metal filled Bavril's head. A Krill claw was coming through the wall next to him. It ripped the panel away exposing him to the corridor that ran alongside the duct. The beast was next to him, roaring and flaying.

Bavril swung the gun up and pumped blast after blast of plasma energy into the creature's trunk. It screamed and staggered backwards. Bavril kept on firing, his eyes shut tight. The blast was burning him, but the creature was retreating. Bavril heard the sound of Cythosi shouting. The Krill staggered to one side as three Cythosi troopers opened fire on it.

Bavril threw himself forward and scrambled through the tangled barrier, severed cables spitting like snakes on either side of him.

The shuttle bay was empty. The quiet felt unnatural after the chaos of conflict. Blu'ip scuttled furtively from a corridor. Six troop shuttles were berthed in the bay. The dolphin approached the first, his twin machine guns sliding from their chest-panel.

He approached the first shuttle and fired with both barrels into the docking mechanism. It broke open, crackling and sparking.

He moved to the next shuttle and did the same. He crippled each of the shuttles in turn, leaving only one – his lifeline. The Cythosi, he knew, would not evacuate; he was determined that no humans would get off the ship.

Glancing with satisfaction at his handiwork, he left the shuttle bay.

The refugees had been crawling like moles through the tunnels for well over an hour. The Doctor could hear mutterings in the column behind him. People were getting nervous. 'We're lost,' somebody said.

'Shut it!' Peck shouted. 'We are not lost. It's a long way, that's all.'

He turned a corner, and froze.

The Doctor could see a service robot directly ahead of Peck, and bearing down on him fast.

For a second, Peck glanced back at the Doctor, a fearful yet determined look in his eyes.

'Get back,' he said, bringing up the laser-cutter as he crawled forwards.

The Doctor could see the beam of the cutter lancing out and severing a robot tendril, cutting into the machine's breastplate. The robot squawked and struck out at Peck, who screamed in pain.

'Back!' the Doctor shouted to the column. He began pushing himself backwards through the tunnel and bumped into the man called Huttle.

'Quickly man! Reverse gear!'

Peck was trying to buy them time – they had to use it.

They scrambled backwards, metre by metre. The Doctor saw the robot's tools cut into Peck, sparking as they did so. Finally the tunnel turned and the sight was taken from him.

The convoy backed into an open area where several tunnels converged. The Doctor tried to think. 'Peck's dead,' he announced. 'And I don't know the way.'

'I do,' said Huttle timidly. 'I was in engineering with Peck. I'll go in front.'

The Doctor looked at the little man. Huttle was terrified.

'Thank you, Mr Huttle,' the Doctor said.

Huttle scrambled around him.

'We can go this way,' he said, and began to crawl down one of the cramped tunnels.

* * *

Ace and Rajiid hit the storm wall of the colony at about the same time as the hurricane. The wind was lifting wet sand and whipping it across the beach. Ace felt her face stinging as sand scoured across it. Rajiid's head was tucked against his chest, his eyes clamped shut.

'Rajiid!' Ace screamed. 'How do we get in?'

He shook his head. 'I don't know. There are hatches, but I don't know the security overrides.'

Ace ran her hands over the delicate outline of a hatch in the smooth metal. Sealed. Solid. She stared desperately at the metal walls, looking for some way over. The storm shutters towered above her. A violent gust lifted her feet from the beach and she scrabbled for a handhold.

Frantically, she hammered at the control panel.

After a while, Huttle stopped.

'We've got to climb now,' he said. 'The command deck and shuttle bay are five decks up from here.'

The Doctor peered up the shaft which extended vertically from the tunnel. A wide rail, serrated with metal teeth like a comb, ran up it. The robots used a sort of ratchet system to haul themselves between decks.

Huttle began slowly pulling himself up the shaft, his feet scrabbling between the metal teeth. The Doctor followed behind him.

Huttle was unfit. After two decks he was already breathless and flagging. He stopped.

'Come on, Mr Huttle,' the Doctor said slowly.

'I don't think I can,' said Huttle.

'You're doing well,' said the Doctor. 'We've come this far... we can't let the others down now.'

He looked below him. The shaft was crowded.

Huttle began to climb again. At last he swung himself clumsily from the shaft into a passageway. The Doctor scrambled after him.

'The command deck's through there,' Huttle said, indicating an access panel at the end of the short passage. 'The shuttle bay's further on.'

'You're a very brave man, Mr Huttle,' said the Doctor. 'Get your people into a shuttle. Get down to Coralee. I'll do my best to contain the situation here.'

Huttle nodded and began to crawl away. The human train followed him.

'Good luck to you all,' the Doctor muttered under his breath.

Lights flickered on in the control centre. There was a sporadic round of applause.

Brenda looked up as Holly appeared, tired and dirty, in the doorway of the office.

'Finished.' Holly shrugged, 'Well, as much as I can be finished.'

'You've got the force field up?' Brenda poured a shot of brandy into a glass.

Holly reached for the brandy. 'No, but you've got power to the surveillance grid, so you can see if the Krill are coming. And you've got partial use of the repulsor field. It won't stop them, but it's something.'

Brenda sat back, nursing her own drink. 'Right then. Let's see what's out there.'

She snapped on the communications console on her desk, cycling through the security channels.

'Good God!' She suddenly sat bolt upright in her chair.

'What? What is it?' Holly scrambled round the desk.

Brenda pointed at the screen.

'It's Ace, the Doctor's friend, and Rajiid. What the devil are...?'

'Well, they're not going to last long out there!' Holly dashed from the room. 'R'tk'tk! Come on.'

Dolphin in tow she bounded from the control room.

Ace's grip on the wall was slipping when the hatch slid open and she tumbled inside. She was suddenly aware of hands pulling her to her feet, of blankets being thrown over her. She reached back weakly for Rajiid, only to see R'tk'tk gathering him up in the metallic arms of his spider-like transporter and scurrying off with him. Then she stopped trying and let herself be carried away.

The command deck, the centre of shipboard operations, was for once almost deserted. Mottrack's command chair was empty. Three Cythosi lumbered from console to console, struggling to stabilise the ship's failing systems.

Garrett took a deep breath and concentrated. He felt the familiar pain of metamorphosis – it was as if his entire body was being pierced by a multitude of needle-beams of laser light – and sensed his skin rippling and folding, flowing, contracting.

He was Cythosi once again. He stepped on to the command deck.

One of the troopers turned his head and regarded him briefly, before returning to his desperate task. Garrett raised his plasma gun and felled all three Cythosi before any of them had a chance to react.

He climbed on to the low dais in the centre of the room and sat in Mottrack's chair, the ancient weapon from the oceans of Coralee draped across his lap.

'Mr Garrett. I expected to find you here.'

Garrett spun round in his chair. The Doctor stepped through a service hatch and dusted himself down.

'Or is it Skuarte?' he continued. 'When you decide which of those you'd like to be, please let me know.' He smiled. 'I am here to destroy the Krill.'

Garrett laughed.

'Only I have the power to destroy them,' he said. 'And I choose not to use it. The Krill are my loyal servants. My bringers of death.'

'What do you hope to achieve by this slaughter?' the Doctor snapped.

'Purification,' whispered Garrett. 'Liberation. An end to the wars and the politics, an end to the spying and the subterfuge. A new beginning.'

'Listen to me,' said the Doctor. 'You've been ill. You are a loyal soldier of the Cythosi war fleet. Do you really want to see your comrades destroyed? Do you want to die? Use the weapon! Destroy the Krill now!'

'I cannot die,' said Garrett, 'though my mortal form may pass away. Do not be deceived by this manifestation.' He rose from his throne, holding the weapon before him. 'I am Treeka'dwra,' he said. 'A god cannot die.'

'Treeka'dwra.'

The Doctor turned. Blu'ip was perched in the shadows. The dolphin scuttled forward.

'The liberator-god of the Dreekans.'

'You recognise me,' said Garrett.

'Indeed,' said Blu'ip. 'Hail, great god. If I could bow... but you understand, it's none too easy in this thing.'

'What do you want, Blu'ip?' said the Doctor angrily. 'What game are you playing now?'

'No game, Doctor,' the dolphin spat.

'Revenge?'

'Revenge against the human scum and cetacean traitors who drove me from Coralee. Who hunted me across the perimeter worlds. You yourself gave me my plan, Doctor. The ship will plunge down into the oceans of Coralee. The Krill will be released. The colony will be wiped out.'

'And you?' the Doctor queried.

'Oh, I shall be long gone. I can't allow the weapon to be used, Doctor. You understand that, don't you?'

The dolphin scurried towards Garrett, his machine guns sliding from their casing.

'No!' bellowed the Doctor – in vain.

Blu'ip opened up with both barrels, pumping bullets into the weapon. Garrett roared and leapt towards the dolphin. Bullets cut into him and he staggered to one side, howling in pain. The Doctor watched in dismay as the weapon's metallic casing cracked and sparked, as its controls shattered.

Garrett dropped the weapon and slumped to the ground, gasping for breath. He was bleeding badly. Blu'ip's guns rattled into silence, his ammunition spent. The Doctor sprang forward and ran his hands over the weapon. The ring of green cylinders was intact – whatever it was made of, the bullets had failed to penetrate it. The controls, though, were utterly destroyed.

'You've wrecked the dispersal mechanism!' the Doctor yelled.

He jabbed at a button. The weapon crackled hotly in his hands.

'Give it to me, Doctor.'

Blu'ip was bearing down on him. Twin metallic tentacles snaked towards the Doctor. From the dolphin's exoskeleton a laser-drill emerged, buzzing with harsh red light. The Doctor felt his shoulders gripped by the tentacles. The dolphin was on him, drawing him forward in a lethal embrace, pulling him towards the laser.

'Think, Blu'ip!' shouted the Doctor. 'If I can't repair this thing you will die along with the rest of us!'

'I think not, Doctor,' the dolphin squeaked. 'My plan's complete. I'm getting out of here. And I want the weapon.'

He pulled the Doctor forward. The Time Lord could feel the heat of the laser. He raised the weapon. The laser beam ricocheted off its green-glowing trunk and back into the dolphin's breastplate. The dolphin chirruped his pain, and scuttled backwards, releasing the Doctor.

'And just how do you intend to escape?' the Doctor shouted. 'By shuttle? The shuttles on this ship are designed for close-orbit flight. The only place you can go is Coralee – and if I can't repair the weapon Coralee will become as infested with Krill as this ship!'

'You underestimate me, Doctor,' said Blu'ip. 'I've escaped from tighter situations than this. There are other planets in this system.'

'You'd never reach them!' the Doctor railed.

'I've flown further in smaller tubs,' said the dolphin. 'I'll make it.'

There was a loud explosion from one of the corridors leading to the command deck. The door slid open and Mottrack staggered through it. The door closed behind him. He was wounded. Thick purple blood oozed from his shattered shoulder. He looked balefully around him. His eyes fell on Garrett, whose body rippled eerily, shifting between his human guise and his Cythosi form.

'Skuarte!' Mottrack snarled. 'You have done this! Traitor!'

Garrett lurched to his feet. The two wounded Cythosi regarded one another with savagery. Mottrack tried to raise his gun. Garrett sprang forward and clubbed the Cythosi general to the ground. He staggered to a door at the far side of the command deck and lurched through it.

As Blu'ip scuttled towards him, the Doctor cursed himself for being distracted. A tentacle swept out and caught his ankles, sending him crashing to the floor. Two more tentacles snatched up the weapon. The dolphin spun round and raced towards another door.

'Blu'ip! No!' bellowed the Doctor.

'Skuarte...' growled Mottrack.

'Never mind Skuarte!' the Doctor shouted at him. 'Blu'ip's got the weapon!'

'Skuarte...' Mottrack growled again.

'Forget him!' the Doctor yelled. 'He's dying! Help me!'

'He has destroyed my ship,' Mottrack snarled. 'He will die – by my hand!' The wounded general stumbled to his feet, picked up his gun, and lurched off after Garrett.

The Doctor sighed and set off at a run. He had to catch Blu'ip.

The corridor leading to the shuttle bay was free of Krill and Cythosi. The Doctor hared along it. His fist slammed against the entry button and he burst through the doors.

The shuttle bay was a mess – the docking controls of the shuttles were utterly destroyed.

No. One was intact. Blu'ip, still carrying the weapon, was entering the emergency launch code into the docking mechanism of one of the shuttles.

'You're not taking the weapon!' the Doctor shouted.

'You again!' Blu'ip chittered angrily. 'You're persistent, Doctor. Face it – you've lost. Coralee is doomed.'

There was a sound to the Doctor's left. A service panel slid open and Huttle crawled out of it, pale and dirty, sweating and trembling. His companions followed him.

'Stop the dolphin!' the Doctor cried. 'You must stop him!'

The humans seemed confused, dazzled by the light.

'The dolphin!' the Doctor yelled again. 'He mustn't get away.'

One of the humans – Bavril – seemed to understand. Weakly he raised his gun and fired an erratic shot in the direction of Blu'ip. The shot ricocheted off the wall and hit the weapon. The dolphin dropped it with an angry screech and looked frantically around. The undocking mechanism was beginning to activate. The Doctor threw himself forward and dragged the weapon away from Blu'ip.

'It won't make any difference, Doctor!' the dolphin laughed. 'The weapon is damaged beyond repair. You will all die!'

A door at the far end of the bay opened. Bisoncawl backed into the bay, his gun blazing. He slammed the door shut behind him.

'I wish you a painful death!' Blu'ip screeched, thoroughly enjoying his own melodrama, and scurried into the shuttle.

'The Krill are everywhere!' Bisoncawl gasped. 'It's finished.'

The Doctor was poring over the ancient weapon. It was

wrecked beyond repair. Bisoncawl was right. Blu'ip had been right. It was over.

There was a sudden high, whistling scream from inside the shuttle, then another, and another. The ragged, bloody bulk of Blu'ip flew through the shuttle door, his metal tentacles flailing uselessly. The corpse hit the deck with a wet thud as a Krill leapt from the shuttle and stood scanning the room, its claws flexing and unflexing, choosing its next victim.

Bisoncawl immediately began pumping plasma charges into the creature's flank.

Bavril began to do the same. Other humans joined in. The Krill went down in a torrent of energy.

'Quickly,' the Doctor said to the humans, 'you don't have much time. The shuttle's about to launch itself. Get to Coralee. At least down there you might have a chance.'

He threw a glance at Bisoncawl, whose eyes flashed between the Doctor and the functionaries.

'They're getting off the ship,' said the Doctor firmly, folding his arms. There was a heavy pause.

'Very well,' said Bisoncawl.

'Go with them,' the Doctor urged. 'The ship's finished.'

'What about you, Doctor?' Bavril asked. 'Aren't you coming with us?'

'No,' said the Doctor. He had the vaguest scrap of a plan. A last, desperate gamble. 'Perhaps there's something I can do, even now. Go!'

With a last glance at the Time Lord, Bavril entered the escape ship. Huttle followed him and the rest of the humans filed aboard.

'Commander?' the Doctor said.

'What are you planning?' Bisoncawl asked.

'If the ship's guidance systems are still operational I'm going to pilot it into the asteroid belt. The Coralee ring. Destroy it up here.'

'There are Krill on the command deck,' said Bisoncawl. 'I shall come with you.'

'Thank you,' said the Doctor, sincerely.

Bisoncawl grunted. 'You remember what General Mottrack said – Cythosi do not abandon their ships.' He hefted his gun. 'Follow me,' he said.

The shuttle doors closed and the crowded vessel slid towards the airlock.

Garrett staggered down endless corridors. He barely heard Mottrack's bellows somewhere behind him. His world was collapsing – without his sceptre the Krill didn't recognise him. He had already narrowly avoided death at their hands.

He rounded a corner, to be confronted by six of the monsters. They turned to face him, spitting and mewling.

'No,' he called. 'I am Treeka'dwra – I am your master!'

'Skuarte!'

Mottrack lumbered round the corner. He was badly wounded now, and weaponless. With a snarl he lurched forward, his mighty hands closing around Garrett's throat. The pair fell to the floor and rolled towards the Krill.

The monsters swarmed over them, claws flailing and slashing.

'There are only three of them,' Bisoncawl whispered to the Doctor.

With surprising elegance the Cythosi commander spun through the door to the command deck, his heavy gun blazing. All three Krill fell back in a volley of plasma fire, snarling and mewling. Bisoncawl slammed the door shut behind them.

'There are more out there,' he said. 'I won't be able to hold them off for long.'

The Doctor was poring over the ship's flight controls.

'The helms have just about had it,' he said. 'But there might still be enough power...'

He began keying instructions into the console. He felt the deep vibration of the huge vessel's engines engaging.

The door to the deck was suddenly sliced through by Krill claws. Bisoncawl opened fire again, advancing on the door. The claws continued to slash the door, combining with the commander's blaster fire to reduce it to strips of hanging metal.

'Hurry, Doctor,' said Bisoncawl, still firing furiously.

The Doctor's hands flew over the controls.

A Krill leaped through the door, to be cut down by Bisoncawl. Another followed.

'Goodbye, Doctor,' the Cythosi commander said. 'I will give you what time I can.'

Bellowing a bloody, guttural oath, he charged through the wrecked door, his gun blazing.

The Doctor stepped back from the console. The ship was turning slowly. He hoped his guess at the coordinates was good enough.

The firing from the corridor stopped.

The Doctor ran across the command deck as the Krill burst in. He dodged into the corridor that led to the shuttle bay and closed the door behind him. He ran into the bay. Why? Trying to delay the inevitable...?

It was what he did.

There was no escape here – but at least he might be granted a short time to reflect, to gather himself, before the marauding monsters tore him to pieces or the ship crashed into the asteroid ring.

For almost the first time since boarding the ship he thought of Ace. He wondered what had happened to her in the jungle of Coralee. She was a woman now – tough and resourceful. If anyone could survive down there, she would. But so many would die...

The remains of the Krill that Bisoncawl and the humans had felled was lying at his feet. Already its hide was thickening, glandular secretions were creating the cocoon in which it would heal itself, waiting for rebirth.

The Doctor was seized by a desperate idea. The front of the Krill had been blown away, leaving a ragged hollow. He dragged it towards the docking bay of the shuttle in which Bavril's people had escaped, and placed it on the launch pad. He keyed the undocking sequence into the pad, then crawled on top of the Krill. He buried himself as best he could inside its shattered trunk and clung on tightly. The body was disintegrating beneath him.

The monster's secretions washed over him. He felt them stinging into his flesh, painfully cold. He began to lose feeling in his arms and legs. The numbness was creeping towards his body and head.

He had no idea whether this process would kill him – or whether the Krill egg would afford him the protection he sought. A hard black carapace was advancing lumpily over him. He closed his eyes as it moved up his chest and neck and folded over his face.

The last thing he was aware of was movement as the launch pad activated and carried him towards the airlock, and cold, empty space.

Out in the cold blackness, the Cythosi ship began to tumble as its navigational systems went offline. It span in an elegant arc towards the rings, dwarfed by them.

Its nose ploughed into the mass of rock and ice crystals and the first explosion tore through the hull. Seconds later, the entire ship was ripped into blazing fragments as the chain reaction swept though it, lighting up the rings like a small sun.

In moments the blaze had died and the ship was gone.

Chapter Twenty-Two

Ace sat on a rock far out on the peninsula watching the cool blue waters of Coralee lap at her feet. It had been two days since the hurricane, two days since the news that the Cythosi ship had broken up in the asteroid belt. She peered up at the sky. You could see nothing in the day, but at night there was always a spectacular display of shooting stars as objects burnt up in the atmosphere.

They had found out from Huttle and the others. The nervous humans had landed on the beach and weathered the storm there. They had told of the Doctor's manic battle to save the planet from the Krill, of everything that had happened since the reactor explosion.

Ace had found it difficult to accept that the Doctor was dead.

After Holly had rescued her from the hurricane she had been told that he had been at the reactor when it blew, but even then she hadn't believed that he was gone. It was only when Huttle and the other humans told her about the battle on the ship that she started to give up hope. Now, two days later, the truth was finally beginning to sink in.

She spent much of her time in the TARDIS, wandering its long corridors, finding things the Doctor had left half done. Rajiid was worried about her, she knew that, but keeping out of everyone's way was for the best. The colony had its own wounds to heal.

When the hurricane had finally subsided the full extent of the damage had been revealed. Most of the harbour quarter was gone, ragged concrete jetties sticking out into the water and buildings piled like matchwood.

The coastguard had been out every day searching for

survivors, responding to emergency signals from all over the planet. A huge military cruiser had arrived from the neighbouring system and now it dominated the bay, a huge grey island of metal. Marines marched everywhere, helping to get the emergency reactor online.

Brenda was still compiling a list of the dead, a list that seemed to include the entire colony. It was difficult to comprehend so many bodies; the number was too big. It made her grief for one person seem so... selfish.

Q'ilp had taken the death of MacKenzie – of *Alex* – hard. He felt responsible for him. Ace knew how he felt. She had been responsible for the Doctor. She had watched as the skimmer returned from the mountain and Q'ilp took the professor's body to the morgue. The funeral was tomorrow, with hundreds of other funerals. Burial at sea.

The cultists were long gone, vanished into the obscurity of their everyday jobs. The commander of the military cruiser had asked her to try and identify them but it was an impossible task. You could have put paint on the faces of any of the Dreekans and they would have looked like the cultists. She had found herself thinking *they all look the same*. The cry of the racist. She had hated herself for it. In the end she had sworn at the commander and run back to the TARDIS.

Now she spent her time on the rock, watching the sea and trying to work out what the hell she was going to do. She couldn't fly the TARDIS, that much was certain. She could stay here, but it was *so far* from her home and, beautiful as it was, it had too many bad memories.

Besides, it was still uncertain that the military were going to let anyone at all stay on Coralee. There were already rumours of more Krill eggs being found out in the ocean.

Q'ilp, R'tk'tk and most of the other cetaceans had been seconded to secret military manoeuvres and were scouring the seabed all over the planet.

Ace pulled a pebble from her pocket, the one she had found on her very first day on Coralee, a day so far away that it scarcely seemed real. She drew her arm back and hurled it with all her might, watching it arc out into the water and vanish with a soft plop.

She suddenly heard her name being called, very faintly, carried down the beach by the wind. She peered through the dazzling sunlight. A figure was running towards her across the sand, shouting and waving its arms.

She clambered to her feet, straining to hear.

'Ace!'

It was Rajiid.

'Ace! They've found him! They've found him!'

Ace started to run.

Light and sound and feeling returned slowly to the Doctor's world. He was lying on an operating table. The shiny black carapace lay on either side of him. A human doctor stood over him, laser in hand. He was on Coralee... he was in the medi-centre. It had worked...

'Professor!'

Ace bounded up to his bedside. He smiled weakly.

'Hello, Ace,' he whispered.

'What happened to you?' she asked.

'I suppose I must have free-fallen back to Coralee. That was my plan, at least.'

'Q'ilp found you,' she said. 'You were floating out at sea.' She grinned, and nudged at the carapace. 'He recognised you at once.'

The Doctor looked at the dead black shell. Etched into one side of it was a perfect image of him, eyes tight shut.

'I might keep that,' said Ace. 'Put it on my wall in the TARDIS.'

'The Krill...' the Doctor looked around, confused, and suddenly panicked. 'The Cythosi ship... what happened?'

Ace shrugged.

'The ship exploded in the asteroid belt,' said Brenda Mulholland, simply. 'Your plan, I take it?'

The Doctor's head slumped back on the pillow, his eyes lightly closed. 'Then it's over,' he said.

Epilogue

Ace lay back on her beach towel and stared across the expanse of gleaming white sand. All around her the colony was slowly returning to normality: even now she could hear the chirp and whir of service robots out in the jungle, repairing the damaged storm shutters.

Everything had taken a severe battering – not least herself. The bruises on her arms were just fading, but every day that she stayed on Coralee the better she felt – and the more of the colony was rebuilt.

Another ship thundered overhead, a gleaming dot in the blue of the sky. The rescue craft had been coming in thick and fast, the colony pad barely coping with the extra demand.

Holly Relf's sister had arrived on the last transport and there, on the baking tarmac landing pad, Holly had finally broken down into floods of tears. That was the point at which Ace had known that the nightmare was finally over. People had the time to grieve.

Rajiid and Greg were at the old shuttle wreck. They were talking about jacking in the tourist business and transforming the shuttle's derelict shell into a beachside bar. A huge awning stretched over the cluster of driftwood tables and stools and a crude sign surrounded in gaudy lights projected from the roof. The Beachcomber Bar and Grill. Ace squinted at it across the glare of the sand. Overnight someone had painted out the G and added a K. One of the kids probably. It never failed to amaze Ace how quickly children could bounce back from tragedy, how quickly they could joke about it.

Ace watched Rajiid's broad back as he carried out another tray of drinks. Leaving him was going to be the hardest thing. She had nearly asked him to come with them. In the end she hadn't, and she still wasn't quite sure why. Was it because she thought he'd say no – or because he might say yes?

She wasn't sure how she would cope with someone else involved in her life style, with having someone else to look after, someone who wasn't the Doctor.

She stared down the beach. The Doctor's City of the Exxilons rose out of the sand again and he was digging an elaborate network of moats and channels, diverting the river that streamed out of the jungle. He had been working on every aspect of the reconstruction of the colony and there were already mutterings from the administration about keeping him on. Ace smiled. The two of them had already agreed that they would just slip off quietly one evening – but not just yet.

She lay back on the towel, looking up at the sky. Troy was playing with the kite again, though from the erratic patterns it was making in the sky he still hadn't mastered it. It weaved against the rings and, as Ace watched it, her eyes grew heavy.

She jerked awake at a cry of alarm from the Doctor. The kite began to plummet earthwards. The Doctor stood defensively in front of his sandcastle, arms outstretched.

The kite swooped lower and lower, skimming the sand, then suddenly swept skywards again in an elegant arc, almost striking the Doctor full in the face, knocking his hat from his head. He stood on the edge of the moat, arms windmilling wildly and, to the cheers of the kids and the helpless laughter of Ace, toppled backwards into his creation.

The noise of the delighted children rang across the beach as they hurried forward to dig the Doctor out. Ace wiped the tears from her eyes, pulled her shades down and settled back on the sand.

High above the oceans of Coralee, NavSat Nine drifted in its elegant orbit checking and re-checking the hundreds of new signals beamed up from the central computer.

It tracked a transport to low orbit, its scanners shielding themselves as the freighter went to warp in a blaze of radiation.

For a microsecond its sensor array swept across the huge chunks of ice and rock that tumbled overhead, checking, as instructed, for debris from the Cythosi ship.

Sweeping clear, it turned its attention to the planet once more and drifted on into the blackness of space.

Nestled in the rings of Coralee, clinging to the rocks, frozen in the ice, the eggs glinted like diamonds.

Inside the glistening skins the cold black eyes of the Krill stared into space.

Unseeing. Eternally patient.

Among them, a single light winking on the cold metal of its surface, the weapon drifted, tumbling gently amid a sea of stars.

BBC DOCTOR WHO BOOKS

THE EIGHT DOCTORS *by Terrance Dicks* ISBN 0 563 40563 5
VAMPIRE SCIENCE *by Jonathan Blum and Kate Orman* ISBN 0 563 40566 X
THE BODYSNATCHERS *by Mark Morris* ISBN 0 563 40568 6
GENOCIDE *by Paul Leonard* ISBN 0 563 40572 4
WAR OF THE DALEKS *by John Peel* ISBN 0 563 40573 2
ALIEN BODIES *by Lawrence Miles* ISBN 0 563 40577 5
KURSAAL *by Peter Anghelides* ISBN 0 563 40578 3
OPTION LOCK *by Justin Richards* ISBN 0 563 40583 X
LONGEST DAY *by Michael Collier* ISBN 0 563 40581 3
LEGACY OF THE DALEKS *by John Peel* ISBN 0 563 40574 0
DREAMSTONE MOON *by Paul Leonard* ISBN 0 563 40585 6
SEEING I *by Jonathan Blum and Kate Orman* ISBN 0 563 40586 4
PLACEBO EFFECT *by Gary Russell* ISBN 0 563 40587 2
VANDERDEKEN'S CHILDREN *by Christopher Bulis* ISBN 0 563 40590 2
THE SCARLET EMPRESS *by Paul Magrs* ISBN 0 563 40595 3
THE JANUS CONJUNCTION *by Trevor Baxendale* ISBN 0 563 40599 6
BELTEMPEST *by Jim Mortimore* ISBN 0 563 40593 7
THE FACE EATER *by Simon Messingham* ISBN 0 563 55569 6
THE TAINT *by Michael Collier* ISBN 0 563 55568 8
DEMONTAGE *by Justin Richards* ISBN 0 563 55572 6
REVOLUTION MAN *by Paul Leonard* ISBN 0 563 55570 X
DOMINION *by Nick Walters* ISBN 0 563 55574 2

THE DEVIL GOBLINS FROM NEPTUNE *by Keith Topping and Martin Day*
ISBN 0 563 40564 3
THE MURDER GAME *by Steve Lyons* ISBN 0 563 40565 1
THE ULTIMATE TREASURE *by Christopher Bulis* ISBN 0 563 40571 6
BUSINESS UNUSUAL *by Gary Russell* ISBN 0 563 40575 9
ILLEGAL ALIEN *by Mike Tucker and Robert Perry* ISBN 0 563 40570 8
THE ROUNDHEADS *by Mark Gatiss* ISBN 0 563 40576 7
THE FACE OF THE ENEMY *by David A. McIntee* ISBN 0 563 40580 5
EYE OF HEAVEN *by Jim Mortimore* ISBN 0 563 40567 8
THE WITCH HUNTERS *by Steve Lyons* ISBN 0 563 40579 1
THE HOLLOW MEN *by Keith Topping and Martin Day* ISBN 0 563 40582 1
CATASTROPHEA *by Terrance Dicks* ISBN 0 563 40584 8
MISSION IMPRACTICAL *by David A. McIntee* ISBN 0 563 40592 9
ZETA MAJOR *by Simon Messingham* ISBN 0 563 40597 X
DREAMS OF EMPIRE *by Justin Richards* ISBN 0 563 40598 8
LAST MAN RUNNING *by Chris Boucher* ISBN 0 563 40594 5
MATRIX *by Robert Perry and Mike Tucker* ISBN 0 563 40596 1
THE INFINITY DOCTORS *by Lance Parkin* ISBN 0 563 40591 0
SALVATION *by Steve Lyons* ISBN 0 563 55566 1
THE WAGES OF SIN *by David A. McIntee* ISBN 0 563 55567 X
DEEP BLUE *by Mark Morris* ISBN 0 563 55571 8
PLAYERS *by Terrance Dicks* ISBN 0 563 55573 4
MILLENNIUM SHOCK *by Justin Richards* ISBN 0 563 55586 6

SHORT TRIPS *ed. Stephen Cole* ISBN 0 563 40560 0
MORE SHORT TRIPS *ed. Stephen Cole* ISBN 0 563 55565 3

DOCTOR WHO: THE NOVEL OF THE FILM *by Gary Russell* ISBN 0 563 38000 4

THE BOOK OF LISTS *by Justin Richards and Andrew Martin* ISBN 0 563 40569 4
A BOOK OF MONSTERS *by David J. Howe* ISBN 0 563 40562 7
THE TELEVISION COMPANION *by David J. Howe and Stephen James Walker*
ISBN 0 563 40588 0
FROM A TO Z *by Gary Gillatt* ISBN 0 563 40589 9